BOULEVARD WOMEN

More advance priase for *Boulevard Women*

Boulevard Women is a mesmerizing collection of linked short stories, with characters so real, so familiar, that they lingered in my thoughts long after I closed the book. Set against the backdrop of race and religion in the contemporary South, this literary debut reveals an impressive stylistic range, from wry social comedy reminiscent of Elizabeth Strout's *Olive Kitteridge* to the poetic lyricism of *To Kill a Mockingbird.* While each story offers its own rewards, together they weave a plot that twists and turns in surprising ways, right up to the deeply satisfying ending. The gorgeous writing vividly evokes small-town life, from lonely midnight trains to a cat that loves thunderstorms and a troubled boy who finds solace from a tree that owns itself—an entrancing world that I didn't want to leave.

–Sheri Joseph
Where You Can Find Me, Stray, and *Bear Me Safely Over*

Boulevard Women is a compassionate and passionate rendering of the lives of the invisible women of a neighborhood in Athens, Georgia that has seen better times. Teenage Layla, just transplanted from California, middle-aged waitress Leona, and Miss Thalia, an elderly Southern Belle and true Steel Magnolia, are the main characters, representing the three major stages of womanhood: youth, middle age, and old age. As they fall into the different traps and dilemmas that present themselves at different points in a fully lived life, we see the strong spirits of these women warriors emerge, asserting themselves as individuals and as a loyal tribe. In a remarkably cohesive weave of interlocking stories, Lauren Cobb gives us a compelling look at our own selves through the Boulevard women, inviting us to ask, as Layla does, "If my life were a novel [would I] get a second chance?"

–Judith Ortiz Cofer
If I Could Fly and *The Line of the Sun*

BOULEVARD WOMEN

Lauren Cobb

Winner of the G.S. Sharat Chandra Prize for Short Fiction

Selected by Kelly Cherry

 BkMk Press
University of Missouri-Kansas City

Financial assistance for this project has been provided by the
Missouri Arts Council, a state agency.

Executive Editor: Robert Stewart
Managing Editor: Ben Furnish
Book Cover Design: Peter Geissler
Book Design: Susan L. Schurman

The G. S. Sharat Chandra Prize for Short Fiction wishes to thank Naomi Benaron,
Leslie Koffler, Linda Rodriguez, Brian Shawver.

BkMk Press wishes to thank Elizaneth Uppman, Grace Sansbery and Marie
Mayhugh.

Library of Congress Cataloging-in-Publication Data

Cobb, Lauren.
Boulevard Women / Lauren Cobb.
    pages cm
Summary: "These ten stories feature the evolving friendships of a teen-aged girl,
a widowed waitress in her forties, and a traditionally minded Southern woman
in her seventies living as neighbors on Boulevard in Athens, Georgia, during the
early 2000s."— Provided by publisher.

ISBN 978-1-886157-90-3 (pbk. : alk. paper)
1. Female friendship--Fiction. 2. Female friendship--Fiction. 3. Athens (Ga.)-
-Fiction. I. Title.
  PS3603.O22553B68 2013
  813'.6--dc23

                                   2013025891

Printed in the United States of America.
This book is set in Quantas and Mistral

ACKNOWLEDGMENTS

My heartfelt thanks to Kelly Cherry for selecting *Boulevard Women* for the 2012 G.S. Sharat Chandra Award for Short Fiction; to Ben Furnish at BkMk Press for his generosity, wit and editorial acumen, and to my dear friend Peter Geissler for designing the book cover.

I received support for this project from the Hambidge Center for the Creative Arts and Sciences and the Community of Writers at Squaw Valley, for which I am truly grateful.

My thanks to the editors who published slightly different versions of the following stories: "Writing on the Wall" (*Green Mountains Review*), "Boulevard Women" (*Another Chicago Magazine*), and "House of Dust" (*Southern California Review*).

I've had a number of inspiring teachers through the years. My thanks to my friend and mentor Lou Mathews, who got me started; to Iowa State University's Jane Smiley, Fern Kupfer, and Joe Geha, who taught me much and kept me going; and to the University of Georgia's Julie Checkoway, the late James Kilgo, and Judith Ortiz Cofer, who saw me through. I'm immensely grateful to Judith for her generous spirit and sage advice; she's an extraordinary mentor.

I'm also grateful to my friends in Lou Mathews' Fine Food and Fiction workshop, who changed my life for the better: Paul Arenson, Bill Audeh, Rhona Blaker, Marc Danziger, Jenny Mead, Rachel Resnick, Phil Rowe, the fabulous Glenda Shaw, and Jennifer Shull. At the University of Georgia, I found kindred spirits in the women's writing group, including Karen McElmurray and Melissa Crowe.

My heartfelt thanks to the wonderful writers who read these stories in various stages. I'm deeply grateful to my talented friend Maureen Gibbon, who read the first story, told me to write more, then read the stories that followed. My indispensable friends Sheri Joseph and Lorraine Lopez read every story, and their astute comments and unstinting friendship are as necessary to my writing life as is their amazing fiction. I can never repay my dear friend Jean Harfenist for her faith in me, the inspiration of her own beautiful writing, and her insightful edits. Dawn Yackzan's generous encouragement and comments helped me to the finish line, and David Masiel and Susan Rebecca White were equally generous in taking time to read the manuscript despite their incredibly busy lives.

My thanks to Virginia Cobb, Beth Cobb, and Anne Monkarsh for reading these stories and cheering me on, and to Charles Cobb and Beth Monkarsh for their love and support. I'll always be grateful to my Georgia family for their love and encouragement: the late Mary Lucy Hill; Mary, Donald, and Deon Hill; Idell Bundrage; and Jeannie Mapp and the dearly missed Louise Mapp. Lastly, and always, my deep gratitude to the gifted poet Sean Hill for being in my life.

For my dear mother, Virginia Cobb,
and in loving memory of my father, Charles Cobb

BOULEVARD WOMEN

FOREWORD

S*how,* writing teachers tell their students, at least their beginning students; *don't tell.* But how often is a story completed without some telling, some assertion of a thought or thesis, even if thought or thesis may be limited to a particular character's point of view? Words, which are what writers work with, coax the writer to reveal secrets, including thoughts and theses. Yet Lauren Cobb, in her first and quite marvelous story collection, has managed to convey setting, scene, description, dialogue, and plot—and thought and thesis—in continuing action that pulls the reader into the very lively world of her "Boulevard women." It is as if she has triumphed over artifice. I say *as if* because, of course, a book of fiction is always artifice. But by triumphing over it, she has given us stories that are infused with life, as natural as life, as real as life. I could not put this book down. I did not want to leave it. I had entered its world of women and was enthralled by them, turning pages to see what they would do next. Which was always a surprise.

The "Boulevard women" include Janice and her daughters, Layla and Summer, who are half-sisters. Layla is already acutely aware of her mother's restlessness and various urgencies; she recognizes "the doomed eager light in her mother's eyes." Summer, the younger sister, searches on the Internet for her biological father. There is Leona, a middle-aged widow who waitresses at the Normaltown Café. Leona lives across the street from Miss Thalia, an elderly churchgoing spinster devoted to her conventional life—until life begins to change her in excellent, exciting ways. There was a time when the Boulevard was a coveted address, but that time has gone. The relationship between Leona and Miss Thalia takes twists and turns, deepening with each twist, each turn. Jody, prostitute and drug addict, has a role to play. Gwen is African American and, with good reason, a little leery of white people. And then there are the men, and though they are peripheral, each is clearly drawn and as fully alive as the women: Paul, the stepfather; Clayton, the brother; Will, the other brother; Harry, the nephew; Dwight, the cop; and Nolan, who is one of the author's surprises.

Each of the stories is a complete whole, and yet they are linked in a sequence. Or maybe *braided* would be a more accurate term, because Cobb's characters interact throughout and in between the stories. This decision on the part of the author works a kind of magic whereby the reader's interest is coolly held by the single story at hand at the same time as it is inflamed by a narrative that races faster and faster, like a spreading fire. With this début collection Lauren Cobb proves herself as a writer who can create suspense, humor, and aesthetic shapeliness out of ordinary materials. I think you will fall in love with her book. I did.

—Kelly Cherry
Final judge
G. S. Sharat Chandra Prize for Short Fiction

BOULEVARD WOMEN

In the false dusk of the living room's lowered blinds, Leona rested her sore feet on the ottoman while her thoughts floated on a gin-tinctured tide through the years with Frank, past the faces she'd known since his death. Smoke spiraled from the ashtray. A few raindrops tapped the windows, and thunder rumbled. God moving furniture, Frank used to say. The air slowly darkened. Rain clattered on the roof, hissed in the trees. Her burly orange cat Henry padded to the front door and meowed. When Leona opened the door he darted past her, the only cat she'd ever known to like storms. She stepped onto the porch, smelled wet air and damp Georgia earth. In the dark magnolia trees a lone blossom glowed like a white star, the wet grass littered with brown petals as soft and leathery as old gloves.

Lightning flickered in the clouds. Across the street Miss Thalia stood in her parlor, a lamp-lit figure shrouded by lace curtains, no doubt watching the yellow pickup idling beside her birdhouse mailbox. Leona waved but wasn't surprised when the old lady didn't respond. They exchanged greetings if they met on the street, but all visiting between them had stopped on a warm Sunday morning, a few weeks after Frank was killed by a drunk driver on the Atlanta highway. When Miss Thalia knocked on Leona's door to invite her to church, Leona was drunk, stark naked under her mint-striped bathrobe, and she'd burst out laughing at Miss Thalia's blanched dismay. "Lemme ask you something, Miss Thalia," she'd said. "You're old as the hills, all alone—so what's the goddamn point?"

"If you're asking why I don't kill myself," Miss Thalia had said tartly, "it's my duty to live out my appointed time. I take each day as a gift from the Lord."

The rain fell harder as a skinny woman got out of the yellow truck and slammed the door. "Screw you!" she shouted. The truck sped off, the scowling driver hunched over the wheel. The woman flung her arms wide and laughed, then fell backward onto the grass. Miss Thalia's shrouded figure retreated behind the lamplight.

Clutching the mailbox's wooden post, the woman climbed to her feet. In a tanktop, miniskirt and knee-high black boots, dark wet hair plastered to her bony shoulders, she was probably one of the streetwalkers from Barber Street, just a few blocks away. Smiling, she hooked an arm around the mailbox and kissed it. Leona's breath caught as she pictured Jody dancing in the Normaltown Café after closing, the radio blasting, the other waitresses grinning as Jody jumped into a booth and go-go danced, shaking her scrawny hips and tossing her black curls. Even the song came back to Leona: "Don't You Forget About Me" by Simple Minds.

Waitresses, Jody had said, were the world's extras—walk-ons who never spoke a line, were never in the spotlight unless they won the lottery or suffered a newsworthy death. Maggie, the café's owner, had called Jody an attractive menace, but Leona had liked the girl's brash honesty. She'd even tried to talk Jody out of moving in with her lowlife boyfriend.

Hugging her elbows, Leona turned and went inside. She should follow Miss Thalia's example, keep her blinds drawn until this woman (could she be Jody?) wandered back to Barber Street to score whatever drug she craved and find shelter from the rain. But Leona remembered Jody coasting up the sidewalk on her black ten-speed, smiling as if a brisk autumn morning were reason enough for joy.

Leona went to the kitchen and pulled a wad of crumpled bills from the purple clown cookie jar. Then she slid her feet into her sneakers and went out the back door. The rain eased to a drizzle as she squelched across the yard to the alley. She hurried past dripping garage eaves, gravel crunching under her feet. At the end of the alley she walked to the corner and crossed to Miss Thalia's side of the street. She was on a fool's errand, she knew that. But she couldn't look the other way, not if it was Jody.

The woman had draped herself over the mailbox, her eyes closed. Leona stopped a few feet away. "Jody?"

The woman gasped and blinked, then lurched forward and flung an arm around Leona, breathing wine into her face. "Leona," she crooned. "My favorite extra."

Leona grabbed Jody's shoulders to steady her. Broomstick thin, her freckled face pale and grimy, but not slurring, not dead drunk. Miss Thalia's lace curtains flickered. Leona said, "We'd better get moving."

"My way or the highway, Maggie always said." Jody's laugh rasped into a cough. "You got a cigarette?"

"Not on me, but I'll buy you a pack. Feel like a cup of coffee?"

Jody swayed, grabbed the mailbox. "I got to get back to work."

Leona pulled a handful of bills from her pocket, counted out ten ones, a five. "What's the going rate these days?"

Jody smiled into Leona's eyes. "I have *no* idea what you're talking about."

Leona smiled right back. "Cut the shit, Jody."

Jody peered around, then snatched the bills and shoved them into her boot. Glancing up through her tangled curls, she said, "You still at the café? Those were good times, at the good old Abnormal Town Café."

"I'm still there," Leona said. "Let's hit the Waffle House, okay? I'm buying."

As they headed down the sidewalk, Jody pointed across the

street. "I always thought your house looked kind of spooky. All those dark trees."

"I don't live there anymore," Leona lied. "I'm over on Cain Street now."

By the time they reached Prince Avenue the sun was blazing through black clouds, the pavement steaming. At the gas station Jody said she'd wait outside, soak up some rays. When Leona came out with a pack of Marlboros, Jody was leaning against the wall, her hair drying into tangled black curls. As they crossed the parking lot, a cloud hid the sun and drizzled rain on the horizon—a faint shadow falling through the air.

The only customer in the Waffle House was an elderly black man reading a newspaper at the counter. Leona steered Jody to a booth, then raised an eyebrow at the two frowning middle-aged waitresses. The skinny one came over, sloshed coffee into their cups, took their orders and stalked off. "She doesn't like me," Jody hissed in a stage whisper. "But I bet her hubby does."

Leona stifled a grin. "Don't get us thrown out."

"Wouldn't be the first time, won't be the last. So, you still raking in the big tips, dating the thick pricks?"

"Tips are all right."

Jody rolled her eyes. "You always made twice as much as the rest of us. Everybody *loves* Leona." She tapped a cigarette from her pack. "In like, two weeks, it'll be illegal to do this. Just one more thing they can bust you for."

The waitress slung down their plates, slapped down the bill and walked off.

"How about you?" Leona asked. "How are you doing?"

"Same old, same old." Jody squirted catsup on her scrambled eggs. "But I'm thinking about moving to Atlanta. I've got a friend who works at a club in Buckhead. She says I'd be perfect."

"A club?"

"Hello? Exotic dancers? Buckhead's where the pro athletes and music moguls hang out. Carrie says the tips are stupid good, and I can stay with her till I get on my feet."

"There are other lines of work."

"Yeah, and they all pay shit. Anyway, once I get my act together, I'm gonna move out West, maybe get an office job. I'm good with numbers. Maybe marry a nice guy and have a bunch of babies." As Jody stared out the window at her future, her smile faded. "Or not. How do you do it, Leona? You've been in love more times than frigging Cleopatra, and when it ends you just crook your finger at the next guy in line."

"I had Frank. Everything else is icing on the cake. So I've got to ask. Whatever happened to that guy you moved in with?"

"Bobby? You sure called that one right. I mean, at first it was great. He said we were gonna get married and move to LA. That's like, three years ago, right? So last summer he brings home this *total* pop tart, Carissa. Boobs out to here and the IQ of a dead moth, but Bobby acts like she's fucking gifted. So now I've got a room on Barber Street." Jody shrugged. "True love, there's an urban legend for you."

Leona didn't ask why Jody had let it happen. Some girls thought turning tricks was exciting at first—endless dating with an illicit, profitable edge. But Jody didn't seem to be doing real well. Leona hesitated. "You aren't hooked on anything, are you?"

"I'm not stupid, Leona. I do a little meth now and then, recreationally, that's all."

Great, a streetwalker who did meth "recreationally." And Jody had barely touched her food. Leona picked up the bill and went to the cash register. As she headed back to the booth a big blond policeman came in—Dwight Jordan, a regular at the Normaltown Café. Keys and flashlight clanking, he sat down at the counter and smiled at Leona. "You get prettier every damn day, girl." He glanced past her. "Who's your friend?"

"This is Jody. Jody, this is Dwight."

Dwight's marble-blue eyes narrowed. "Seems I've seen you before, Jody."

Leona smiled at him. "Of course you have. She used to work at the café."

Jody made the Jedi hand gesture. "This is not the droid you're looking for." Her giggles eroded into hoarse coughs.

As Dwight plucked a menu from the rack, Jody slid out of the booth. Leona touched his shoulder. "See you around, Dwight." He nodded without looking up.

When they emerged into sunlight, Jody said, "Thanks for telling him my name."

"What does it matter?"

"I don't need to be on a first-name basis with law enforcement, if you follow me."

"Sorry." Leona stepped around a puddle. "I wasn't thinking."

"Yeah, well, what am I supposed to do now? Sure as shit, next time he sees me he'll bust me. Fucking cops. Like they don't have anything better to do."

"The guilt-trip thing? It's not working, Jody."

"I'm just saying, the boys in blue aren't my best friends."

They turned down a narrow street overhung with trees. The air grew muggy, and midges swarmed in the warm shade. Halfway down the block Jody said, "So you want to go hang out at your place? Have a drink, catch up some more?"

"I think the party ends here."

"Some party." Jody licked her lips. "I hate to ask, but could you loan me twenty?"

Leona pulled a couple of fives from her back pocket, handed them to Jody. "That's all I have." She studied Jody's mascara-smudged eyes, the faded yellow bruises on her arm. "Well, try to take care of yourself, okay?"

"I'm fine, Leona. But thanks for the loan." Jody winked, stuffed the money into her boot. "Next time I'm on Boulevard, I'll look you up. The house with the trees."

As Jody crossed the street, a cough shook her thin shoulders. She walked into a patch of shade, disappeared around the corner. Staring after her, Leona wished she could fix Jody's train-wrecked life. Failing that, she wished Jody had believed her lie about Cain Street. Because sooner or later Jody would show up on her doorstep. And Leona would probably let her in.

The shadows were lengthening when she got home. She opened her faded purple mailbox and pulled out a few bills, a postcard from Frank's sister, who was vacationing in Acapulco, and a flyer advertising tune-ups at the Chevron station. A screen door creaked open, slapped shut. When Miss Thalia called to her, Leona crossed the street and said, "Afternoon, Miss Thalia."

"Warm, isn't it?" Miss Thalia said in a voice that scratched like starched lace. "Tell me, do you know that unfortunate girl?"

"She used to work at the café."

Miss Thalia opened her mailbox, then peered at Leona over her spectacles, her pale blue eyes clear as water. "I don't like to call the police, because a girl like that, the minute she gets out she's back on the streets anyhow."

Leona sighed. "I sure hope she doesn't start hanging around here."

Miss Thalia gave a thin-lipped smile. "It doesn't do any good trying to help that kind, does it?"

"She didn't used to be that kind."

"We're all born innocent." Miss Thalia's bony finger tapped Leona's arm. "But the devil lays his snares."

"Well, I'd better get going." Leona brandished her mail. "Bills to pay."

Miss Thalia pulled out the Chevron flyer. "There ought to be a law against putting such trash in people's mailboxes. Well, I won't keep you, dear."

Henry twined around Leona's legs as she opened the front door. She sank into her armchair, lit a cigarette, and envisioned Jody in a damp room crawling with cockroaches. If Frank hadn't paid off the mortgage, Leona might be living in a dank hole, too. As it was, she could barely pay her property taxes, didn't have health insurance. But although years of waitressing had riveted pain into her shoulders, mapped varicose veins on her thighs, her muscles were still strong, her heart unfaltering.

Hard to believe Frank would have turned fifty this fall. They'd met when he was in the Navy, stationed in San Diego. With dark blue eyes that spoke more than his mouth did, he'd looked like a good time to a nineteen-year-old waitress. When he got out of the Navy, they'd married and moved to Georgia so he could work in his family's hardware store. At first she'd missed San Diego's sea breezes, its red tile roofs, the musical Spanish street names. Leona sipped her watery gin and tonic, remembering their raucous parties, weekends in bed drinking beer and making love, crossing the railroad tracks to shoot his Colt revolver, the gun's sharp crack, beer bottles exploding, turkey vultures circling in a blue sky. On summer nights they'd strolled the dark streets, fireflies glittering in the shadows.

This white clapboard house shrouded by magnolia trees was where she'd been happiest. Wet summers and winter ice had grayed and splintered the clapboard, and the porch roof was rotted in one corner, but this was home. As was Boulevard, the broad shady street where she'd spent most of her life—the last twelve years alone but not lonely. She wasn't beautiful, she knew that. But her auburn hair and sleepy smile had drawn men to her bed until she grew weary of what passed for love, stopped bringing home the men who flirted with her at the café. She'd slept with them to fend off grief, and none ever lasted more than a few weeks, as if Frank's lingering presence in her bed cast a pall over any passion or affection she tried to ignite there. Until Jesse, ten years younger than she was, the exception. Maybe a mistake.

Henry leapt onto her lap, his fur still damp, his green eyes staring into hers. She ran her finger down his spine. "Don't tell me you're hungry again." He rasped a meow, his front claws pricking through her jeans. "You're just like Frank," she said. "When you want something, you want it now."

෨෨෨෨

On Friday night Leona cut across the café's back parking lot to Foxy's Bar and Grill, where she was meeting Jesse. The basement bar was crowded, Percy Sledge on the jukebox, the low ceiling creaking as people milled about in the restaurant upstairs. She ordered a gin and tonic from the bartender, lit a cigarette and glanced around. This was where she and Jesse had first set eyes on each other, so now it was "their place." But she couldn't look across the dim, smoky bar without seeing her younger self leaning over a pool table to line up a shot, Frank's hand on the bare skin above her tight jeans.

"Been waiting long?" Jesse sat down beside her, shoved his dark hair out of his eyes and leaned in for a kiss, then ordered a hamburger and a Corona. They took their drinks to a booth, and he told her about his day. The construction job was behind schedule, the foreman riding their asses from sunup to sundown. He took her hand, rubbed his thumb across her knuckles, over her thin gold wedding band. "Since I'm the new guy, I get the shit jobs like hauling shingles and lumber up ladders to the other guys. Most days I'm so beat, I'm asleep as soon as I walk through the door. Wake up around midnight tired and dirty and hungry as hell."

"But it'll get better, won't it?" Leona interlaced her fingers through his. "After a while you won't be the new guy, won't have to do all the shit work."

"Yeah. If I don't get laid off or fall off a ladder first."

After Jesse ate his hamburger and fries, they went back to Leona's house, drank whiskey in bed, made love with the windows open to the cool night. Lying beside her, his head propped in his hand, Jesse talked about his restaurant back in Savannah, tourists standing in line for catfish po-boys, crab cakes, shrimp and grits. He hadn't said how he lost the place, and she hadn't asked. His hands were nicked and calloused but gentle, and his dark eyes said she was beautiful. It was enough for now.

On Sunday he said he was too tired to come over, he'd call her in a few days. Leona said she understood, but as the week wore on, he didn't call and he didn't call. When she left a message on his cell phone it went unanswered.

On Saturday morning she went for a walk without admitting

where her feet were taking her. She ended up in front of the duplex Jesse shared with two guys from his construction crew. The third time she knocked, a bare-chested young man in drawstring pants opened the door, his sleep-messed hair a pale halo. Trevor, that was his name. He'd been at Foxy's the night she'd met Jesse. When she asked if Jesse was home, slow recognition widened his eyes. Then he looked at his feet and said, "Jesse's gone."

"Oh, I didn't know," Leona stammered. "Did he say where he was going?"

"Atlanta." Trevor scratched his head as if trying to remember more, but Leona had heard enough.

Walking home, she told herself she'd known it was only a fling. But her younger self rose in her throat clamoring that she wasn't done yet, he couldn't leave her, not yet. She dug her nails into her palms and walked faster. She was forty-six. Had her last kiss come and gone without her knowing it?

As she crossed her front porch, a flute's slow notes drifted from Miss Thalia's upstairs windows. Leona sighed, unlocked the door. These days she heard the flute less often, those gnarled fingers getting too stiff, maybe, to press the keys.

Leona was roused from sleep by someone pounding on the front door. Pressing the light on her alarm clock, she squinted at the glowing green numbers. Nearly two in the morning. Maybe drunken frat boys, but it was only July, not many college kids around yet. She opened the nightstand drawer and took out Frank's revolver. Fists hammered on the door as she pulled on jeans and a sweatshirt, tiptoed downstairs.

The living room blinds were closed, so no one could see her standing alone at the bottom of the stairs. She thumbed back the revolver's hammer, heard muffled voices on the porch. A fist thudded on the door. She crept closer and pressed her ear to the wood, flinched when someone rattled the doorknob. A woman gave a hoarse cough, then shouted, "God damn it, Leona, open up!"

Leona was scared and angry, but not surprised. She'd always known Jody would turn up again. When footsteps tromped down the porch steps she ran to the kitchen. She was lifting the wall phone from its cradle when glass shattered behind her. As she whirled around, a branch nosed through the backdoor window, pushing aside the curtains and poking out the windowpane's jagged shards. Glass tinkled onto the floor. She dropped the phone and gripped the revolver in both hands the way Frank had taught her. "I've got a gun," she called. "Get the hell out of here or I'll shoot."

Voices muttered and the branch withdrew. The dangling phone bleated. As she reached for it, a bearded man peered through the curtains. His eyes widened at the gun and his face disappeared. Henry crept into the kitchen and leapt onto the counter to stare at the broken window as if expecting a bird to fly in. A deep voice said, "We've got Jody. Let us in or we'll hurt her."

"God damn it, they mean it, Leona!"

"Tell that to someone who gives a shit."

A slap followed by an anguished yelp made Leona wince, but Jody had brought trouble to her door. She steadied the gun, felt the old weary anger at Frank.

Jody gave a muffled shriek. "Get your hands off me, motherfucker!"

If she pulled the trigger she might scare them away. At the very least someone might call the police. But what if the bullet found Jody, or ricocheted and hit Henry? She pictured the headline: Woman Shoots at Burglars, Hits Cat.

The deep voice said, "Fuck it." A meaty freckled arm reached through the window, and wiggling fingers groped for the dead bolt. Her heart pounding, Leona stepped closer, aimed, squeezed the trigger into deafening noise, blood mist and screaming, the man jerking his arm back through the jagged glass. Dogs barked up and down the street and footsteps pounded across her yard. She hung up the phone, dialed 911. Her voice shook as she told the dispatcher what had happened.

"You *shot* somebody?" the dispatcher asked. "I'll send over a squad car. Please stay on the line, ma'am."

When the dispatcher finished with her, Leona slid to the floor with her back against the broom closet, the Colt on her knee, its barrel aimed at the door. A breeze fluttered the curtains. Outside, a woman sobbed in the dark. She'd asked Frank not to go to Atlanta on Labor Day, all those drunks on the road. Leona raised her voice. "You'd better go, Jody. I called the police."

"They hurt me. They punched and slapped and pinched me till I said I could get them some money." Jody gasped a sob. "I bet they're waiting back at my room."

"Then I guess you'd better stay here. If you're hurt, the cops will take you to the hospital."

"Are you mad at me?"

"What do you think?"

"I'm sorry."

"And I really don't give a shit." Leona's knee cracked as she stood up. She unlocked the door and inched it open. Crouched on the steps, Jody squinted into the light, her face swollen and bruised, red welts on her cheeks. Blood dripped from her puffy upper lip. One of the bastards must have worn rings.

"Come on in," Leona said. "You need some ice on that lip."

Jody groaned as she got to her feet. Leona pulled her inside, locked the door, then sat her down at the kitchen table. She poured a few fingers of the Maker's Mark she'd kept for Jesse and set it in front of Jody, then folded a dish towel around a frozen chunk of ice cubes and told Jody to hold it on her swollen lip. Sirens wailed in the distance.

"I really stepped in it this time, didn't I?" Jody mumbled. Leona hesitated, then said, "I'll say they forced you to bring them here, and maybe the cops will let you off. But they'll probably want names."

Jody took the ice from her lip, gulped some bourbon. "I can't do that."

Leona opened her mouth to argue, then thought better of it.

Taking the gun, she went to the hall linen cupboard and rummaged through frayed guest towels until she found the white metal box with a flaking red cross on its lid. Jody's cuts might scar less if they were smeared with antibiotic ointment. Stealthy sounds—a drawer shutting, the clink of china—drew her back to the kitchen. Jody was tiptoeing toward the door, the whiskey bottle in her hand and the cookie jar under her arm. The purple clown head grinned on the counter. Leona dropped the first aid kit to the floor. Jody spun around, her eyes frightened. Then she sneered and blood trickled from her lip. "You'd shoot me for your goddamn tip money?"

"Don't get me wrong, Jody. I'd love to see you in a world of hurt."

"I *said* I was sorry." As the sirens screamed closer, Jody's voice grew urgent. "Come on, Leona. I need it more than you do. I owe that guy two hundred. I've got to give him something."

Leona lowered the gun. "If you've got any brains left, you'll put down that bottle and run for the next bus out of here. Because that wonderful life you're planning out West? You keep this shit up, your life won't be worth living—not anywhere. And it won't last long either."

Jody stared at Leona, a startled question in her eyes, as if she'd glimpsed death peeking around a corner at her.

"You're young," Leona said. "You've still got choices."

The sirens grew louder, then squealed into silence. Car doors slammed. When someone rapped on the front door, Leona went to answer it, the gun in her hand. It looked like half the Athens police force was on her porch. Three squad cars were parked haphazardly at the curb, their red lights smearing the darkness. She switched on the porch light, and the crowd dwindled to six men who blinked and shaded their eyes. Of course one of them was Dwight. "Must be a slow night," she said. "Come on in."

As they tromped inside, Dwight said quietly, "Let me guess. Your little friend?"

"Yep." She pointed toward the kitchen and raised her voice. "They broke in through the back door."

Dwight rubbed his mouth. "You shot your little friend?"

"No, one of her little friends."

"You're really something, Leona."

"Yeah, I'm something."

In the kitchen, the back door stood open to the night. The Maker's Mark was on the counter, the cookie jar gone. It had been a good week, nearly two hundred dollars in the jar after she'd stocked up on cigarettes and gin. She hoped Jody was running through back alleys to the Greyhound station, climbing aboard a bus to Atlanta, New York, Miami, wherever two hundred bucks would take her. Leona smiled her sleepy smile, asked if anyone wanted coffee.

For the next hour she worked a graveyard shift in her own kitchen, pouring coffee and answering questions until only Dwight and his pimpled young partner were left. When Dwight asked if she had any plywood to cover the broken window, she went out to the garage. Nervous, startled by shadows, she came back with a hammer, a coffee can of nails and a cobwebbed piece of chipboard. Dwight held the board up to the window. "It'll do. Can I get some more of that coffee?"

As she refilled his cup, weariness dragged at her muscles, sank into her bones. "Those men beat her up pretty bad, Dwight." *Run,* she thought, run *now.*

He hammered in a few more nails. "They won't be back, not after the can of whoop ass you opened up. But better safe than sorry. You ready to roll, Brad?"

When she walked them to the door, the eastern sky was turning gray, sparrows twittering. Dwight paused on the steps. "You all right, Leona?"

"I'll be all right."

She watched them leave, then went inside and sat at the kitchen table with a cup of coffee. But the chipboard on the window unnerved her—an ugly intruder blocking out the dawn. She picked up her coffee cup and went upstairs to the front balcony. Henry was hiding somewhere, would come out when he was ready. She sank into a wicker chair and lit a cigarette with trembling fingers. She'd always felt safe in this house, had never felt alone. She had memories to populate every room, voices she could hear—even talk to if she felt like that. Now her memories hung about her like a tattered spider web. But she'd kept the bastards out. They'd scared her but they hadn't hurt her. She'd try to get the broken window replaced today.

Miss Thalia's screen door creaked open, and Leona glimpsed the old lady stooping to pick up the *Athens Banner-Herald* from her front porch. At least Jody hadn't led those men to Miss Thalia's house, though for all Leona knew, the old lady had a gun, knew how to use it—the only real security for a woman living alone. Her eyes half-closed, Leona summoned Frank's shadowy presence to the balcony, sleep-tousled, scratching his bare belly. She murmured, "Why'd you have to go to Atlanta?"

Henry padded onto the porch and jumped into her lap. "You were a lot of help," she told him. "I should trade you in for a Doberman." She rubbed behind his ears until deep purrs rumbled in his chest, and he butted his head against her ribs. Stroking his soft fur, she hoped Jody was on a bus heading into the night's last shadows.

You couldn't save other people, or even keep them by you. She knew that. But as she stood up, the cat in her arms, she saw them all in a dim distant land, saw herself running toward them through the years, past graying hair and arthritic knees, a thousand more wait-ress shifts and whatever else life brought to her door. "But there's no hurry," she whispered. The sky grew brighter as the sun cleared the rooftops and rimmed the world in silver light. Below her the avenue murmured awake, the shadows receding.

WRITING ON THE WALL

On a warm breezy Saturday in June, Layla, her little half-sister, and their mom moved from the San Fernando Valley to a housing tract in the hills. The next day the other two moms and their kids arrived, nine people in all. While movers stomped through the rooms, the moms drew plastic straws snipped different lengths. Layla's mom, Janice, drew the longest straw and got the master bedroom. The middle straw went to Toni Nolan, who had two bleach-white streaks in her spiky black hair like a skunk. Sweet-faced Lisa Mayer drew the shortest straw and was stuck with the bedroom next to the "communal spaces." The six kids would share the big dormer-windowed room that, along with a small bathroom across the landing, took up the whole second floor.

"We'll hang curtains for you if you want more privacy," Toni Nolan said at the inaugural house meeting that afternoon—a meeting enlivened by her eight-month-old son's incessant wails. He was teething, which Toni said felt like razors slicing through your gums. Layla raised her hand and waved it back and forth until Toni looked at her.

"The baby's not sleeping upstairs, is he?" Layla asked.

Toni clasped her hands between her knees and leaned forward.

"He needs to sleep apart from me," she said earnestly, "for his successful individuation. The family bed has its merits, but individuation is *vital*."

Sixteen-year-old Beth Mayer muttered, "That means we get to smell his dirty diapers." Without raising her hand, she said, "I'm sixteen, so my individuation is at a crucial stage. I'm sleeping in the garage."

Toni shot a reproachful look at Beth's mom, Lisa, who said, "It'll get cold in there this winter, honey."

Beth shrugged. "I'm not sharing a bedroom with a bunch of little kids."

Janice rubbed her nose, her expression thoughtful. "Beth has a point. Remember when you were sixteen, Toni? That's dream time, alone time, poetry time. I think Beth needs her own space."

Layla hated it when her mom talked like that. And if anyone said *communal space* or *personal space* one more time, she'd puke all over the ugly shag carpet that, along with the avocado kitchen appliances, carbon-dated this house to the 1960s. Which was why her mom had gotten the place so cheap—plumbing shot, furnace gasping its last breaths, the backyard fence sagging every which way like it couldn't make up its mind where to fall. Though Layla had to admit that a blue sky and oak-dotted green hills were an upgrade from smog, strip malls and traffic noise.

Sitting beside their mom, Layla's nine-year-old half-sister Summer chewed on a strand of her long blond hair, her eyes soft with daydreams. The little twerp didn't realize how horrible it was going to be, sharing a bedroom with a screaming baby and moon-faced twelve-year-old Ben Mayer who hadn't said a word so far—not to mention Toni's daughter Ashley, who was thirteen, just a few months older than Layla, and wore lipstick on her fat lips and makeup on her dark sullen eyes.

After dinner the moms helped the kids shove their beds and nightstands into the dormer nooks and push the dressers against the walls. The air conditioning was feeble, and the dormer windows didn't open, so it was hot upstairs under the roof. Sticky with grime and sweat, Layla watched her mom rummage in a storage closet. Janice finally emerged with dust in her long brown hair and a pole with a metal hook that opened the skylights so the heat could escape into the night. When Ashley asked her mom about the privacy curtains, Toni, who was struggling to set up Zach's crib, said she'd get right on that, just as soon as she finished doing a zillion more-important things.

At bedtime Layla went into the bathroom to change into her pajamas. In the mirror her nipples were shadowy bumps under her thin nylon top. Clutching her clothes to her chest, she scurried back to her bed—the last nook on the left. Ben was sitting cross-legged on his bed picking at his toes, his shaggy dark hair in his eyes. "You through in there?" he asked. "Finally?"

Ashley grabbed her pajamas and got to her feet. "*I'm* going next."

When it was Summer's turn, she insisted that Layla come with her. Then Janice came in and kissed them goodnight. A little while later Toni came upstairs to put the baby down. She tiptoed back to the door and said softly, "Lights out."

Layla hunched a shoulder. "I'm reading."

"Mom," Ashley whined, "you *know* I can't sleep with the light on." Toni flicked the light switch and the room went dark. Layla closed her book, making a mental note to scrounge up a flashlight so she could read under the covers. She'd barely fallen asleep when the baby started squalling. He screamed until Toni climbed the stairs, plucked him from his crib and paced the floor between the beds, murmuring, "Hush, hush." When he shrieked louder Layla bunched her pillow over her ears. Moving them into this zoo was *so* typical of her mom, who was born way back in 1962, the last of the hippie-dippies. That was why Layla and Summer had stupid names and dads they'd never met, why they'd grown up in an apartment draped in Indian-print bedspreads, Joni Mitchell's twittering voice the soundtrack of their Sunday mornings.

At breakfast the next day Layla wondered if Beth Mayer's gentle brown eyes and sweet smile meant she was a kind, gentle person. As she and Beth cleared the table, Layla asked if she could share the garage with her. Beth pretended to consider it, then shook her head. "It's my dream time, my alone time, my poetry time—"

"Your touching-yourself time?"

"Watch your mouth." Her cheeks pink, Beth stalked out of the kitchen.

怀 怀 怀 怀

Gradually they established a summer routine. Saturday mornings they grumbled through chores, and in the afternoons two of the moms took the kids to the beach, a movie or maybe the Oaks mall while the third mom had the afternoon and evening off. Sundays were spent playing video games and watching television, or if you were Ashley and thought you were God's gift to boys, locking yourself in the bathroom to preen.

Weekdays were less regimented, but a lot worse. When Janice first proposed her "concept for communal living," she'd said the key ingredient was Toni, who got child support *and* alimony from the dickhead who'd cheated on her while she was pregnant. A stay-at-home mom, Toni could watch the kids while Janice and Lisa were at work. This, according to Janice, was the brilliance of her plan. Their children wouldn't be latchkey kids, and their combined incomes would more than cover the mortgage and expenses. So they'd be better off together than they'd been on their own.

But it wasn't long before Layla hated the commune house. Lisa Mayer was cool—she didn't mind if they got loud, and she cooked the best dinners. But Toni kept threatening to chop off Summer's tangled blond hair. And she was full of bullshit theories to justify being mean, like when she screamed at Ben for splattering the toilet, AKA *behaving like a typical male-hauvinistic pig.* Hell, he was only twelve, even if he was a snot-nosed moron who left his smelly socks all over the house.

Layla escaped as often as she could, wandering the streets in search of friends with normal families. But the neighborhood kids had heard about the strange setup at 1014 Oak Knoll Lane. They asked if the commune moms were dykes, if their kids came from sperm banks. The boys asked if Layla wanted to fuck, if she could score them some weed. She ended up spending July and August under an oak on the hill behind their house, reading *The Chronicles of Narnia* to her sister while the tall grass turned to straw in the sun. They'd just started the second book, *Prince Caspian*, when Summer put her hand on the page and asked, "Do you think it'll be like this forever?"

Layla sighed. "Well, not *forever.* In fact I bet we're out of here by spring, next summer at the latest." She watched a small white butterfly climb a grass stalk. "Remember when Mom started talking about the commune house?"

Summer nodded. "But I didn't really understand what it meant."

"Yeah, I don't think I did, either. Anyway, she said her biggest concern was their periods. You know what a period is, Summer?"

"It's when Mom gets crabby and uses tampons."

Layla nodded. "She said when she worked at Dark Star Films, all her coworkers started having their periods at the same time." Layla grinned. "Picture it—all the moms bitching about whose turn it is to do the laundry. Toni will call Lisa a lard-ass, and Mom will say Toni's selfish, and balooey, the whole thing will blow up like a Wile E. Coyote booby trap."

Summer gave a wan smile and murmured, "Stupid Coyote." She always rooted for the Road Runner while Layla kept hoping Coyote would nab the smug bird. "What'll happen then, Layla?"

"One of the moms will move out. Pretty soon they'll explode again, blam! And we'll lose the other mom."

"Will we have to go back to the apartment? I don't like it here, but I like coming to our tree."

"I don't *think* we'll go back, but who knows? Maybe Mom will sell you to the circus. You know, as a baboon."

॰ఢ॰ ఢ॰ ఢ॰ ఢ॰

The last Sunday of summer vacation, the moms decided to spend some "private time" with their kids. After lunch Layla woke up from a nap in the blessedly empty "children's space" and went downstairs, yawning and rubbing her eyes. The house was quiet except for the television's murmur in the family room and an odd *ffht, ffht* coming from the living room, where Layla found her mom spray-painting big yellow letters on the wall behind the couch. Janice had shoved the couch aside and was standing on clear plastic sheeting. As she sprayed she sang, "Well there's a hmm, and a distant hmm, and the eagle flies, with the dove. If you can't be, with the one you love, hmm, love the one you're with." She shook the paint can, its insides clacking like castanets, and sprayed another word. Yellow paint dribbled down the wall. When Janice stepped back, the big letters spelled TOLERANCE + PATIENCE = SERENITY. "Well?" she asked. "What do you think?"

"Graffiti's *so* played, Mom."

Janice squirted paint thinner on a rag and wiped off the drips. "It expresses my hope—my lodestar, if you will—for social evolution, starting right here in this house."

"Just so you know, graffiti's an *outdoor* sport—at least for normal people."

Janice squinted at her handiwork. "Do you think it needs an exclamation point?"

The front door opened and Lisa Mayer came in, her arms full of shopping bags, her elbow propping open the door for Beth and Ben. "We've been to the mall," she said breathlessly. "Back-to-school clothes." Her voice faltered. She thrust the shopping bags at her kids. "Go put these in my bedroom, okay?" Beth strolled off swinging a Charlotte Russe bag. Moonfaced Ben trudged after her with the rest of the bags.

Janice smiled, her hands on her hips. "What do you think, Lisa?"

"I think you should have brought this to a house meeting." Lisa stepped closer to read the yellow words. "It's a nice sentiment, but this is communal space."

Janice narrowed her eyes. "I didn't think there'd be any objection."

The Road Runner beeped from the family room. Any minute Wile E. Coyote would blow himself to smithereens. But Layla didn't want to miss any real-life explosions, so she backed into the rocking chair by the front window.

"Why don't we just wipe it off before Toni gets back," Lisa suggested, "and vote on it at the meeting tonight?"

"Why don't we leave it and see if Toni objects?"

Lisa shrugged. "Fine. Don't say I didn't warn you." As she went down the hall she glanced back and said, "Don't forget, it's your turn to make dinner tonight."

When Lisa's bedroom door shut, Layla said, "You own this house, don't you, Mom? I mean, they pay you rent, but it's our house. So if you want to write shit on the walls, they can't stop you."

"You think you're a regular Svengali, don't you? Rasputin without the beard."

Layla eyed her mother. "Am I supposed to know what you're talking about? Because if so—not."

"You'd just love me to get into it with Lisa and Toni. Well, if they want me to wipe it off, I will. I just want Toni to see it first—get the impact before they decide."

"We hate it here," Layla whined. "Toni's a bitch when you and Lisa aren't around. She screams at Summer all the time, Mom, and at Ben, too."

Janice hesitated. "Well, school starts tomorrow. You won't have to put up with her so much then. Tolerance plus patience, Layla. We can change the world."

Layla rolled her eyes. "Whatever."

That night the moms held the weekly house meeting in the master bedroom, kids excluded. Layla heard shouting, but they emerged an hour later, smiling and misty eyed, their commitment to communal living undiminished. Soon they were laughing, drinking wine and blasting Macy Gray while they scrubbed off the yellow paint. Then they pushed the couch farther back and danced in their socks on the plastic sheeting. Summer, Ashley and Beth giggled and nudged each other, then hurried onto the impromptu dance floor.

Peering into the living room from the stairs, Layla watched Summer twirl in slow circles, her long yellow hair fanning out. To join them would be to admit defeat, so Layla went into the kitchen, poured a glass of wine, stole three Virginia Slims from Beth's purse and went outside. She shut the sliding glass doors behind her, muffling the music and laughter. Sitting cross-legged in the shadows on the concrete patio, she gazed up at glinting stars and sipped her wine. It tasted like paint thinner, and the cigarette made her queasy. But she kept sipping and puffing until she felt giddy—tipsy, she decided.

Ben pushed open the door and shuffled out onto the patio. He sniffed the air, then came over to Layla, his face a plump moon peering down at her. "You got any more?" he asked.

"Any more what?"

"Cigs. Duh."

Layla held out her half-empty glass. "Fill this up and I'll give you one."

"Consider it done." Ben went inside and returned a few minutes later with two full glasses. He pushed back his bangs and smiled. "They opened a ginormous bottle." Layla gave him a cigarette and the matchbook she'd found in Beth's purse. Ben finally got a match lit, sucked on the cigarette and coughed up the smoke.

"First time?" Layla asked scornfully.

"What, you're an expert?"

She grinned and lit her last cigarette, watched their mingled smoke arabesque into the night.

"Do you like this?" Ben asked.

"The wine?" Layla wrinkled her nose.

"No, living here."

"Are you kidding? It's the summer camp that wouldn't die.

Schedules and field trips, lining up with paper plates for dinner." Layla hunched a shoulder. "I just want it to end so I can go home, but I'm *already* home. Now you're gonna tell me you love it."

"Not hardly." Ben puffed gingerly on his cigarette. "Toni can't stand me, in case you didn't notice. But hey, if the Momsters are gonna throw parties like this, it won't be so bad."

Layla smiled. "The Momsters, that's good. Can I ask you something, Ben? Do you, well, do you and Beth have a dad?"

"Yeah, but we hardly ever see him." Ben picked up a pebble, tossed it onto the dark lawn. "He's living his own life, I guess, and that's cool. But Beth hates him."

Layla had to admit Janice was right, life did get easier once school started. Dispersed into elementary, middle, and high school, from Summer to Beth they embraced their anonymity. As Ben said, his eyebrows scrunched in imitation of Toni's earnest look, "Separation is beneficial to individuation." Ashley and Layla were in the same class, but Ashley was one of the popular girls who ignored Layla— which was *totally* fine. Layla made friends with three smart, disgruntled girls and spent as much time as she could at their houses.

That was why she didn't notice the storm brewing until the first blast swept through the house in late October. It was a Saturday night, cold and rainy, so Lisa Mayer lit the family room's gas fireplace and made a huge batch of buttery, salty popcorn. The younger kids were sprawled on the couch watching *Harry Potter and the Prisoner of Azkaban* on HBO while Lisa and Beth worked on a jigsaw puzzle at the kitchen table. When Janice appeared in the doorway wearing tight jeans and a red sweater, her dark hair shining, Layla whispered to Summer, "Mom's got a date." Summer nodded, her mouth open as she watched Harry Potter race through Hogwarts.

"I'm going out for a while," Janice announced.

Lisa frowned. "But it's Toni's night off."

"I didn't think you'd miss me if I went out for a bit."

Beth flapped her hands as if shooing a cat. "Go. We'll hold down the fort."

"Thanks, I love you both!" Janice blew them kisses, then tossed a kiss to her daughters and rushed out. The front door slammed behind her.

Later on, Lisa grumbled to herself while she herded the kids to bed, and her mutters increased as she tromped up and down the stairs to stop giggling and squabbles. Around midnight Layla woke up to Toni yelling about irresponsible people who didn't answer their cell phones. It might have blown over if Janice had come home, but she didn't show up until the next afternoon. Lisa was ready to call the police when Janice drifted into the family room, her lips parted in a dreamy smile. Lisa and Toni were sitting at the kitchen table, their arms folded and their faces stony. Janice flung up her hands. "I know! I know! I'm sorry, but it was a magic night."

Toni aimed the remote at the television and clicked it off. Lisa shooed the kids out of the room and shot a stern look at Beth, who said, "I want to hear all about it later, Janice."

"You, too, Layla," Toni said. So Layla went upstairs, then crept back down to the bottom step in time to hear Lisa say, "Of course we understand love. In fact, didn't I say at the start that the biggest threat to our stability was romantic involvement?"

"It was just one night," Janice protested.

"You had a one-night stand?" Toni sounded outraged.

Janice laughed. "Oh, like you've never had one, Toni. But no, it wasn't like that. I met him at a studio screening. We're going out again next weekend."

"Excuse me," Lisa said, "But next weekend's *my* turn."

"Well it's not like you ever go anywhere," Janice snapped.

Layla heard rustling, turned to find Ashley crouched on the stairs above her, her dark eyes shining. She nudged Layla's shoulder with her knee, and they both smiled.

"So the rules apply to everyone but you, is that it?" Toni asked.

"Toni, this is supposed to make our lives better, not turn us into Nazis. I can't believe you guys are making such a big deal out of this."

"You broke the rules," Lisa said in a stern mom voice. "That's a big deal."

"And excuse me," Toni snapped, "but did you just call me a Nazi?"

"I didn't *call* you a Nazi, Toni. I said I don't want us to *turn into* Nazis. Look, how about if we change the rules so Saturday nights it's only one of us on duty, two of us off, and maybe one of us off Friday nights, too."

Layla pictured their thoughtful looks and tilted heads as they pondered Janice's suggestion.

"Well," Lisa said grudgingly, "that sounds reasonable."

Layla whispered, "Shit." Ashley rose silently and went back upstairs.

"But what about staying out all night?" Toni asked. "And all the next day. You didn't even bother to pick up your cell. What if Summer or Layla got sick?"

"I'm sorry." Janice's apologetic tone didn't quite hide her elation. "I was irresponsible. It won't happen again."

That evening Janice told Layla that she was in love with a film writer named Paul Beauvais, who'd moved to Los Angeles from Georgia three years ago to pitch his screenplays. When Layla and Summer met Paul over hamburgers and fries at Dupar's in Thousand Oaks, Layla wasn't impressed. Freckled and nervous, he had stringy arms and a narrow chest, and just like their mom he tried to look younger than he was—tight black tee-shirt and jeans, his thin ginger hair in a straggly ponytail. But Summer looked into his kind green eyes and said, "I like him," which was all the approval Janice seemed to need.

"What if he's playing you?" Layla asked on the drive home. "Just using you to get a screenplay optioned?"

"You're such a worrywart. As a matter of fact, the only scripts he's got out right now are at Cinebar and FilmWest." Janice glanced at Layla. "Anyway, he's thinking about moving back to Georgia."

"You aren't serious."

"About what?"

"You want to go with him, don't you?"

Janice glanced into the rearview mirror. "Keep your voice down."

Layla twisted around to look at Summer asleep and drooling in the back seat. "Answer my question, Mom."

"Jesus, Layla, it's complicated, okay? The whole house thing is just—well, complicated. I thought Toni would drive me nuts, but Lisa *grills* me every time I leave the house." Janice gave a tight smile. "I guess now we know why her husband left her."

Layla rolled her eyes. "So much for feminist solidarity."

"I know, baby, but solidarity doesn't mean ignoring the facts."

"So when are we leaving?"

Janice reached over and smoothed Layla's hair. "We're a long way from a decision, honey. We've only been dating a few weeks."

The following Friday Janice stayed out all night again. When Layla came downstairs Saturday morning, Lisa and Toni were folding laundry in the living room. Hearing her mom's name, Layla sank down on the stairs and hugged her knees.

"She gets us to move in with her and cover her mortgage, then she parks her kids with us and takes off," Toni said.

Layla pressed her forehead to her knees. She was a stray dog, fed and sheltered out of pity. Her mom had parked her, and her dad was only a few old photos and her mom's reminiscences. In some of Janice's stories he was a fiery idealist, in others a hound dog who got Janice pregnant, then trotted off wagging his tail. Either way, he was long gone.

"Janice didn't plan on falling in love," Lisa said. "It just happened. But I wish she'd come down from cloud nine. I mean, I've already got my hands full, and Layla's thirteen now—that's when Beth started fooling around with cigarettes and boyfriends."

"Tell me about it. All Ashley ever thinks about is guys and

makeup. But what really gets me is that tonight's *our* night off. And it doesn't matter that you weren't going anywhere, Lisa. You still deserve a night to yourself." Toni lowered her voice. "The thing is, I think..." As Layla strained to hear the rest of it, the garage door slammed and Ben thundered down the hall into the living room. "Mom!" he hollered, "Beth's picking on me!"

Beth was spending the night at a friend's house, so Toni cancelled her plans and stayed home to help Lisa get dinner on, both their faces grim. Even the baby sensed the tension. He sat quietly in his highchair while his big sister Ashley fed him mashed peas and carrots, his round eyes following his mom. Watching television after dinner, the kids kept glancing uneasily at the two women, who were sharing a bottle of wine at the kitchen table, their low voices edged with anger. Around nine Janice breezed in, her cheeks flushed, raindrops spangling her dark hair. Toni said, "We need to talk."

Janice gave a wry smile. "My bedroom?"

As soon as they shut themselves into the master bedroom, Layla, Ben, and Ashley tiptoed down the hall to listen at the door. Lisa's voice was a soft mumble, but they heard Toni insist that Janice had an "ethical obligation" to sell the house to Lisa and get the hell out. "Oh, and don't forget your kids," Toni added, "because we're tired of raising them for you."

"That's harsh," Ashley whispered.

"Actually, that's perfect," Janice said. "Paul's asked me to marry him. He's moving back to Georgia in November, and the girls and I are joining him at Christmas. So, hey, the house is yours, Lisa."

They all gabbled at once, Lisa high-pitched and congratulatory, Janice excited, Toni still angry. As the clamor neared the door, the eavesdroppers ran upstairs and flopped onto Ben's bed. Rain drummed on the dormer windows. Ben switched on his bedside lamp, and they looked at each other.

"That sucks," Ashley said glumly. "Ben and me are still stuck here."

"And I have to move to some bogus town in Georgia so my

mom can marry some random guy." Layla shook her head. "I never thought I'd say this, but I'd rather be here."

Once Lisa and Janice agreed on a price and signed the papers, the moms became better friends than ever, as if they were already nostalgic for the good old days that would end when Janice moved out. For Thanksgiving, they planned a feast with as many friends as they each wanted to invite—a festive open house from early afternoon until, Lisa said, the cows came home.

In the days before Thanksgiving, the moms bustled around, cleaning, decorating, running to the grocery store, asking each other how many sweet potatoes to buy, and should they get a ham, too? Laughing and squabbling like grownup sisters, they drank wine and played music late into the night—Sheryl Crow and Tracy Chapman, the Doobie Brothers, Fleetwood Mac. Toni put on the Pretenders and danced around the family room playing a mean air guitar—her fingers frenzied, her spiky black hair bouncing to "Back on the Chain Gang" and "Middle of the Road." Beth and Summer got the giggles, and the baby beamed astride Ashley's hip. Even Layla felt the sense of anticipation.

And when Thanksgiving arrived it was a wonderful day, the house fragrant with pumpkin and cherry pie, roast turkey and sweet potatoes. The moms laughed and flirted and let the kids run wild. After dinner Layla and Ben pilfered cigarettes from several coats and purses and a wine bottle from the counter, then met on the patio. Their backs against the house, they squatted on their heels above the cold concrete while they drank red wine from plastic cups, lit their cigarettes with kitchen matches. Layla held a match while its flame dwindled. "Why does it have to be so confusing?" she asked.

Ben shifted on his heels to face her. "Come again?"

"All I've ever wanted is a normal family—a house with a mom and dad. But now that it's happening, I don't want it anymore."

"That's what the Momsters never think about," Ben said. "What *we* want. They throw us together and tell us to get along, then they rip us apart. And if they feel guilty for like, a second, one of them says, oh kids are tough, they'll get over it."

Layla glanced at his pale pudgy face. "You're so smart," she said. "That's exactly what I mean." She was just tipsy enough to lean forward and kiss him on the lips. His eyes widened. When he opened his mouth to hers, his breath stank of smoke and his tongue was sour but she wanted more. Like alcohol and cigarettes, it was disgusting at first but then you wanted more. When Ben closed his eyes, she closed hers too. His hand touched her cheek. The sliding door scraped open and they turned to blink into the light.

It was Ashley, clutching a glass of wine and frowning into the darkness. When Layla hissed, "Over here," Ashley joined them in the shadows. She'd filched a cigarette from Beth, who, she said, was flirting with some hairy old guy from Lisa's office.

"A Momster in training," Ben scoffed. "You want to play spin the bottle, Ash?"

Ashley pouted. "I'm not kissing you."

Ben leaned forward and kissed her on the lips. She gasped and jerked away, then tilted her head, her dark eyes considering. Eyebrows raised, she smiled at Layla, who promptly kissed her. Ashley's mouth was softer than Ben's, a small pillow. Layla pulled away and reached for Ben. Their lips and tongues touched. Then they were laughing and Ashley was lighting a cigarette while Ben poured more wine. Huddled against the cold, they held their own farewell party, and Layla knew that their miserable, giddy joy meant they'd found something at the very moment it was lost to them forever.

ৡৡৡ৶

Lisa and her kids were spending the holidays with her parents in Palm Springs, and Toni had taken her kids to her sister's house in San Francisco. A few days before Christmas, Layla watched a moving van pull into the driveway to haul her family's belongings to a

far-off place called Athens, Georgia. The next morning she helped
her mom search the house for forgotten items like Summer's mermaid night light and Janice's ratty old pink slippers. Finally they
got in the car, Layla in the front seat, Summer in the back in a nest
of pillows, blankets and coloring books. They'd spend Christmas
with their grandmother in Phoenix, then follow Interstate 10 clear
across the country.

"I'm glad it turned out this way," Janice said. She backed down
the driveway into the street, dead leaves crackling under the tires.
"I started something good here. I'm glad they'll keep it going when
we're gone."

As they drove away Layla twisted around for a last glimpse.
The house looked dead, no lights shining through the curtained
windows. When they turned the corner Summer said, "We're a family again."

"What did you say, baby?" Janice asked.

"Nothing, Mom."

Her forehead pressed to the cold glass, Layla stared bleakly out
her window as if she already knew about the flat tire in El Paso, the
rainstorm that would strand them in Houston for three days, her
mom's regret when she realized she was stronger and smarter than
the man she'd married. But even if Layla had known, she wouldn't
have said a word because she recognized the doomed eager light
in her mother's eyes. As they drove east into the rising sun, Layla
faced forward and fastened her seat belt.

HOUSE OF DUST

On a hot, still afternoon with heavy white clouds shadowing the town, a two-story clapboard house on Boulevard groaned, its frame shuddering as an interior bearing wall buckled. The wall's slow collapse pulled down two upstairs rooms and dislodged the ridge beam from the roof. The massive beam plunged through the broken floorboards and slammed into another bearing wall. Stricken, the house heaved forward onto its knees, then imploded in a billowing cloud of dust and shrieking birds.

Across the street, Miss Thalia was in the kitchen watering her African violets. At first she thought the low rumble was a passing freight train. Then screeching birds and snapping timbers drew her into the front parlor to peer through her lace curtains. Tawny dust billowed up from the magnolia trees in Leona Davis's front yard. When the dust thinned, a mountain of rubble appeared where Leona's ramshackle clapboard house had stood, disgracing Boulevard's historic elegance with its peeling white paint and sagging green shutters.

Pleased that Leona wasn't immune to divine retribution yet mindful of her civic duty, Miss Thalia dialed 911. Then she called the Normaltown Café and left a message for Leona that her house was gone. Her conscience appeased, she returned to the window.

Leona ran across the back parking lot to the road that wound past the creek and over to Boulevard—a mile in the sticky heat. Out of breath, she trudged along the road, her mouth pinched and her vision blurred. Forty-seven years old and homeless—what was she supposed to do? She kept picturing her house. What did that mean, *gone?* Had it burned down? She pressed her clasped hands to her mouth and whispered, "Let Henry be okay."

When she got home she hurried past a fire truck and started up her front walk, then stopped to gasp at the mound of rubble. The chimney had gaping holes she could see the sky through. Shattered glass glinted on broken boards, twisted rebar, and chunks of brick. A red lace bra dangled from an exposed pipe, and a splintered chest of drawers teetered halfway down the staircase. A fireman clambered down from the rubble to meet her. Under a mask of dust his face was young, his blue eyes earnest. "You live here, ma'am?"

Leona nodded, transfixed by the monstrous pile. "Have you seen a big orange cat?" she asked. The fireman smiled and patted her shoulder. "Cats spook at the first sign of trouble. It'll turn up."

She gestured toward the rubble. "Can I see if there's anything left?"

"Better wait a while, ma'am. We've turned off the gas, but we still don't know what happened."

All afternoon and into the dusk Miss Thalia glimpsed Leona clambering around the rubble, lugging what she could salvage into a pile in the grass. Common decency demanded that Miss Thalia offer Leona shelter for the night, but decency also forbade letting a woman like Leona cross her threshold. Why didn't Leona just go to a motel, Miss Thalia thought fretfully. The mosquitoes were going to eat her alive.

As darkness fell, bats swooped around a streetlamp and the night buzzed with cicadas. Leona got a flashlight out of her car, and its beam flitted through the shadows like a monstrous lightning bug. A car pulled up and a heavyset couple got out. Squinting, Miss Thalia recognized Frank's older brother, Jed, and his wife. Jed switched on a flashlight, and they helped Leona stow her belongings in her Thunderbird. Then they got in their cars and drove off. Miss Thalia let the curtain drop. At last she could go to bed.

వ్ వ్ అ్ అ్

Termites, thousands of the tiny white grubs, had infested Leona's house for at least a decade, soundlessly munching support beams and floorboards from the inside out. The *Athens Banner-Herald* ran an article about the collapsed house, listing the warning signs of eastern subterranean termite infestation and urging readers to have their homes inspected. Apparently everyone in town read the article. At the café Leona couldn't help noticing the mild contempt in her customers' eyes as they questioned her. Was she home when it happened? Did she have somewhere to stay? And the unspoken question, don't you know these old wooden houses get infested? Leona had always prided herself on her self-reliance, but Frank had taken care of things like plumbing and termite inspections. In the years since his death she'd grown used to the house's slow decay, the long list of things that needed fixing.

When Maggie, the dark-eyed whirlwind who owned the café, asked if she planned to rebuild with the insurance money, Leona sighed. "We paid off the mortgage before Frank died, but I couldn't keep up with the insurance on my own."

Maggie sat down beside Leona, who was folding napkins at the bar before the lunch rush. "So what are you going to do?"

"I don't know. I still can't find Henry." Leona stared at the napkin in her hands. "And the city's threatened to fine me if I don't clear away the rubble. They say the chimney's an attractive nuisance."

"Not a problem," Maggie said cheerfully. "I'll ask Tom to do it."
"I wasn't hinting, Maggie."
"What good is it being married to a contractor if you can't help out your friends?"

Leona thanked Maggie, though accepting charity galled her, as did the glass jar Maggie set by the cash register for donations to the Leona Davis Fund. But the jar did some good. Foxy's Bar next door set out a jar too, and so did the antique shop and the beauty parlor. In three days, the combined donations were nearly three hundred dollars. Not enough to build a house but enough to replace some clothes, buy a new alarm clock.

After her Friday lunch shift Leona drove over to Boulevard. Grass was sprouting between the splintered planks and broken bricks Tom's crew had missed. Squatting on her heels, she opened a can of cat food onto a pie tin and called for Henry, as she had for the last three days. This time she heard a raspy meow, then two pale green eyes peered from the hedge and the cat crawled out. He was thin, the pale tufts under his flanks matted and dirty, but purrs rumbled in his chest as he crouched over the food. When he finished Leona picked him up, and he buried his head in her armpit. "What am I going to do with you?" she muttered.

She stood up, her knee cracking. Henry wriggled loose and leapt to the ground. Her hands in her pockets, she walked through the vanished house and out the invisible back door, then sat down on the picnic table under the mulberry tree. She lit a cigarette, looked around. She could pitch a tent beside the picnic table, buy a charcoal grill to cook on. The Chevron station had a bathroom, and she could beg showers from Deb or one of the other waitresses. But north Georgia winters were cold. What would she do then?

She hadn't cried yet and she didn't feel like crying now. Tears were for your husband killed by a drunk driver on the Atlanta highway. Yet the house had become a part of her, like her teeth or fingernails or a tortoise's shell—her refuge from the world's harsh light. Its dim high-ceilinged rooms had witnessed her happiness with Frank, and after his death, when she'd gone wild with grief, the house had waited until she subsided into gin and memories.

Last summer a pair of drug addicts had broken in through the back door and she'd had to shoot one of them. The experience had shocked her awake, and she'd finally noticed her own life tiptoeing past her. So she'd enrolled in an art class, volunteered at the animal shelter. But the apples she painted were misshapen red blobs, and caring for the shelter's doomed cats and dogs depressed her. Discouraged, she'd returned to her cool quiet rooms, but they no longer lulled her into a waking trance.

The red flicker of a cardinal swooped past, trailing a low, sweet whistle. She should have counted her blessings, should have been grateful for a roof over her head.

The swath of pale blue beyond the magnolias was Miss Thalia's house, a stately Victorian with white gingerbread trim built by the old lady's grandfather in 1889. For nearly twenty-five years Miss Thalia had peeped through her lace curtains, deploring the scandalous goings-on across the street and watching Leona's house fall into disrepair. But there hadn't been any goings-on since Jesse skipped town last summer after heating her bed and her heart. And now even the house itself was gone, all traces of her lovers crushed to dust. Gazing through the magnolia trees, Leona wondered if Miss Thalia had already climbed the stairs for her afternoon nap.

When the doorbell chimed Miss Thalia laid aside the *Smithsonian* magazine and rose from her wing-back chair. Beyond the locked screen door Leona Davis hugged her elbows and stared down at the welcome mat. Raffish as usual, a loud floral shirt tucked into tight jeans, her pale auburn hair an unruly mop to her shoulders—unbecoming on a woman her age. When Leona glanced up and saw the old lady through the screen, she hastily stepped back. "Afternoon, Miss Thalia."

Miss Thalia's hand rose to her throat. "Yes, Leona?" she asked in a dry, raspy voice. "I'd ask you in, but I'm about to lie down for my nap."

"This will only take a minute. Would you rent me the carriage house? You don't have anyone in there now, do you?"

"Not at the moment, no. Callie graduated in May, and I've not found anyone suitable yet."

Leona spoke in a rush, her eyes downcast. "I hate asking you, Miss Thalia. It's hard, begging a favor like this, from you—"

"I'm sure it is."

"It's just that I can't bear to leave here."

Miss Thalia hesitated, then unlocked the screen door and pushed it open. "You'd better come inside." She blinked at the bright day. "Warming up, isn't it?"

As she led Leona into the parlor, she said, "To own the truth, I've been thinking of making some repairs before I rent it out again. The stove's almost as old as I am, and the paint's peeling in the bedroom. Sit down, won't you?"

Sitting on the edge of the couch, Leona ventured a smile. "I'd feel right at home with peeling paint and a cranky stove."

"Don't you have any other options? Where are you staying now?"

"With Frank's brother and his wife, but they don't have much room and she's allergic to cats."

Miss Thalia twitched aside the lace curtains and peered out. "Wouldn't you be more comfortable in an apartment, dear?"

"I've lived on Boulevard *so* long, I'd be homesick anywhere else." Leona met Miss Thalia's unyielding gaze. "Please. I'd be *so* grateful."

The old lady turned away to stare grimly out the window. Outrageous to be importuned by such a woman. On the other hand Jesus himself had let a prostitute dry his feet with her hair. She signaled her decision with a faint sigh. "You can stay for a while. A very short while."

"Thank you." Leona bit her lip. "I'm afraid I can't afford to pay you much."

"How does twenty-five dollars a week sound?"

Leona flushed. "I can manage more than that, Miss Thalia."

"Twenty-five is fine. And a fifty-dollar cleaning fee, for the cat." Miss Thalia walked over to the spindle-legged table by her chair, opened her handbag and pulled out a large silver key. "Just leave it as clean as you find it, and no smoking."

Leona groped in her purse for her checkbook. As she wrote out the check, she asked, "Can I smoke on that upstairs porch?"

Picturing cigarette burns on the white wicker porch furniture, smoke befouling the scent of wisteria, Miss Thalia opened her mouth to say no. But Leona's downcast eyes and tight smile revealed how humiliating this interview was for her. "If you must," Miss Thalia said. "Here's the key. You can move in when it suits you. Now, if you'll pardon me—"

Leona grabbed her purse and stood up. "Of course." She went to the door and stepped out onto the porch. As the screen door slapped shut, Leona turned and met the old woman's mildly affronted gaze. "How can I ever thank you?"

Miss Thalia sniffed. "Just don't burn the place down, is all I ask."

Leona nodded, then ran down the walk, her footsteps light as a girl's. A home on Boulevard, right across the street—even if it was temporary. She hurried across the avenue and into her front yard, calling for Henry. As she emptied another can of food into the pie tin she told the cat their good news. "She made me grovel, but it's got a kitchen, a bed, a washer and dryer. We can sleep there tonight, Henry."

She knelt to pet him, curving her hand over his back. Then she rose and walked swiftly through the trees to her yellow Thunderbird. As she opened the car door she glanced across the street, picturing the old lady lying rigid on her bed praying for deliverance from her new tenant.

Miss Thalia lay on her back under a faded patchwork quilt praying for guidance. The ornate little china clock that had been her mother's ticked steadily on the bedside table beside her old Bible, its black leather cover faded gray at the corners. She already regretted her decision, but if the good Lord saw fit for her to shelter a loose woman, then it was her duty to figure out what His plan was.

For twenty-five years now, Leona had been a blight on Miss Thalia's immediate horizon. When the young couple first moved in she'd paid them a visit, bearing a peach pie warm from the oven. She'd known Frank since he was a teenager working summers in his father's hardware store, a quiet, respectful boy, and he'd returned from the Navy a good-looking young man. But his barefoot bride, in her dungarees and skimpy blouse, a cigarette jutting from her reddened lips, had no manners at all.

And then the parties—blaring music and drunken laughter, cars coming and going at all hours. And on hot summer nights the whole street had to listen to love noises coming from their dark bedroom. Oh, she'd pitied Leona when Frank died so young, but it wasn't long before there were men, one after another, half-naked on the front balcony, or drinking beer from a can on the front porch, laughing with Leona, slapping her on the behind. Almost like living across the street from a bordello. Though Leona had settled down in the last few years, no longer dragged home every Tom, Dick and Harry. Well, her house falling down surely was a judgment on her, but it might also be the Lord's way of leading her to salvation.

The next morning, Leona sat on the upstairs porch of the carriage house reading Colleen McCullough's *The First Man in Rome*, a much pleasanter way to broaden her horizons than painting misshapen fruit. A mockingbird sang in the azalea hedge. Turning the page, she felt the tension seep out of her neck and shoulders.

A screen door slapped shut, and Miss Thalia crossed the side lawn. Hands on her hips, she stared over the hedge at the brick house next door, her lips pursed in disapproval. Sunlight shone on her thin white hair and pink scalp. Beyond the hedge a lanky man with a ponytail and a woman in tight jeans and a tank top were hauling boxes from a U-Haul van into the house, assisted by two adolescent girls, one small and blond, one with long brown hair like the woman, who was probably their mother.

Miss Thalia spoke without looking at Leona. "That house used to be the Tate mansion's servants' quarters. I don't know how you can stand it, sitting outside in this heat. You'd be better off inside where it's cool."

Why on earth, Leona wondered, did it matter whether she was hot or cold? Why didn't people leave each other alone? She held up her cigarette. "I was having a smoke."

Miss Thalia sniffed. "Coffin nails, my daddy called them. By any chance are you going by Kroger's today?"

Leona asked if she could pick something up for Miss Thalia, who, it turned out, needed eggs to bake a cake for church tomorrow. "You're welcome to join us," Miss Thalia added as if it were an afterthought.

"Thanks, but I always work brunch on Sundays."

"Well, I won't keep you." Miss Thalia shot a hard look at her new neighbors, then turned away. She meandered across the lawn toward the front porch, pausing every few feet to uproot a weed and fling it onto the brick walk that led from the street to the carriage house.

৬৯ ৬৯ ৵৩ ৵৩

The donation jars collected another two hundred dollars before contributions dwindled to nickels and dimes. Leona put the money in a savings account earmarked for rebuilding—probably an act of futility. The truth was, she thought as drove home from the bank, she needed to find a place to live, not daydream about rebuilding. The carriage house already felt like home, but she couldn't stay there forever. And no bank would loan her the money to rebuild unless she mortgaged her vacant lot. And even then, she couldn't make the payments, not on her waitress's salary.

As Leona went up the brick walk, Miss Thalia came to the door and invited her in for a glass of sweet tea. Leona didn't much like iced tea, but she couldn't refuse her landlady's invitation any more than she could refuse to fetch her groceries. Besides, Miss Thalia made her tea the old-fashioned way, filling large mason jars and letting them brew in the sun. Leona climbed the porch steps and opened the screen door. Miss Thalia bade her sit down in the front parlor and handed her a cold slick glass. Sitting on the edge of the couch, Leona sipped her tea.

"Sweet enough for you?" Miss Thalia asked.

"It's perfect."

Miss Thalia's grim mouth relaxed. She sat down, smoothed her housecoat over her bony knees. "Orange Pekoe, with just a squeeze of lemon. That's the way to make sweet tea. I have a proposition for you, Leona. Our church holds Bible study every Wednesday evening." She held up a hand to forestall Leona's protest. "You attend Bible study, I'll lend you the money to rebuild your house, interest free, with your property as collateral of course. I've discussed it with my pastor and lawyer, and they approve."

Leona opened her mouth, then shut it. Miss Thalia was offering her a way to get her house back, but the price, it seemed, was her soul. She took a deep breath. "It's a generous offer, Miss Thalia. I need to think about it."

๛ ๛ ๛ ๛

"Yes indeed, it's a generous offer," Miss Thalia muttered as she feebly attacked the hydrangea with her pruning shears. It was one of Ester's days, and Miss Thalia was gardening as much to get out of her cleaning woman's way as because the hydrangea needed tending. Her shears drooped as she glanced at the carriage house. She'd been sure she was doing the Lord's work, but there'd been a quiver of resentment in Leona's voice, as if she thought Miss Thalia were a Christian Mephistopheles, an evangelical devil in the guise of a wrinkled old woman.

A scream shattered the afternoon. Miss Thalia jerked around and clutched the shears tighter. Another loud shriek sputtered into giggles. Twigs crackled as the little yellow-haired girl crawled through the hedge, then scrambled to her feet to stand, dirt-smudged and grinning, on Miss Thalia's lawn.

"Summer!" called a high, clear voice. "I told you not to go over there! She'll turn you into a toaster!"

The girl's soft blue eyes widened in dismay. "Oh," she gasped, "I'm sorry, lady. She's kidding, is all."

"Are you aware that you're trespassing?"

"We're playing fox and rabbit," the girl said earnestly. "I'm the rabbit."

The older girl's thin face appeared above the hedge. Under thick eyebrows, cool blue eyes met Miss Thalia's. "I'm sorry," she said. "Summer, get over here, now!"

"That's quite all right," Miss Thalia replied, liking the older girl's direct gaze. "Why don't you come around the hedge and introduce yourself? I promise I won't turn you into a kitchen appliance."

The girl bit her lip, then walked around the hedge and across the sunny lawn. She was dressed in grubby shorts and a tee-shirt like her little sister, with leaves and twigs tangled in her long dark hair.

Miss Thalia introduced herself and shook their dirt-smeared hands, thankful she had on her gardening gloves. The older girl was thirteen-year-old Layla. Her little sister Summer had turned ten in March. When Miss Thalia remarked on their pretty names, Layla looked glum. "They're like, totally embarrassing."

Summer flipped back her tangled gold hair. "I like my name."

"That's because you're too dumb to know how lame it is."

"At least I'm not named after some stupid song." Summer elbowed Layla and sang under her breath, "Lay-ay-la. Got me on my knee-ee-ees."

"And at least you're not named after the comic muse," Miss Thalia said.

Summer looked puzzled. "Comic amuse?"

"No," Layla said impatiently. "Remember the nine ladies dancing in a circle in the Big Golden Book of Myths?"

Summer nodded, her attention wandering to the bumblebees droning above the pink and blue hydrangeas. Her mouth hung open. Clearly not very bright. Miss Thalia turned to Layla. "So, are you all settled in, you and your parents?"

"I guess so." Layla pushed her big toe into the grass. "There don't seem to be many kids around here."

"No, this is an old neighborhood—the houses and the people in them."

A door creaked, and a reedy voice called, "Summer! Layla!"

"That's Paul, the stepdad." Layla rolled her eyes. "We'd better go."

"I like your garden," Summer announced. "It's all flowers and grass and sunshine."

"Thank you, dear."

"Come on, Summer. No, not under the hedge. You're not a rabbit anymore." As they hurried toward the sidewalk, Layla hollered, "Coming, Paul!"

Miss Thalia shaded her eyes against the sun. Nice enough girls, but noisy, and no manners. She hoped they wouldn't be a nuisance. Still, their young voices might be a pleasant change from the habitual quiet of her days.

A window sash rattled, and Ester's wrinkled brown face appeared. "You should come in out of that sun, Miss Thalia. I've got sweet tea and vanilla wafers set out for you on the side porch."

She should have offered the girls some cookies. On second thought, they were too dirty to let in the house. And they'd probably think she was fattening them up for the oven like Hansel and Gretel. Slowly pulling off her gloves, she smiled at her cleaning woman. "Thank you, Ester. I'll be in directly."

ও ও ও ও

After her dinner shift Leona ran into Dwight Jordan in the back parking lot the Normaltown Café shared with Foxy's. "You working vice now?" she asked. "I almost didn't recognize you in street clothes."

The big blond cop smiled. "I'm off duty, and it looks like you are, too. Why don't you let me buy you a drink?"

So she accompanied him through the back door into Foxy's dark basement bar. Seated at the bar with their drinks, Leona told him about Miss Thalia's proposition. When she finished he asked, "So are you gonna do it?"

Envisioning her house reborn, with fresh white paint, dark green shutters and shining hardwood floors, Leona said, "One minute I think I'd be a fool to turn her down. But then I think about being in her debt for the rest of my life."

The bartender set down a bowl of popcorn. Dwight grabbed a handful. "Seems likely you'll outlive her."

"She'll probably live another twenty years. I'll die of lung cancer before then."

"Not if you quit smoking."

Leona stared at the bubbles in her gin and tonic. "If my dad were alive, he'd be shouting hallelujahs right about now."

"How's that?" Dwight glanced around the bar. Leona wondered if he was bored.

"My folks were hardcore bible-thumpers." She shrugged, forced a smile. "I bet they'd think a weekly bible class was the perfect punishment for my sinful life."

Three young men thumped down the steps from Foxy's upstairs restaurant and sauntered over to a pool table. As the billiard balls scattered across the green felt and tumbled into pockets, Leona said, "Frank and I used to play pool here."

"You still miss him."

"I'm used to it."

"A fact of life?" he asked.

"I guess you could call it that."

"What happened to that guy you were with last summer?"

"Jesse? He moved to Atlanta." Leona forced a smile. "I don't seem to have a lot of luck with men."

"That's not what I hear."

When Leona punched his shoulder he grabbed her wrist and

swiveled her barstool toward his, their faces close. As she stared into his blond-lashed eyes, he smiled, let her go. "Sorry, but you ought to know better than to startle a cop."

"I do now." She scowled and rubbed her wrist. "I bet that leaves a bruise."

He lifted her wrist and lightly kissed it. Flustered, she said, "Is that what you do when you make an arrest?"

"Only when they're as pretty as you."

"You must not think I'm all *that* pretty. You've never asked me out."

Dwight grinned. "What do you call this?"

"Two friends having a drink after work."

"Maybe that's why," he mused. "Because I like you. I don't want to mess with our friendship."

"So, you don't like the women you go out with?"

"I'd have to say they're both more and less than friends." He cleared his throat. "Do you *want* me to ask you out?"

"To tell the truth I never thought about it till now. No, a drink with a friend is fine." She gave him a shy, pleased smile. Her relationships with men had always tended toward one goal, her bed. The stasis of friendship, that was a new idea.

 co co co co

Miss Thalia was spending "a fortnight" with her older brother in Charleston and expected Leona's answer when she returned. Sitting on her upstairs porch, Leona wished she could just stay in the carriage house. Fragrant wisteria overhung the porch, the lavender blossoms cascading down the white latticework screen, a shady bower where she could read and think. Hearing whispers and giggles below, she rose and leaned over the rail to find the girls from next door peering up at her. "Hello," she said. "What are you two up to?"

"We wondered what happened to Miss Thalia," said the taller girl. "We haven't seen her in a while." She brushed back her dark bangs. "So we came over to find out."

"Have you found out?"

"We thought maybe you'd tell us."

"Sure, but there's not much to tell. The door's open. Come on up."

Leona stubbed out her cigarette and dumped the overflowing ashtray into the wastebasket while trying to invent a mysterious fate for Miss Thalia. Henry was sprawled in a patch of sunshine, but as the girls' footsteps sounded on the stairs the cat yawned and stretched, then leapt to the porch rail and disappeared into the wisteria. The girls came through the French doors, breathless and fanning themselves. "It's hot up here," exclaimed the smaller gold-haired girl.

"Would you like something to drink? Some 7-Up?" Leona asked.

The little girl nodded, but her sister elbowed her and said, "No thank you."

"Well, have a seat." The girls sat down, hands clasped primly on the table. Leona introduced herself and asked their names and ages. They told her, talking over each other until Leona said, "You don't sound like Georgia peaches."

"We're not," Layla said. "We moved here from California last Christmas, when Mom and Paul got married. We were staying with Paul's parents, but that *clearly* wasn't going to work. So now we live here."

"I'm from California, too, but I've been here, gosh, twenty-six years."

Summer's eyes widened. "You're old. Do you pluck your white hairs like Mom does?"

"Shut up," Layla hissed.

Leona smiled. "I've got bigger things to worry about than a few gray hairs."

"What's the matter?" Summer asked.

"Oh, just grownup problems."

Layla gave a sharp sigh. "Grownups always think their problems are worse than ours. You'd think they'd remember."

"Well, thirteen's a long way from forty-seven. I guess I've forgotten what it's like."

"At least grownups can *do* something. If you're a kid, you can't do a thing if your mom decides to haul you across a million states to a hot, muggy town in the middle of nowhere, where everyone talks like they've swallowed a ton of syrup."

"I like it here," Summer said. "Except how sweaty everything is, and the bugs. I hate bugs, except bumblebees. They're cute. So what happened to Miss Thalia?"

"She's visiting her brother. She'll be back in a few days."

"Is she a witch?" Summer asked.

Leona stifled a grin. "Miss Thalia's nice, but she's, well, strict. Old-fashioned." Pointing across the street, where her mailbox stood orphaned at the curb, she said, "I used to live over there, but termites chewed up my house and it collapsed. Miss Thalia's letting me live here for a while."

Layla sat up straighter. "Do you still get your mail over there?"

When Leona nodded, the girl pushed back her bangs and said, "I think that's cool. A mailbox without a house."

Leona reached for her cigarettes, set the pack down. "Yeah, cool."

꙳ ꙳ ꙳ ꙳

Miss Thalia was due back on Sunday and Leona still hadn't reached a decision. She yearned for the cool dim privacy of her house with its shady magnolia trees. But weekly Bible study, sitting in a folding chair surrounded by the sanctimoniously intolerant—Miss Thalia would own her soul and never let her forget it.

She worked the Saturday dinner shift, and when her last table, a family celebrating a grandmother's birthday, finally left, she carried a tray of empty wineglasses to the café's bar. Dwight was drinking a Pabst Blue Ribbon beer and watching CNN on the television mounted above the bar. A reporter was standing in front of a bomb blast in Baghdad. "God, it's so terrible," Leona said as she set down the tray. "So many people dying when they just want to live their lives."

"I've got a nephew over there," Dwight said. "In the National Guard."

Leona glanced at his freckled weather-beaten face. She guessed he was about fifty, knew he'd been married once. "You have any kids, Dwight?"

"A girl. She's a teacher up in Gainesville." He smiled. "You know you're getting old when you start wishing your kid would settle down and give you some grandchildren. Though you can't help wondering what kind of world they'll live in."

"I don't think about the future much," Leona said. "At least I didn't used to. Now I think about it all the time. And it's one big question mark."

"You haven't made up your mind?"

"I keep swinging back and forth. I want my house, my old life back. But the price tag's pretty steep." Leona shrugged. "Well, I'd better clock out."

"Did you walk to work? I'll give you a lift home."

"You don't have to do that."

"What are friends for?" He drained his beer, put a five on the bar and stood up.

They went out to the parking lot and got into his big black truck. On the drive home Leona gazed out at the wilderness of kudzu along the road. Frogs and rasping cicadas sang in the long summer twilight. Dwight cleared his throat. "If you need someone to cosign a loan, I'd be willing."

Another generous offer, maybe with a different price tag. "That's sweet of you, Dwight. But even with a cosigner, I can't see how I'd make the payments."

Darkness cloaked the street when they reached Miss Thalia's house. Dwight went around to open Leona's door, then took her hand and helped her down. They stood at the curb gazing up at the cloud-wracked moon. When Leona turned her head Dwight's lips brushed hers. He stepped back. "Sorry. I was aiming for your cheek."

She didn't think, just stepped closer and kissed him on the

mouth. When he stiffened she backed away, her face hot with em-
barrassment. A light flared in an upstairs window and Miss Thalia
appeared like an elderly Juliet, a dark silhouette against the lamplight. When the old lady shook her head, Leona hastily thanked
Dwight for the ride and said he'd better go.

"Leona—"

"Please, just go. Damn, I didn't think she'd be back till tomorrow."

"I guess you've made your decision then." When Leona didn't
answer, he said goodnight, climbed into his truck and slammed the
door.

As his truck roared off she looked up at the window. Miss
Thalia's shadow moved across the far wall, then the light went out.
Hard to believe the old lady had ever been young, had ever been
kissed in the moonlight. At least Leona had known love, fifteen
years of it with Frank. She still missed his eyes watching her face,
her gestures. Her life had been beautiful, important, because he
witnessed it. And who were Miss Thalia's witnesses? Her congregation maybe, the brother in Charleston.

Like a teenager sneaking home after curfew, Leona quietly let
herself into the carriage house. No doubt Miss Thalia would ask
her to move out now—not that Leona could blame the old lady for
objecting to a tenant who kissed men right under her bedroom window. Climbing the stairs, Leona wondered if this was her last night
in the carriage house.

Miss Thalia stood in her dark bedroom, listening to Leona's
stealthy footsteps, the carriage house door squeaking open, clicking
shut. Startled awake by slamming car doors, she'd been confused,
thinking her younger brother was coming home late, drunk again.
When she'd seen Leona and that man, she'd shaken her head not
so much at Leona as at her own addled thoughts. Wide awake now,
she groped for her flute on the dresser and raised it to her lips. She
played a few notes, but it was no good, her fingers too arthritic to
make music. She sighed and got back into bed. Between the parted
curtains, stars glimmered in the cloudy night sky, and beyond the

stars God watched over his creation. She pressed her hands together and prayed for the wisdom to do what was right.

In the morning Leona carried her coffee upstairs to the porch, lit a cigarette, and gazed across Boulevard. Through the trees she could see tangled green kudzu where her house had stood. Maybe she could rent a trailer and put it on her lot—if it wasn't against the zoning laws. Depressing, the thought of living out her life in a trailer, fading into a defeated old woman shuffling around in slippers, scraping by on social security. Better to sell her land, put the money in a retirement fund—something she should have done years ago— and move into an apartment. She glanced at the cat lying in his morning patch of sunlight. Henry would miss his hunting grounds, but they'd both just have to adjust.

When Layla called to her from below, Leona ground out her cigarette and called back, "Come on up, Layla!"

"Me too," piped Summer. "I'm coming up, too."

Leona smiled as she heard them scampering up the stairs. She'd miss her morning visitors. Henry, accustomed to the girls now, yawned and blinked. Layla trudged onto the porch and flung herself into a chair, her thin face wearing its habitual look of discontent. "It's only eight-thirty," she said, "and I'm already bored." Summer knelt beside Henry and stroked his flank. He purred without opening his eyes.

"It'll be better when school starts," Leona said. "You'll make friends."

"But that's like, almost two months away. What am I supposed to do till then?"

"Leona?" Miss Thalia stood on the brick path, shading her eyes as she gazed up at the balcony.

Leona rose and hurried to the railing, the girls trailing after her. Beaming at Miss Thalia, Summer said, "Welcome back, Miss Thalia. Did you know Leona's from California, just like us?"

Miss Thalia's hand rose to her throat. "You mean Miss Davis?"

Summer looked inquiringly at Leona. "Is that your last name, Leona?"

Miss Thalia made a sound in her throat—annoyance or a stifled chuckle. "You can't help being Yankees, but here in the South, young ladies respect their elders."

Her eyes mischievous, Layla said, "We aren't really Yankees, Miss Thalia. A lot of people in Los Angeles were on the South's side. In fact a militia troop, the Los Angeles Mounted Rifles, rode clear across the country to fight with General Lee. It was in our history unit last year."

Amusement flickered in Miss Thalia's pale eyes. "Is that so? Leona, could you stop by this afternoon? I'd like to have a word with you."

After the old lady left, Leona sank into her chair and put her head in her hands. Summer came and sat beside her. "What's wrong?"

"I think Miss Thalia's going to make me leave."

"You can come stay with us, can't she, Layla? We'll ask Mom when she gets home."

"Thanks, but it wouldn't work out." As Summer's lips formed another question, Leona said, "Families work better with just two grownups in the house."

"But what's gonna happen?" Summer asked.

"I won't know for sure till I talk to Miss Thalia." Leona patted Summer's knee. "Don't worry about it, honey. Nothing very terrible's going to happen. I promise."

Thunderheads loomed on the horizon when Leona left the café. She'd walked to work that morning, needing the time and solitude to weigh her options. She'd pretty much resigned herself to selling her property and finding an apartment, though when she thought about leaving Boulevard, it felt like she was losing Frank all over again. Maybe Miss Thalia was right: the lord worked in mysterious ways. Losing her house had forced her back into the world. She glanced at the clouds and quickened her steps despite the muggy heat; if a storm broke she'd get soaked.

The first raindrops splattered the bricks as she hurried up Miss Thalia's front walk. The old lady was seated in a rocking chair on her front porch, a black shawl around her shoulders. As Leona climbed the steps, Miss Thalia said, "I adore watching a storm blow up."

Leona smiled. "Henry loves storms, too. Maybe it's a Southern thing."

"Don't you like them? Have a seat, dear."

"Yeah, I guess I *do* like them." Leona sat down beside Miss Thalia. "We didn't get much lightning back in San Diego."

"I was deadheading the roses, but these—" Miss Thalia held up her hands and shook her head. "They do less and less, and do it more slowly, every day. I can't play my flute anymore, you know."

"I know," Leona said. "I miss it." Rain pattered on the porch roof, as loud as that summer storm in the house she and Frank rented when he'd first brought her here. They'd been sprawled naked on the bed, a floor fan beside them and another fan on the dresser, when the storm hit. Rain had clattered on the tin roof, and they'd run outside and danced around the muddy backyard, laughing at each other while raindrops flowed in cold beautiful rivulets on their bare skin.

"So have you made up your mind, Leona?"

Thunder rumbled. Lightning split the dark clouds. Leona stared at the gaunt, wrinkled face close to hers. "I thought you'd tell me to pack my bags."

Miss Thalia raised her eyebrows. "Now why ever would I do that?"

Leona clasped her hands in her lap, stared down at them. "Because of last night."

The old lady shrugged, her voice amused. "A goodnight kiss isn't exactly a sin." Rain wafted onto the porch. She hitched her shawl closer around her shoulders.

"Miss Thalia." Leona's hands clutched each other. "I'm truly grateful to you. You've been kinder than I've any right to expect. But I can't accept your offer." She lifted her clasped hands, let them fall into her lap. "My soul's not for sale." When Miss Thalia's grim mouth tightened, Leona's hands stilled. "How soon do you want me out?"

"You can rent the carriage house for as long as you wish." Miss Thalia looked at her with something like affection in her eyes. "I may be too old to play my flute, but I can still enjoy your antics. And now if you'll excuse me, it's time for my nap."

Leona rose from her chair. "I'm so grateful—"

"No, don't thank me. Gratitude has a way of becoming resentment. Anyway, as long as you pay your rent on time you don't owe me a thing." Miss Thalia got up and walked slowly to the door, a hand pressed to her hip. "Dratted arthritis. Take my advice, Leona. Don't get old."

As the screen door slapped shut the rain abruptly ceased. Water dripped from the porch eaves, and a small green frog hopped across the brick walk. Leona went down the steps and across the street. Standing beneath her magnolia trees, she squinted up the front walk to the empty space where her front porch had been. A squirrel leapt onto a branch overhead, and cold raindrops spattered her face. Blinking the rain from her eyes, she saw her white clapboard house, its windows lit in an imaginary dusk. Inside, the girls chattered to Miss Thalia, and Dwight sat on the couch with Henry curled on his lap. Clasping her hands to her mouth, Leona gazed at the vision of what she couldn't have. Then she sent up a prayer through the drifting clouds and sunlight, thankful for what she'd been given.

COME LOOK AT THE MOON

Layla's mom and stepdad didn't shout or hurl things. They quarreled upstairs in their bedroom late at night, their voices hushed. Roused from sleep by their harsh whispers, Layla sat up, yawned and pushed her hair out of her eyes. A breeze had come up, and dim shadows flickered on the walls. She got out of bed and tiptoed to the door. Wary of the hall's creaking floorboards, she leaned out her door and listened to the darkness. It was clear, Janice hissed, that Paul's family thought she and her girls were trash. If Paul had the balls of a goddamned chipmunk he wouldn't expose her *or* the girls to that kind of emotional abuse.

Layla smirked as Paul begged Janice to give it some time. It served her mom right for dragging them clear across the country to this sweltering bug-infested town, all to marry a guy she'd been dating for like, ten minutes. Layla was only fourteen, and even she knew her mom's rash marriage wasn't turning out so hot.

Lying on Miss Thalia's porch swing the next day, her chin in her hands and her feet kicking the air, Layla wondered if all married people were discontented, if true love was the same as religion—

something people believed in because the alternative was unbearable. On this warm September afternoon, they were having tea on the side porch, a ritual Miss Thalia had inaugurated during the summer. Layla had accepted the first invitation out of boredom but soon found herself enjoying the old lady's company. They talked about books, argued politics, discussed the ineffable charm of carousels and pondered the whereabouts of butterflies at midnight. And when Layla had problems with her stubborn mom or her stupid little half-sister, she profited from Miss Thalia's tart advice.

Miss Thalia had gone inside to answer the phone. When she returned, Layla pushed back her dark bangs and said, "Can I ask you something sort of personal?"

"You can *ask*." The old lady refilled their cups, then sat down and smoothed her housedress over her knees. "Sit up straight, child. Don't lie there thrashing your legs like you've got ants in your pants."

Layla hunched a rebellious shoulder, then sat up with her feet on the floor, her knees together. She picked up the Wedgwood cup, blew on her tea and watched the dark surface ripple. "I just wondered, well, why you never married."

"Did you, now?" Miss Thalia's pale eyes became thoughtful. "I suppose the wrong men asked me. The first one was a lawyer. He was nice enough, but he had bad breath and his eyes bugged out like my Aunt Lilly's bulldog. The second one, Tom Gordon, was my older brother's friend, and from a prominent family. His great-great-grandfather was a Civil War hero and a state senator. Now Tom *was* attractive. Dark hair and eyes, good cheekbones."

"Like Mr. Darcy." Layla had just read *Pride and Prejudice* on Miss Thalia's recommendation. Now Leona, the waitress who rented Miss Thalia's carriage house, was reading it.

"But unlike Mr. Darcy, Tom would have made an awful husband. A domestic tyrant *and* unfaithful, a horrible combination." Miss Thalia rubbed her arthritic thumb. "There are far worse fates than spinsterhood."

"And then?" Layla asked.

The old lady withdrew her gaze from the past. "And then, nothing. I was twenty-three when Tom proposed, and the women in my family fade quickly." She sipped her tea. "So, no more proposals. Mother kept hoping, but I didn't, not after I refused Tom. That was back in 1955, over fifty years ago." She narrowed her eyes in a sly smile. "I'd guess your mother wasn't even born yet."

But Layla knew better than to blab her mom's age, especially to Miss Thalia, who Janice called a meddling old snoop. "What did you look like, back then?" she asked.

Miss Thalia thought for a moment, then set down her teacup and left the screened porch. When she came back she handed Layla a framed photograph of three young people standing on her front steps. "I was seventeen there," she said. In the picture Miss Thalia had thick dark curls, a lovely smile and a thin nose. Behind her stood a young man with pale eyes and a tightlipped smile. Beside her, a brown-eyed teenage boy stared somberly into the camera. "Wow," Layla said. "You were so pretty."

"I was, wasn't I? But age pares us down to the essentials. That's why the elderly look as much alike as a litter of purebred puppies, the same way newborn babies look alike." She pointed at the pale-eyed young man. "That's my older brother, Clay, the one I visit in Charleston. And that's my younger brother, William." Miss Thalia sighed. "He turned out so wild our daddy disinherited him. Of course Will was living in Galveston by then, and we hadn't seen him in years."

Layla nodded. She knew her father only from photographs and her mom's stories, so she understood about family members who acted like they had amnesia and didn't know they were related to you.

Miss Thalia straightened her spine, her voice brisk. "Well, it's time for my nap—another way old people are like puppies."

Layla set the photograph on the table and gathered the tea things onto the silver tray. As they went into the kitchen, Miss Thalia asked, "Have you made any friends at school yet?"

"No." Layla lowered the tray onto the counter, her long hair hiding her face, then looked up with a bleak smile. "When I started middle school here last January? Everybody already had their cliques. And it turns out that high school's just more people in a lot more cliques. Anyway I'd rather hang out with you and Leona." Miss Thalia raised her eyebrows. "Hang out? Is that what we do?"

Layla grinned. "Spend time with. Is that better?"

"You'll make friends. And then you won't want to visit me so often." Miss Thalia smoothed Layla's hair. "Don't you feel guilty when that happens. It's natural to want friends your own age, and guilt doesn't do anyone a lick of good."

Surprised by the tender gesture, Layla smiled uncertainly. "Well, thanks for tea, Miss Thalia."

After Layla left, Thalia washed up the china, glad that her older brother couldn't see her right now. No doubt Clay would say she was going soft in the head, first letting Leona rent the carriage house when her own house was destroyed by termites, then befriending the smart-mouthed little hoyden who'd moved in next door. But Layla had a quick mind and an affectionate heart, and the Lord said we should love our neighbors.

She remembered the photograph and returned to the porch to retrieve it. Pressing the picture to her chest, she gazed out at the side street. The maples along the curb were starting to turn, the leaves light yellow or pale pink like tender skin. Soon they'd be fiery red and orange, brilliant as the stained glass windows at Emmanuel Episcopalian Church, where she still sat in the pew her family had always occupied. On the Sunday after she'd rejected Tom, she'd gazed at the north transept's glowing stained glass window, which depicted Jesus visiting two sisters—dutiful Martha and spiritual Mary. Ever since Thalia was old enough to see over the pews, she'd admired the stained-glass Mary, a woman who neglected her housework to talk with Jesus. But on that Sunday morning it was Martha who epitomized Thalia's future—an old maid doomed to household cares and church bazaars, tedious evenings at home with her aging parents.

Clay scowled and fidgeted in the pew beside her, still furious that she'd rejected his friend. Beyond him their father's thin face was rigid with disappointment. Will had stayed home again, yet another black mark against him. Still, she wished her little brother were beside her, stifling bored yawns and nudging her when Father Stanton extolled the womanly virtues of patience and obedience.

After church she stood blinking in the sunlight while her mother chatted with a neighbor. A gust of wind fluttered the women's dresses and tore the blossoms from a dogwood tree. The white petals swirled around Thalia, beautiful as snow, though in retrospect they were an ill omen.

But it did no good to dwell on the past. Just look where it had gotten Leona. Widowed young, instead of asking the Lord's help to get on with her life, she'd drowned her grief in gin and fornication. Now she faced a penurious old age. And getting old was bad enough when you *had* money—sore joints and feeble muscles, wrinkled skin, hair thin as dandelion fluff. Thalia sighed, glanced at her watch. And you tired so easily, especially when you missed your nap.

Lying under a faded blue quilt, her hands clasped on her stomach, she stared at the ceiling and saw Layla's clear, direct gaze staring back. The girl's eyes were the dark blue of that artesian well, what was it called? The Blue Hole, that was it, in Santa Rosa, New Mexico. She'd seen it on a trip out West with her parents in 1965, the year before they both passed on. Her father had fussed and fretted the entire trip, but she and her mother had enjoyed seeing such entirely different country—red plateaus, antelope, distant mountains that seemed close enough to touch in the clear desert air. They'd been discussing another trip, to the Oregon coast, maybe, when her father died of a sudden stroke. A few months later her mother caught pneumonia, which led to acute respiratory failure. She passed on after three days in intensive care, Thalia holding her frail hand.

❧ ❧ ❧ ❧

As the autumn days shortened Layla did make friends, though not the sort Thalia approved of. Barely in their teens, they were pierced and tattooed, flaunted rainbow-colored hair. The boys' jeans hung down below their underpants, and the girls wore gauzy tops that exposed their pudgy bellies.

On a warm afternoon marbled with gray clouds, Thalia was checking her curbside mailbox when a negro boy came out Layla's front door. His dreadlocks bobbing, a bandanna around his head like those hoodlums on the evening news, he slouched toward Thalia. It wasn't so much that he was colored; it was his bored, bitter glance that alarmed her. She climbed her porch steps feeling beset from all sides. First Leona wheedling her way into the carriage house, now hoodlums next door. Nearly as bad as the summer before last, when those thugs and a prostitute Leona had befriended broke into Leona's house. Leona had shot one of them in the arm—something Thalia had to admire. It was one thing to keep a gun in your bedside drawer, another to aim straight, pull the trigger.

The week before Halloween, Thalia was sitting on her front porch sipping a glass of sherry. A thin stream of evening traffic trickled up Boulevard from downtown, and neighbors were out strolling in the day's last warmth. "Miss Thalia!" Layla called from the sidewalk. She came up the front walk dragging the negro boy by the hand. Thalia didn't have to think. She stood up and moved to the steps, blocking their way. "Evening, Layla."

Layla beamed at her. "Miss Thalia, I'd like you to meet Sterling. Sterling, this is my dear friend Miss Thalia."

The boy's gaze flicked from the porch to the windows. Good heavens, was he planning to rob her? Trying not to seem flustered, she said, "How do you do, Sterling?"

"I'm doing good, real good. And how are you doing"—he gave an insolent smile—"Miss Thalia?"

"Fine, thank you." Her lips felt stiff, her palms damp. She heard herself ask if they wanted something to drink, a ginger ale maybe.

"No thanks," he paused, gave another mocking glance, "ma'am."

"We're going downtown," Layla explained. "But I wanted to introduce you."

"Well, have a good time." Thalia forced a smile. "Nice meeting you, Sterling."

He nodded, his jaw masticating. She half-expected him to spit a wad of chew into her hydrangeas.

A few days later Layla stopped by on her way home from school. While Thalia made tea, Layla set out the Wedgwood china. The day was cool so they sat in the parlor, Layla curled on the couch in her sock feet, Thalia erect in her wingback chair.

"So how did you like Sterling?" Layla asked.

"He's got mighty big feet."

Layla laughed and hugged her knees. "He gets me. Who I am."

"I see. And do you get him?"

"I know he's my friend," Layla said slowly.

"Hmm. Have you been friends long?"

"About a month, maybe? We met at the food bank, during service-learning week." Layla smiled, shook her head. "At first we argued nonstop, but now it's like we can tell each other anything."

Thalia raised an eyebrow. "Anything?"

"Like, how much I still miss California, and sometimes he talks about his ex—this girl Keisha who broke his heart last summer."

"You know, dear." Thalia paused, choosing her words. "Sometimes it's unwise to confide in a new acquaintance too much, too quickly." She picked up a book from the table beside her armchair. "Have you ever read *Jane Eyre*? I think you'd enjoy it."

Layla stared at her. Then she set her teacup in its saucer. "Sterling's an A student, Miss Thalia, from a good family. His dad's a doctor and his mom's a school nurse. He's named after a famous black poet you probably never heard of." She slid her feet into her clogs. "I thought you'd *understand*. I thought you'd *like* him." She stood up and put on her coat. "Thank you for tea."

Thalia rose as quickly as her arthritic hip allowed. "Sit down and finish your tea, dear. I'm sure he's a nice boy. I just wanted to drop a hint, caution you."

Layla picked up her book bag from the floor. "I'm sorry, but I can't stay." A moment later the front door slammed. Alone in the parlor, Thalia stared at Layla's abandoned teacup, saw the girl's gaze hardening into anger. She'd seen that look before—in her brother's brown eyes—and she'd never been able to forget it. She'd been sitting before her bedroom mirror after church, pondering her bleak future, when chairs scraped and china clinked in the dining room below. She'd hastily brushed the white dogwood petals from her hair before she ran downstairs to Sunday dinner.

Thalia closed her eyes, remembering Wedgwood china gleaming on a white damask tablecloth, Clay forking a slice of rump roast onto his plate, its pink juice seeping into his mashed potatoes. Too angry to heed their father's pinched nostrils and thinned lips, Clay said, *I hope you're happy now, Thalia. I hope you like being an old maid.* Will smiled and said she was better off a spinster than married to a pompous asshole like Tom, who kept half the whores on Barber Street in garter belts. Their father dabbed his mouth with his napkin. Then his fist slammed the table. "You will apologize now, sir!"

"Charles," their mother pleaded, "it's Sunday."

"I don't give a damn what day of the week it is." He narrowed his eyes at Thalia. "Is that why you rejected Tom Gordon? Because of William's filthy innuendoes?"

Thalia's face burned with shame. Will *always* did this. Always opened his mouth and set ugliness loose among them. "As if I'd listen to Will," she said with a tight smile. "That was Ettie I saw you with, wasn't it, Will? Kissing in broad daylight?" She instantly regretted it. Dismayed, she watched the shock in his dark eyes harden into anger. Their mother gasped and said, "*Our* Ettie? You were kissing *our* Ettie?"

Will sighed. "We don't own them anymore, Mama."

"In broad daylight." Their father closed his eyes. "Are you crazy, son, or just plain stupid?"

"Neither, sir." Will pushed back his chair and dropped his napkin on the table.

"I don't believe you've been excused," Clay said. But he was talking to Will's back. A moment later the front door slammed. Rapid footsteps crossed the porch and faded down the front walk.

That afternoon Thalia tapped on Will's bedroom door, gingerly pushed it open. Even now the scene was a bright vignette surrounded by the darkness of the intervening years. Will was studying at his desk, a nimbus of sunlight around his head, a cigarette smoldering between his fingers. When he looked up, she said, "I'm sorry I lost my temper."

His arm on the chair back, he contemplated her, then said, "You know Mama's going to fire Ettie."

"Oh, she wouldn't—"

"Daddy will make her whether she wants to or not."

"Well, I'm sorry, but you should have known—"

"Known what? That you'd rat me out the first chance you got?" He stubbed out his cigarette. "You can shut the door on your way out."

Tears blurred her sight as she hurried to her bedroom. She sank onto her bed, the back of her hand pressed to her mouth. When Will was small, she'd pulled him in their Ryder wagon, read him Peter Rabbit stories. When he'd had nightmares he'd crawled into her bed and snuggled his warm little body close to hers. But in her teens she'd sensed that Clay was the favorite son, the family's next patriarch. Gradually, almost unconsciously, she'd closed her heart to Will, adopting the family attitude that he was turning out badly. But until last week she hadn't really believed it.

She'd been reading in the grape arbor when Tom came by to invite her to a dance, and when he left she went outside to retrieve her book. Distracted by the lingering feel of Tom's lips, and wondering why the prospect of marrying him frightened her, she stumbled on Will kissing Ettie, their maid, under the oak tree. All three of them froze. Then Ettie smoothed her hair and hurried across the grass to the house. Will smiled and shook his head—as if he'd caught *Thalia* doing something wrong. Then he thrust his hands in his pockets and sauntered off. Thalia sat down on the carriage house steps, nauseated by what she'd seen—her little brother kissing a *negro's* lips—almost as revolting as watching him kiss another man. Not to mention he was leading Ettie on, tempting her to sin. If he cared about her at all he'd leave her alone.

After that awful Sunday dinner, Will avoided the family, and when he couldn't escape them he listened politely, then went his own way, usually to the Hot Corner's negro juke joints and pool halls. By Christmas, Rosa Parks had refused to give up her bus seat, and Will had moved to New Orleans in defiance of their father, who expected Will to go to law school. Only Thalia saw a connection between the two events: the world had shifted on its axis, the old familiar landmarks erased.

The parlor was full of shadows now. As Thalia reached for Layla's teacup the doorbell chimed. She went to the front door and peered through the peephole, hoping Layla had come back. But it was Leona standing there with a hip jutting out, her red sweater too tight across the chest, her hair in a messy bun. Thalia sighed and opened the door.

"Evening, Miss Thalia." Leona held out a plastic grocery bag with the loaf of bread and package of lemon cookies she'd picked up for Thalia at Kroger. As Thalia took the bag, Leona said, "Are you all right?"

Thalia forced a smile. "Come in, won't you?" Remembering the dirty teacups in the parlor, she nodded for Leona to follow her into the kitchen. "Have a seat while I put these things away," she said. "Can I get you a glass of sherry?"

"I'm fine, thanks." Leona sat at the table and glanced around the kitchen. The white tile countertop gleamed, and the red-checked floor was immaculate. "Your place is always so spotless."

"That's Ester, not me. She's been with me forty years, and a finer woman, white or colored, I've never known." Correctly interpreting Leona's silence, she asked sharply, "Well, what am I supposed to call them?"

"Black or African-American, I think."

"I had words with Layla this afternoon, about one of her, um, black friends. The truth is, he reminded me of your streetwalker, that skinny little white girl."

"Jody."

Thalia nodded. "Layla says he's a good boy from a decent family, so no doubt I'm mistaken, but I meant it for the best. The Lord knows her mother doesn't heed what that girl is up to. Barely fourteen and already running wild. I don't know what the world's coming to. Time was, Boulevard was a respectable street, and now look at it."

Leona shook her head. "Terrible, isn't it? Ever since Frank and I moved in, the whole neighborhood's been going to hell in a handbasket."

Thalia smiled. "It's been slower than that. And Frank, God rest his soul, was from decent people, no matter how wild you two were, keeping me awake all hours with your parties and your rock and roll."

"Layla's stepdad's a high school teacher. That's pretty respectable."

"Now you just tell me why he wears his hair in that scrawny little ponytail when it's clear as day he's going bald, and why Layla's mom wears her jeans so tight, and why those girls have different fathers they don't even know, and maybe I'll agree they're respectable." Thalia sighed and sat down, one finger tracing the tablecloth's embroidered pink roses. "But it grieves me that I upset Layla, and I'll admit she upset me."

"If you think you were wrong about this boy, why not say so?"

"I wish I hadn't said anything at all." Thalia stood up. "No doubt I'm keeping you from your dinner." She closed her eyes. "Thank you for your advice, Leona."

After Leona left, Thalia poured a glass of sherry, put on her black shawl and went out to the screened porch. It was getting dark, a nip in the air. A streetlamp lit the side street like a stage, the maple trees aflame with orange and red leaves. At any moment, an actress might step from the shadows and recite a few lines from *Our Town* or a tragic soliloquy by Tennessee Williams. Leaning against a porch post, Thalia let old memories throng her—playing the Barrère nocturne on her flute, seeing Lillian Hellman's *Toys in the Attic* on a trip to New York, kissing Tom on this side porch, playing hide-and-seek in the house on rainy days—each recollection like a small perfect scene inside a snow-globe. And if there were darker scenes as well, it did no good to recall them.

No good at all. And it wasn't as if she'd lost touch with Will completely. From time to time he scrawled her a note on a picture postcard of his saloon in Galveston—the Blues Palace, a big ramshackle building photographed against a wide blue sky. The postcards could have been sent by a stranger. *The weather's been fine and except for a head cold I'm well. The bar's been overrun by tourists all summer which is good for the till but hard on the rest of us.*

Nevertheless, she'd formed the habit of writing him long letters, especially when she was lonely. But she'd never told him that after their parents died she'd rehired Ettie at twice the usual wage for domestic help—a private, belated act of atonement. By then Ettie Harris had become Ester Johnson, a married woman with four children, her childish nickname set aside long ago.

Curled on the couch under a plaid blanket, Layla skimmed a page in her history book about the War of 1812. It was getting dark outside, the wind roaring through the trees. On the muted television Marilyn Monroe was dancing in a pink evening gown with a phalanx of tuxedoed men. Layla's mom came in from checking the mailbox, her nose and cheeks flushed from the cold. She flopped down on the couch and held out a lavender envelope addressed to Layla in spidery handwriting. Layla took it, ripped open the envelope and pulled out a note that read, *Dear Layla, May I take you to lunch at one o'clock this Saturday at the Normaltown Café? It would give me great pleasure to do so. Cordially, Miss Thalia Henderson.*

Janice picked up the remote, her finger poised above the mute button. "Who's that from?"

"Miss Thalia. She wants to take me to lunch on Saturday, at the café where Leona works."

Janice set down the remote. "I'm all for respecting your elders, but I hope you don't tell that old busybody everything that goes on over here."

"Believe me, Mom. I don't."

"So why the lunch date?"

Layla bit her lip. "We had an argument. Maybe she wants to make up."

"What did you argue about?" Janice pulled a fold of the blanket over her knees. "Let me guess. She doesn't approve of your romance with Sterling."

"It's not a romance, Mom."

"No, you two just"—Janice made quotation marks in the air —"hang out."

Layla bit back a grin. "Whatever. How did you know that's what ticked her off?"

"It's not rocket science, babe. Sterling looks like such a badass, I bet she's scared shitless he'll mug her while she's peering over the hedge at her disreputable neighbors."

"She doesn't think we're disreputable. In fact she's never said a word about you or Paul."

"I rest my case. When Southern ladies don't say anything, they're thinking the worst." She glanced up and smiled as ten-year-old Summer wandered into the living room. "Hey there, sweetie."

Summer plopped onto the couch next to her mom, her soft blue eyes fixed on Marilyn, now talking to a statuesque brunette. "Turn on the sound, Mom."

"Did you finish your homework?"

"Uh huh."

Janice gave her daughter a skeptical look, then pressed the mute button. Summer smiled and patted her mom's hand.

Layla slid Miss Thalia's note into her history book. "So where's Mr. Wimpy?"

"He's at a school board meeting. It's loud enough, Summer." Janice moved the remote beyond Summer's reach. "And I wish you wouldn't call him that."

"Why not? It's what he is."

Janice reached over and squeezed Layla's knee. "Admit it," she coaxed. "We're happier now than we were in LA."

"Yeah, but, Mom? Are you, like, actually in *love* with Paul?"

"I've been in love a thousand times, Layla, and all I have to show for it are you and Summer. Maybe I'm not crazy about Paul's parents, or his sisters for that matter. But he adores us and he treats me like a queen. That's good enough for me."

Miss Thalia drove with her head craned forward like a turtle, her foot hesitant on the gas pedal. Layla tried not to fidget, but she could have walked the mile from Boulevard to the Normaltown Café in less time. The trees were leafless and gray, the kudzu withered into snarled brambles along the creek. While Miss Thalia chatted about her cleaning woman's new grandson, Layla ran her hand over the caramel-colored leather upholstery and wished her mom had married someone rich. A floral printed gift bag sat on the back seat, and its pink tissue paper rustled invitingly whenever they hit a pothole.

Miss Thalia nosed the car into a slanted parking space, took the gift bag from the back seat, and ushered Layla into the café, where they halted before the *Please Wait To Be Seated* sign. When the dark-eyed, energetic woman who owned the café bustled over, Miss Thalia asked that they not be seated in Leona's section. "She's our friend," Miss Thalia explained. "She might not like waiting on us."

Ensconced at a small table by the front window, Miss Thalia held out the gift bag. "For you," she said. "A peace offering. Careful, it's heavy."

Layla pushed apart the tissue and pulled out a hardcover

edition of Emily Dickinson's poems. "Oh! Thank you!" She clasped the book to her chest. "Next to Sylvia Plath she's my favorite poet." Miss Thalia sniffed. "Plath. That poor benighted soul."

"At least she didn't lurk in her house dressed in white like a ghost."

"No, she swallowed a bottle of sleeping pills and stuck her head in the oven. I'm glad you like the book, dear. Now, what shall we have?"

After serious discussion, Layla ordered a cherry Coke and fried chicken, and Miss Thalia asked for the pan-fried trout and sweet tea. Leona came over to say hello, Layla showed her the book, and she exclaimed over it, then admitted she hadn't read Emily Dickinson since high school and hadn't understood any of it then.

"*I heard a Fly buzz,*" Layla scoffed. "The best ones are about lonely nights and heartbreak."

"That sounds right up my alley," Leona said. "You'll have to read me the good ones. Enjoy your lunch." She smiled at Thalia, who felt more gratified by Leona's approbation than she'd have thought possible in the days when Leona was merely that trashy widow living across the street.

After Leona left, Layla opened the book and became absorbed in it. When their food arrived she closed the book and snatched up a drumstick, then set it down.

"Too hot?" Thalia asked.

Layla nodded. "And I wasn't sure. Should I use a knife and fork?"

"Lord no. The only way to eat fried chicken is with your hands." Thalia beckoned a waitress over and asked for some extra napkins. "Just don't let me catch you licking your fingers."

While Layla squished butter into her mashed potatoes, Thalia ate a few string beans, then set down her fork. "Layla, dear."

Layla looked up apprehensively. "I can't apologize, Miss Thalia."

"I don't expect you to. After all, I'm the one at fault. When I first saw your friend, I was misled by his appearance. I thought he was a hoodlum." Thalia held up a hand. "Let me finish, child. This isn't easy, so I want to get it said. I'll admit I judged him hastily, though I'm still a bit worried about you spending so much time with a boy who's older than you—he is, isn't he?"

Layla cocked her head, wondering what Miss Thalia was up to. "He's fifteen," she admitted. "But I'm fourteen now."

"Be that as it may—whatever are you grinning at?"

"It just hit me that when you say *be that as it may*, it's the same as when I say *whatever*. You know. What*ever*." Layla rolled her eyes and shrugged.

"Be that as it may," Thalia said with a smile, "I respect you for sticking up for your friend." She stared out the window, collecting her thoughts. Three young women in heels and business suits hurried up the sidewalk toward the café, talking and laughing as they passed the window. Thalia's gaze returned to Layla, who was gnawing on the drumstick. With a stifled sigh, Thalia cut off a piece of trout. Her taste buds were withering along with the rest of her, but the pan-fried fish was tender and juicy. She took another bite with more relish and kept nibbling at it while Layla devoured her chicken and mashed potatoes, though the mushy gray peas went untouched.

"Sorry," Layla said as she wiped her hands on another napkin. "I was starved. That's the best fried chicken I've ever had."

"I'm glad you liked it."

"So, what were you saying, Miss Thalia?"

Staring at the blue-checked tablecloth, Thalia explained that a long time ago she'd seen Will kissing the family's black maid and had told her parents, who fired the girl. "It's true he didn't turn out well," she concluded. "But I've never forgiven myself for our estrangement. It was my fault, you see—partly because I was what you'd call a racist. Well, nearly everybody was back then, and you can say we should have known better but the fact is we *didn't*. The point is, Will trusted me, and I betrayed him." Thalia reached across the table and touched Layla's hand. "I was not loyal, as you've shown yourself to be."

Layla ventured a smile. "Guilt doesn't do anyone a lick of good. You said so yourself."

"But sometimes it's a fit punishment."

"It's not like you committed a sin or anything."

"That's between me and the Lord. But I want to make things right with you. I've missed our talks." She cleared her throat. "I apologize for offending you, and for misjudging your friend."

"Thank you," Layla said gravely. "I accept your apology."

"Now can I interest you in dessert? The pecan pie here is almost as good as homemade."

It was nearly three when they pulled into the gravel driveway behind Miss Thalia's house. Layla walked Thalia to the back door and surprised her with a hug. "I love the book," she said with a quick smile. Then she turned and ran across the grass to the sidewalk. Watching her go, Thalia hugged her own shoulders, feeling the lingering warmth of the girl's arms.

Janice was in the kitchen cutting up potatoes, the knife's quick hard chops betraying her dislike of the task. Layla set her book on the table, opened the refrigerator and took out the grape juice.

"So how'd it go?" Janice asked.

"Fine. I had some killer fried chicken, and she gave me that."

"She *would* give you a book." Janice wiped her hands on a paper towel, picked up the book and read the title. "Poetry, huh? If you're not careful you'll turn into a mini Miss Thalia."

"You'd rather have me drooling in front of the TV like Summer?"

"I just want you to be yourself." Janice scooped up handfuls of chopped potatoes and dumped them into a pot of boiling water.

"I *am* myself. Who else *could* I be?"

"What other people think you should be, what society tries to turn you into—the deadening mediocrity of the norm."

"That's deep, Mom." Layla set her glass in the sink, grabbed her book, and headed toward the door, where she pirouetted, holding the book above her head. "One thing's for sure, I don't plan on being mediocre."

Janice gave a tight smile. "Nobody plans on it, Layla."

A breeze rattled the dead wisteria vines as Thalia unlocked her back door. She let herself in and set her purse on the kitchen counter, then went into the parlor and sank into her wingback chair, too weary to climb the stairs for her nap. At least she'd mended things between herself and the girl. And maybe someday, years and years from now, Layla would understand the struggle it was to keep up with a world that kept rushing forward, the floodtide of change sweeping away everything familiar until you were alone in a world you no longer recognized.

She dozed for a while, then awoke to birds twittering. On an evening like this, the parlor hazed in apricot light, Tom had asked her to marry him, and in all the years since, only once had she known love, felt a man's lips on hers, his naked body against her skin making her feel vibrant, desired. A late and lovely deflowering—odd word for an act that had felt as if she were a flower, a blossom spreading its petals to the sun's dazzling heat. After the first time, she'd gone home and wept, prayed long and hard for forgiveness. But she hadn't been able to resist temptation, and they'd become lovers. To her surprise, the sin had rested lightly on her soul, as if God forgave her for it. She closed her eyes, conjuring memory. George Webber, a beautiful man with deep brown eyes, a sad smile and a black mole beside his nose, pipe tobacco redolent in his clothes and hair. They'd kept company all one winter, had even sneaked away for a week in New York, snow falling as they strolled down Fifth Avenue.

George was a law professor, and when the University of Chicago offered him an endowed chair, he asked Thalia to move north with him as his wife. But she'd been wise enough to know—or foolish enough to think—that at forty it was too late; she'd wilt, a pale limp stalk, if she uprooted herself from her native soil. She'd visited him twice that spring, and he'd come back to see her a few times, but she couldn't overcome her nervous distaste for Chicago's roar and bustle, its gray pavements. Eventually the phone calls grew further apart, and even the gorgeous letters she'd saved, even those ceased. Inevitable, she supposed, and just as well. Birdsong and cicadas, magnolias and crepe myrtle, this was home. All she regretted was that he hadn't wanted to stay. Odd that she hadn't mentioned George when Layla had asked about her suitors. Or maybe not so odd—the memories too personal, too private, to share, even with Layla.

It was getting dark. Time to think about dinner, but she wasn't hungry, not after that late lunch. She put on her shawl and went out onto the front porch. Dusky yellow light paled the eastern horizon. As she sat down, a harvest moon edged above the trees. Far away in Galveston, was her brother watching the same moon rise above the dark ocean? She could see his pale narrow face, but she couldn't tell if he was alone or with someone—as if he'd shut her out so completely that even her imagination couldn't intrude on him. One ill-judged burst of temper fifty years ago and she'd lost him forever. No, she'd done worse than lose her temper. She knew that now. She'd betrayed what was innocent and good in both of them. Beyond the hedge Layla's front door creaked open and footsteps crossed the porch. Thalia heard Layla call, "Summer, come look at the moon," then Summer's high voice crying, "Coming! I'm coming!"

FIRE AND ICE

When Paul and the girls got home from the mall, Janice was in the kitchen dicing an onion for the spaghetti, the radio tuned to a local rock station. Paul turned down the radio and lowered the flame under the sizzling hamburger meat. He kissed the back of Janice's neck and asked, "Need any help, baby?"

Janice hunched her shoulder and kept chopping. Paul ran a hand through his hair, then turned and headed for the den. Layla grabbed an apple and ran upstairs to her room, followed by her half-sister, Summer, who winced as Layla slammed her bedroom door. Layla didn't have to bother with a keep-out sign, Summer thought. Like their mom, she had the family well trained. Alone in the upstairs hall, Summer went over to a door that looked like a cupboard and opened it. She flicked on the light switch, stepped inside and climbed the narrow stairs to the attic, a big dusty room with cobwebs on the ceiling and sunlight slanting through one of the four large porthole windows, one at each compass point. Kneeling beside an old steamer trunk, its black leather cracked and flaking, Summer heaved up the lid and groped through the pile of moldy old shoes a past tenant had left behind. When she found her diary she crossed the bare floor to a couch under the west window and curled up in a patch of sunlight.

A birthday present from Paul, the diary had a gold pencil that fit into a pocket in the cover, and a gold hasp that locked with a tiny gold key. Not that anyone was interested in her secret thoughts, except Layla might read them to tease her. Paul said the distance between ten and fourteen was greater than any other age gap, but on the other side of their teens the years would shrink and they'd both be grownups, on a level playing field. He'd been trying to cheer Summer up, but waiting a decade to be friends with Layla again— when you were ten years old that was a lifetime away.

Summer chewed on a strand of her blond hair, then wrote,

> *Dear Diary, I wish things were like before. Not that exactly. I just wish Layla didn't treat me like a dumb baby. I can't help it if I like pretty things and don't know a bunch of big words like she does. Mom used to call me a day-dreamer like my dad but now she doesn't talk about our dads because it might hurt Paul's feelings but I think it hurts his feelings when she says she still misses Los Angeles. I don't miss it not at all. Mom going off all the time and leaving us alone in the apartment, then that stupid commune house. There's no smog here and we have rabbits and squirrels in the backyard. Paul says he'll build me a tree house next summer but Layla says don't hold your breath. She calls him Mr. Wimpy behind his back but I think she's afraid like I am. Afraid that mom wants to go back to our old life.*

Writing it down made it real, scary. A door slammed downstairs. Summer shut the diary, locked the hasp.

Janice stood at the front window clutching her coffee cup and watching a flock of grackles on the lawn, their black feathers gleaming in the sunlight, their raspy chirps and whistles muffled by the windowpane. It was quiet inside, the girls sleeping late, Paul at the kitchen table doing the Sunday crossword puzzle over his second cup of coffee. Janice had told him she had to go into work for a few hours but really she just needed to get out of the house. In her uncluttered office, with Chinese brocades on the walls and a view of the creek, life seemed cleaner, simpler. And maybe *he*'d be there, would stop by to chat, make her breathless with his dark bedroom eyes.

Long and lean in tight jeans and a black tee-shirt, ginger hair in a ponytail, his green eyes watching her like a cat, Paul had made her breathless when they'd met at a screening on the Paramount lot. He'd told her he was a high school math teacher turned screenwriter, that he had an agent but hadn't sold anything yet. The next weekend they went on their first date, and that night in his rented house in Laurel Canyon he'd held her down by her wrists, their sweat-slick bodies entwined. In the morning, cool sunlight filtered through the oak branches. They'd had French toast on the front porch, his smile so sweet she'd thought, *at last, at last.* How could desire make you feverish for months, every inch of your skin yearning for one man's touch, and then poof—it vanished, and sex became a chore like folding laundry. Maybe she'd feel differently if Paul hadn't decided to move back here. She'd fallen for a hip, sexy Hollywood screenwriter who rode a Triumph, but now she was married to a nerdy schoolteacher who drove a pickup.

Janice set her coffee cup on the fireplace mantel and hugged her elbows. Yesterday while Paul and the girls were at the mall, she'd glimpsed Leona through the hedge and invited her over for a glass of wine. A lanky woman with unruly auburn hair, Leona took people as she found them, which made her easy to talk to. And like Janice, she'd grown up in Southern California and married a man from Athens, Georgia. But that was really all they had in common. Leona was a small-town waitress, probably pushing fifty, while Janice was a youthful forty-three, a producer for the local television station—different worlds. Yet as they sat on the patio drinking Merlot, Janice pushed back her hair and said, "I'm starting to wonder if I made the right decision, marrying Paul. I mean, it made sense back in California, but now, I don't know."

"I did the same thing, minus the kids, and it turned out alright."

Janice hesitated. "You think it turned out alright?"

A smile crept into Leona's eyes. "I know, I'm a dirt-poor widow. But I wouldn't trade my years with Frank for anything." She lit a cigarette, blew out a stream of smoke. "I figure every decision has a price, and sooner or later we have to pay up."

"What if the price is too high?"

"You still have to pay." Leona glanced at her watch. "I have to get ready for work. But whenever you want to talk, I'm right next door."

Janice nodded, though she didn't think a woman who still mourned a husband she'd lost over a decade ago could understand what it was like to be restless your whole life—always yearning for a new man, a greater love, another adventure just down the road. She'd been foolish to think a ring on her finger would change that.

The grackles took flight, a flurry of black wings. Janice didn't hear Paul come up behind her, and when he slid his arms around her she gave a guilty start, then leaned back against his chest, her hands clasping his arms.

"The girls still asleep?" he asked.

"I think so."

"How about we sneak back upstairs?"

Janice turned in his arms and smiled. "I have to go to work, remember?"

"Then kiss me first."

She closed her eyes, felt his thin lips press themselves to the shape of her mouth. Yesterday Layla and Sterling had chased each other in the front yard, faded red leaves eddying at their feet, and Janice had wondered if her daughter was falling in love. When Paul nibbled her earlobe, she sighed and pushed him away.

He blinked nervously. "You used to like that."

"I know. I can't explain it but I don't anymore."

"Do you still love me?"

"Of course. It's just—"

"Just what?"

She smoothed his thinning hair. "Nothing. They say the first year of marriage is the toughest, and we've nearly made it through that." He still looked anxious, so she smiled and took his hand. "Come talk to me while I get dressed."

᠗᠗᠗᠗

It turned cold the next week—a good thing and a bad thing, Summer thought. Ice etched white fern fronds on the windows, and silver frost glinted on the grass. But as she trudged home from school on Thursday, rain needled her skin and she yearned for California's blue skies, winter just brisk enough to make you want to run and shout. Still, she didn't want to go back to LA, at least not without Paul.

That evening she curled up in an armchair by the fire to read *Harry Potter and the Chamber of Secrets* and eavesdrop. Layla was sprawled on the couch twirling a strand of her long dark hair and gabbing on her cell phone. Their mom was upstairs getting ready for a girls' night out with her coworkers. When Janice came running down the stairs, her slim legs sheathed in tight jeans, a black sweater hugging her chest, Layla and Summer exchanged looks. Janice's eyes sparkled just like they had when she'd rushed out of the commune house back in California for a date with Paul, only tonight Paul was in the kitchen with an apron around his waist making sloppy Joes. Layla murmured, "I'll call you back."

Their mom went into the kitchen. The girls listened, relieved when Paul laughed. Then Janice strode to the door, put on her coat and wriggled her fingers into black leather gloves. "You guys be good," she said. "Don't give Paul a hard time."

"You be good yourself," said Layla.

Janice raised her eyebrows. "Excuse me?"

"You heard me, Mom."

Janice bit her lip, then yanked open the door. Cold air rushed in. The door slammed, and a minute later the Honda's engine revved. Its headlights flared through the front window as Janice backed down the driveway. When Summer peeked over her book, Layla said, "Don't say anything to Paul."

"About what?"

Layla rolled her eyes. "How Mom looked, doofus."

Summer returned to her book, but the black print was a blurred jumble. "Layla?"

"*Now* what?"

"What's going to happen?"

"I don't have a clue." Layla flipped open her phone, glanced at Summer, flipped it shut. "Don't worry about it. Mom's got a bad case of arrested development, is all. Nothing's going to happen."

Around midnight a loud bang jerked Summer out of sleep. Unsure if she'd dreamed the sound, she strained to hear through the darkness. Paul grumbled something and her mom shouted, "Don't tell me what to do!" When their voices dropped to angry whispers, Summer pulled the covers over her head and closed her eyes.

In the morning while Janice and Paul chatted over toast and coffee Summer searched their faces for signs of discord. Although her mom was too lovey-dovey, jumping up to refill Paul's cup, leaning down to kiss his cheek, at least she wasn't wearing her hard, defiant look. Paul exclaimed at the time and they all rushed around, Janice telling Layla to hurry so she wouldn't miss the school bus again. As Summer ran upstairs to get her book bag she wondered if she'd dreamed it after all.

ço ço çò çò

"Layla!" Janice called up the stairs, "If you're not down here in ten seconds, we're leaving without you!" She smiled at Summer. "Aren't you supposed to be the slowpoke in this family?" Then she raised her voice again. "*Now* means *now*, Layla!"

Summer wandered into the living room, picked up the remote and clicked on the television. A blond lady pointed at a colorful map while explaining that the pink mass over the Gulf was a warm front, the blue one over the Midwest a cold front caused by an Alberta clipper. "When these fronts meet up in the next few days, we can expect unsettled weather across the South and up into the mid-Atlantic states." The lady smiled like a toothpaste commercial. "If you have travel plans, be sure and keep an eye on this unstable weather pattern."

When Layla thumped downstairs, Janice hustled the girls into the car, loudly complaining that she must have given birth to snails, glaciers, three-toed sloths, because no human children could be so slow.

The parking lot was so crowded they had to drive around and around to find a spot. Inside, the mall was decorated with snow-flocked trees, and Christmas carols floated from hidden speakers. Summer slowed her steps when she saw Santa on his big gold throne. "Aren't you a little old for that?" Janice teased. Summer nodded, her cheeks hot with confusion. She wasn't too old for the American Girl paper dolls she'd gotten for her birthday back in March, and though she wasn't allowed to have Barbie dolls because her mom said they caused "self-esteem issues," she still played with her other dolls. But it seemed Santa was just for babies.

Layla took off on her own while Janice helped Summer choose a pair of bedroom slippers for Paul and a pink hoodie for Layla. After buying a tortoiseshell hair clip for Leona, Summer spent her last three crumpled dollars on catnip for Leona's big orange cat. As they left the pet store she stooped over a pen of yellow puppies, some sleeping, some staggering around on big adorable paws. She put her hand in the pen, and a yellow puppy licked it, its long tail whipping back and forth—love at first sight. She looked pleadingly at her mom, who smiled and shook her head.

"I'd feed him and take him for walks, clean up the poop and everything, Mom!"

"Maybe next year, when things have settled down."

"Things *are* settled down."

"No they're not." Janice pulled her away, then tousled her hair. "We haven't even been here a year, baby. We've got a new house, and new jobs, you and Layla have new schools—a puppy's just too much on top of all that."

When they met up with Layla at the Dairy Queen, Summer asked for a cheeseburger and onion rings. They carried their trays to a table and were chowing down when a deep voice said, "If it isn't my favorite cougar." Janice set down her fish sandwich, dabbed at her mouth with a napkin, then turned and smiled at the man looming over their table.

Summer paused with an onion ring halfway to her mouth, wondering what a cougar was. The man looked younger than their mom, though there were a few lines around his big dark eyes. His head was shaved bald, his full lips smiling as if he and Janice shared a private joke.

"Girls," Janice said, "This is Aaron, one of my coworkers. These are my daughters, Layla and Summer."

He nodded, then raised an eyebrow at Janice. "Guess who your secret Santa is."

"Really?" Janice laughed and shook her head. "You're not supposed to tell."

"I wouldn't if it were anyone but you." He glanced at the girls. "Well, I'll let you finish your lunch. See you Monday."

As he sauntered away, Layla said, "That's him, isn't it?"

Janice picked up her sandwich. "Him who?"

"Um, hello?" Layla curled her fingers into air quotes. "Girls' night out?"

Janice gave an exasperated sigh. "I don't know what you think you know, Layla, but there's nothing going on between me and Aaron."

Layla narrowed her eyes. "You better not mess things up with Paul."

"I *said* nothing's going on. And what's with the attitude? You don't even like Paul."

Layla shrugged. "He's okay." Meeting her mom's irritated glance, she said evenly, "The point is, we like it here, and Summer loves Paul. So if you think you're gonna drag us back to California or wherever—"

"Nobody's going anywhere, Layla. Calm down."

"*Me* calm down? I'm not the one drooling over some Vin Diesel wannabe. Jesus, for once in your life why don't you act your age?"

Their slate-blue eyes and hard mouths mirrored each other. Summer wished she could crawl into the big shopping bag under the table, hide until it was over. Her mom glanced at her and said, "Damn it, Layla. Now look what you've done."

"What *I've* done?"

Janice rubbed Summer's back and said, "It's alright, baby. Don't cry. Everything's okay."

Summer tried to still her trembling chin. "I *like* Paul, Mom. In fact I *love* him."

"I do too, bunny. That's why I married him. Now finish your lunch."

৬৯ ৬৯ ৬৯ ৬৯

Sprawled at opposite ends of the couch, their feet entangled on the coffee table, Layla and Sterling were watching *Jurassic Park* with the sound turned low. The Christmas tree stood in the window, its blinking lights dimmed by the sunlight. "So you think she's lying?" Sterling asked.

"I don't know why she'd bother," Layla said. "She knows I wouldn't tell Paul if she was fooling around. But she's up to something. And that night she stayed out so late? They had a big fight when she got home. Door slamming, angry whispering, etcetera etcetera."

Crouched on the stairs with her diary on her lap, Summer watched a Tyrannosaurus rex, its tiny front legs close to its chest like a prissy lady clutching a purse as it lurched after a stumbling man who screamed and screamed. It was only a movie monster but still scary, like the grinning fears that trailed her to school. The fears had to do with her mom and the man at the mall, something secret and threatening like the tyrannosaurus lurking in the trees before it attacked.

She looked at Sterling and felt safer. His dark eyes were kind and his voice smiled—even when he'd pulled her hand from his dreadlocks and said they were off-limits to white girls, which confused and embarrassed Summer but made Layla laugh. Back in LA, all the kids Summer knew were white or Chicano or Asian. Now she went to school with black kids, most of them from the projects. In class she sat next to a night-black girl named Natalie, but on the playground everybody stayed with their own kind like Neapolitan ice cream flavors. The black kids called each other the N word, but if she said it she'd get in trouble. Sterling seemed different from the project kids, maybe because his dad was a doctor and his mom was a nurse. If he and Layla got married, he'd be her brother and she'd feel safe all the time.

The couch creaked as he leaned toward Layla. Summer held her breath. But he just grabbed the remote and turned up the sound. She opened her diary and wrote,

Just now I thought Sterling was going to kiss Layla but he didn't. So maybe they really are just friends like mom and that guy at the mall. My teacher says a cougar's the same thing as a mountain lion so I don't know why he called mom that.

The fears grinned their jagged teeth. She shut the diary. From the backyard came the rhythmic thunk of Paul chopping firewood. The temperature was dropping, and drifting clouds shrouded the sun. She hoped it snowed for Christmas. Then everyone would be happy, and the only secrets would be wrapped in shiny paper under the tree.

❧ ❧ ❧ ❧

The first day of Christmas vacation Janice turned on the faucet to brush her teeth, but only a few rusty drops trickled out. "Paul?" she called.

He came to the bathroom door, yawned and zipped up his jeans. "What's up?"

"There's no water."

"Christ, I forgot to run the faucet taps. It's probably that damned PVC pipe on the outside of the house between the kitchen and the basement. I bet it's frozen solid."

Janice set down her toothbrush, careful not to smear the toothpaste on the counter. "I have no idea what you're talking about."

"The water pipes. They can freeze if you don't drip the faucets."

"Now you tell me." The alarm radio clicked on, a low murmur of breaking news. Janice went to the closet and rifled the hangers for something to wear. Paul reached in front of her and yanked a sweatshirt from a hanger, tugged it over his head. "The thing is, I meant to wrap that pipe but I never got around to it."

Janice feigned astonishment. "Really? *You* didn't get around to something?"

"I'd better turn off the water so we don't have a flood if the pipes burst."

"Mom! Paul!" Summer ran into the bedroom. "Look!"

Janice let Summer drag her over to the window. She was irritated with Paul and impatient to get to work, but her breath caught as she gazed at a dazzling world of glass. The patio furniture, the back fence and trees and shrubs—everything was encased in ice, each branch, twig and leaf sheathed in crystal. The patio gleamed like a frozen pond. Even the power lines glinted. Cold seeped through the windowpane. Janice rubbed her arms. "It's beautiful, isn't it, baby?"

Summer nodded. "Like the Snow Queen's palace."

With a loud crack an oak branch crashed onto a power line and dragged it to the ground. The radio sputtered out; the digital clock clicked twice and went dark. Janice turned to Paul. "No water, no electricity. What do we do now?"

He chewed his lip. "Daddy wouldn't forget to run the taps, and chances are they've still got electricity. We could go over there for a while."

"Your mom hates me, Paul."

"No she doesn't. She's just—"

"I'd rather freeze to death."

"Fine." He ran a hand through his hair, then smiled at Summer. "Guess we'll have to live like pioneers today. You want to help me get a fire going downstairs, honey?"

As he led Summer out, he glanced over his shoulder. "You'd better call the station, say you're not coming in. It's too icy to drive."

Janice nodded, but he'd already turned away—something he did more and more now. Ever since she'd stayed out so late, he'd walled some part of himself off from her. She'd been *trying* to make it up to him—biting back sharp comments when he irritated her, cooking his favorite meals. And it wasn't like she'd actually *done* anything. Just that one night, the dark alley behind the bar, Aaron's cold hands under her sweater and his feverish kisses on her mouth until she'd breathlessly pushed him away. The funny thing was, now that Paul had grown distant, her desire was veering back to his lean freckled body, his hot breath on her skin. Maybe that was all desire really was—wanting what you couldn't have. Or what you were afraid of losing.

When she called the television station manager he said the ice storm was downing trees and power lines all over town, nobody was coming into work. Shivering, she got dressed, then hurried past Layla's door and down the stairs. Summer was reading in an armchair by the roaring fire. In the kitchen she found Paul on his knees dragging plastic water gallons from under the sink. "We need to save most of this for drinking and flushing toilets," he said, "but you can use some to brush your teeth. Want to take a couple gallons upstairs?" He stood up and handed her two big plastic jugs. "Don't look so worried, Jan. We'll be fine."

That was another thing. He'd started calling her Jan instead of baby or honey. Cradling a gallon in each arm, she raised a sarcastic eyebrow. "Always look on the bright side, right? Doesn't anything get to you?"

He narrowed his eyes. "A lot of things do. Wondering if my wife's been lying to me all this time, saying she loves me so she'll have a dad for her kids. That bothers me."

"You really think that?" Her voice shook. "You really think I've never loved you?"

He crouched down to pull out another plastic jug. "I don't know what to believe. If I did, maybe I wouldn't be here."

"If you're looking for an excuse to leave me, why don't you man up and say so?"

"If I decide to leave you, Janice, you'll be the first to know."

She stared at his hunched shoulders and bowed head, then turned and stalked out of the kitchen and back upstairs to her bathroom. She poured water into a glass, dribbled some on her toothbrush, and brushed her teeth until her tongue and gums tingled. She rinsed and spat, then picked up her comb and yanked it through her long dark hair. Her whole life, she'd followed her heart, which was why her daughters had different fathers. Hell, she'd followed her heart all the way to Georgia, and now Paul had the nerve to say she didn't love him. She set down the comb and bent forward, her hands flat on the counter.

"What's wrong?"

Layla was leaning against the doorjamb, one bare foot rubbing the other. Janice tried to smile. "Just having a little breakdown, is all."

"Why's it so freaking cold?"

Janice told her about the ice storm, the downed power line and the frozen pipe. "Paul's got a fire going. It's warmer downstairs."

Layla pushed her dark bangs out of her eyes. "Is that why you're upset? Because the power went out and a pipe froze?"

Janice bit her lip, then put an arm around Layla and led her to the bed. "Let's get under the covers so we'll be warm. I want to tell you something." She was surprised that Layla came willingly. When they were snuggled under the blankets, Janice confessed that she'd kissed Aaron and now she was afraid Paul might leave her, wasn't sure how to make him stay.

"You have to tell him the truth, Mom."

"You're kidding, right?"

Layla rolled her eyes. "He knows you're lying about *something*, and he probably thinks it's worse than it is. So just tell him what happened, and that you love him and it'll never happen again." She raised an eyebrow. "Unless you don't."

"Don't what?"

"Love him. Duh."

Janice sighed. "I don't know if you can love someone every single day of your life. Except your kids. That's different."

Layla nodded. "You don't have any choice, just like we don't. Except, Mom? *Do* you love us every day?"

The doubt in Layla's voice made Janice remember all the nights she'd left her daughters alone. "Baby," she said hesitantly, "just because you have kids, it doesn't mean you give up your dreams, your own life."

"But what about us? What we want?"

"When you grow up you can follow your own dreams. Till then you get to tag along on my adventures."

"Yeah, that's been great so far. We *loved* the commune house."

"Enough with the sarcasm, already."

"Want to hear about our adventures? Like when you left us with old Mr. Carey and took off with some random guy to Las Vegas? I walked in on him jerking off in front of Summer."

"Jesus, Layla, why didn't you tell me?"

"I yelled at him and it scared him so bad he let us do whatever we wanted all weekend if we promised not to tell. How's that for an adventure?"

Janice thrust a hand into her hair. "What was I supposed to do? Shelve the rest of my life? I was twenty-nine when you were born. Do you have any idea how young that is?" Propping herself on her elbow, she studied Layla's stubborn face. "No, of course you don't." She brushed back Layla's bangs. "Maybe you'll understand when you're older."

"Or maybe you will."

The front door slammed. Janice and Layla exchanged blank looks, then flung back the covers and scrambled out of bed. As they hurried downstairs, Paul's truck started up. A moment later they heard a loud crunch, the engine revving, then the truck rumbling down the street. "He told me it was too icy to drive," Janice said, "and now he's taken off somewhere."

Summer was standing by the Christmas tree, looking out the front window. "Where did Paul go, bunny?" Janice asked.

"He didn't say. He just grabbed his coat and gloves and left." Summer touched a shiny red Christmas ball, watched it wobble. "His truck slid into the pine tree. There's a big gash in the bark."

"Probably running home to mommy," Janice said bitterly. When Summer looked dismayed, she forced a smile. "I'm teasing, baby. Tell you what, we'll get blankets and pillows and put the couch cushions on the floor in front of the fire, and play Monopoly."

Behind her on the stairs, Layla muttered, "That'll rock our world." Janice whispered, "Please, Layla."

"Whatever."

"Summer, can you get all the candles and bring them into the living room? There's a bunch under my bathroom sink." When Layla opened her mouth, Janice flung up a hand. "Give me a minute, okay? Put a log on the fire or something."

Janice hurried into the den, closed the door and leaned against it. The room was cold, the windows glazed with ice. She called Paul and got his voice mail. "Where the hell are you?" she asked. Sliding her phone into her pocket, she wandered over to his desk, which was piled with schoolbooks, books on screenwriting, the latest issues of *Variety* and *The Hollywood Reporter.* A legal pad was covered with notes for a screenplay about a Savannah museum curator whose daughter, a nine-year-old math prodigy, gets kidnapped, and the curator has to solve a mathematical equation to discover the kidnapper's identity. Maybe she should have urged Paul to hang in there for another year or two before he threw in the towel. But as the head of script coverage at Galaxy Studios she'd understood the odds against an unknown screenwriter ever selling anything. And the truth was, of all the men she'd ever loved, only Paul had asked her to marry him, and after all those years as a single mom she'd been eager to escape into a new life. If it had occurred to her that she might miss her old life, she'd brushed the thought aside.

When she left the den, Layla was lurking nonchalantly in the kitchen doorway. Together they dragged the girls' mattresses downstairs to the living room while Summer trotted after them with pillows and blankets. Soon the floor between the fireplace and the denuded couch was a nest of mattresses and cushions, with the coffee table jutting out of the middle. Through the front window Janice saw Leona slipping and sliding up the driveway, her big orange cat peeking out of her coat, his litter box cradled against her hip. When Janice opened the door, frozen air stung her face and scalp.

"I hope you don't mind," Leona said as Janice pulled her inside and shut the door. "The carriage house is like, zero degrees."

The cat sprang out of her arms and dashed behind the couch. Summer, busily arranging blankets and pillows, smiled at Leona. "You can play Monopoly with us."

"We'll play in a minute, baby." Janice went upstairs and called Paul's cell phone again, then hung up on his voice mail and tossed her phone onto the unmade bed. Layla was right, he was spineless, abandoning them when they needed him most. Well, they'd be frigging pioneers without him. She went to the window and looked out. The whole world was frozen. No cars, no radios or barking dogs, just silence. She glanced around the room and her mouth went dry. Paul's reading glasses were folded on the nightstand, his boxer shorts crumpled on the floor, a long strand of ginger hair on his pillow. She'd been so sure that if their marriage fell apart, *she'd* be the one to walk out.

She came back downstairs to find Leona sitting with her back against the couch, her long legs stretched toward the fire. Summer sat beside her, the big orange cat curled in her lap. Layla was standing at the window gabbing on her cell phone. Leona smiled at Janice. "Anything I can do?"

"Not a thing, unless you can tell me where my husband's run off to."

Leona glanced at Layla, who shrugged, then at Summer, who didn't look up. With a sigh, Leona got up and took Janice's arm, marched her into the kitchen and gently pushed her into a chair. "I don't know what's going on, Janice, but those girls are handling this better than you are. You need to get your shit together."

"Oh, so now *I'm* the bad guy? Paul strands us here in this frigging icebox, and *I'm* the bad guy?"

"You think this is an icebox? Try no heat, and no fireplace, either." Leona opened the refrigerator and looked inside. "Let's see. Cheese, turkey, bread, lettuce, mayo, meatloaf. I guess we won't starve." She pulled out a wine bottle, uncorked it and poured a few inches into a glass. "Drink this, then tell me."

Janice took a sip, set the glass aside. "I've just bitched things up, per usual."

Leona leaned a hip against the counter. "Care to be more explicit?"

So Janice told her about kissing Aaron, and Paul's suspicions. "So now I don't know *what* to do."

"I'd say you need to come clean to Paul."

"That's what Layla says."

"That kid's smarter than your average bear."

Janice gave a grudging smile. "Smarter than me, you mean. But it's not easy, you know? I'm not saying it was easy being a single mom, but at least I had my dreams, the excitement of never knowing what was around the next corner."

Leona sat down, folded her arms on the table. "Sounds like things are pretty exciting right now."

"Yeah, but not in a good way."

"Look, Paul's not the kind of guy who goes out for cigarettes and never comes back, so you can stop worrying about that. But you've made him doubt you, and if you screw up again, he probably *will* leave you."

Janice made a wry face. "That's not exactly a game plan, Leona."

"You want a game plan? First off, quit acting like you're the only woman who's ever pissed off her husband. We're gonna have lunch by the fire, play Monopoly, and when Paul comes home, you'll confess your sins and give him the best make-up sex he's ever had—and *keep* giving it to him until he forgets what you were fighting about. Then you never, ever cross that line again."

Janice gulped some wine. "Did you always have the hots for your husband?"

"Love isn't just about having the hots for someone."

"So, I take it that's a no?"

"It comes and goes." Leona smiled, her eyes full of memories. "Just when you think it's gone for good, wham, you're like horny teenagers, making out in public, doing it on the kitchen table. Geez, Janice, you ought to know that by now."

Janice chewed her lip, stared off into space. "Maybe I never stayed with anyone long enough to find that out."

They were setting up the Monopoly board when Paul's truck rumbled into the driveway. A minute later he pushed open the front door and set two bulging grocery bags on the floor. He rushed back outside and returned with another bag, shut the door and hung up his coat. Squatting by the grocery bags, he pulled out four thermoses and said, "Two hot cocoa and two coffee."

Summer squeaked and clapped her hands. Even Layla grinned as Paul displayed his plunder. A pecan pie and a big pot of chili, marshmallows, chocolate bars and graham crackers—all the ingredients for smores. He winked at Leona. "Glad you could join us."

"Paul," Janice said, "wherever did you—"

"Well, Kenny—that's my brother-in-law, Leona—came by and nabbed Daddy's spare generator first thing this morning. So Mama heated up the chili and made coffee and cocoa while I raided the pantry." Paul kicked off his shoes and stepped across the cushions to set the chili pot on the hearth. Janice took the bag of thermoses into the kitchen. She was getting mugs out of the cupboard when Paul came in with the other grocery bags. She smiled over her shoulder. "I never knew pioneers had it this good."

He set the bag on the counter, ran a hand through his hair. "Listen—"

"Paul, please—"

"Please *what*, Janice? What *else* can I do for you today?" His eyes shut in a quick grimace. Then he walked out of the kitchen. She followed him down the hall into the den and shut the door behind her. The room was freezing, the backyard trees dim blurs through the icy windows. Paul stood with his back to her, his hands flat on his desk. Then he turned and said, "Just because I love you doesn't mean you can walk all over me, Jan."

"I don't walk all over you!"

"Well, it's not for lack of trying. And could you keep your voice down?"

Janice hugged her elbows. "So you're fine with being a doormat for everyone but me, is that it?" She flattened her voice, mimicking his drawl. "Yes Mama, No Mama, I'll get right on that, Daddy."

"Sneering at my folks, that's real nice, Janice." He rubbed a hand over his face. "You know what your problem is? You mistake love for weakness."

"*My* problem? *I'm* not the one—"

"Or maybe you're just selfish. You do what you want, and you never count the cost to me—or to your girls. I mean, do you ever stop for one minute to think how *I* feel? *Nothing* I do is good enough for you. And now this—whatever it is—you're doing behind my back."

Her chin went up. "I'm not cheating on you, Paul. I was tempted—"

"That's supposed to make me feel better?"

"But I *didn't*." She stepped closer, touched his arm. "Please, don't be mad at me."

"How would you like it if I went sneaking around behind your back?" He shifted his arm away. "I was just gonna drop this stuff off, go to a motel or something."

Janice swallowed. "I don't want you to go. And the girls don't, either."

He gave a wry smile. "Layla's wanted me gone since the day we met."

"She's coming around, Paul. Just give it some time."

He shrugged, walked past her and opened the door. Unsure what else she could do or say, Janice followed him back to the kitchen, where he poured coffee for the grownups, hot cocoa for the girls, while she got down the sugar bowl and took a carton of half-and-half from the refrigerator. They went back to the living room, Paul carrying the steaming mugs on a tray.

He passed around the mugs, then lowered himself onto the cushions beside Summer, who grabbed his hand and kissed it. When she glanced at Layla, expecting a snide remark, she saw a look pass between Layla and Janice—mouths relaxing, slate eyes smiling. It reassured Summer that their makeshift family would hold together, at least for a while. But she wished she had someone to mirror her soft blue eyes back to her, the way her mom and sister mirrored each other.

Paul smiled at her. "Is your cocoa too hot?"

Summer shook her head, picked up the mug and blew on the cocoa. Then she put her hand on Paul's knee, claiming him—an unexpected gift, the present she hadn't asked for but that was nevertheless exactly what she wanted.

Layla grabbed the top hat from the Monopoly board and said, "Are we playing or what?" So they gathered around the coffee table, and as the afternoon light faded, Leona coached Summer while Paul and Layla ganged up on Janice. After quashing their mutual opponents, Layla gleefully bankrupted Paul, who grinned, flung up his hands in defeat and went outside for more firewood. Then they ate lukewarm chili by candlelight and toasted marshmallows for smores until everyone got so sticky they had to use some of the bottled water to wash up.

Summer dozed off first, the cat curled beside her. Then Layla burrowed into a nest of quilts with a flashlight and a book. Paul brought out a bottle of Scotch, and they talked softly about the war in Iraq, whether Hillary Clinton would become America's first woman president. Eventually Leona wrapped herself in blankets and stretched out by the couch. Paul put another log on, and the flames blazed brighter. He and Janice gathered the rest of the blankets and lay down. When she snuggled closer he stiffened. She rolled onto her side and waited. Firelight licked up the wall to the ceiling. After a while he sighed, spooned his body to hers. She pressed his arm to her ribs, felt his breathing deepen into sleep.

When she woke in the blue darkness that presaged dawn, the fire was dead but the house was warm, the Christmas tree lights blinking. She closed her eyes, snuggled closer to Paul. Soon, gray light would seep into the room and they'd get up, put back the cushions and drag the mattresses upstairs, wash the dishes. Layla would whip out her cell phone while Summer sprawled on the couch watching cartoons. Paul would probably go into the den to work on his screenplay. Standing in the living room with her coffee, Janice would try to picture the rest of her life while beyond the window-pane the gleaming mirrors of ice turned to water, the streets full of dark puddles reflecting dripping trees, the clouds and sky.

STILL LIFE WITH MOON AND STARS

I

Layla hadn't ever been to church, much less to a funeral, so when Sterling missed school on Tuesday to attend his grandfather's funeral, her compassion was tinged with awed curiosity. That evening Sterling whistled a familiar ripple of notes under her window, and she slapped shut her math book and ran downstairs. Her mom was in the living room, reading a spy thriller on the couch. "Sterling's here," Layla said on her way to the front door. Surfacing from her novel, Janice blinked at Layla. "Tell him how sorry we are, okay?"

Sterling stood in the front yard, a silhouette against the streetlight's haze. He was fifteen, just a year older than Layla, but tonight he seemed a lot older. His thin black eyebrows were furrowed, his shoulders slightly hunched, his hands deep in his pockets. Without saying anything, they headed down the driveway and walked through the dim streets to the edge of town, then followed a dirt path to the railroad tracks. A full moon cast black tree shadows across the long grass. A train hooted in the distance. As they stepped onto the crossties Layla said, "I've never lost anybody close. I mean, not like that."

His dark eyes bright with tears, or maybe moonlight, Sterling said, "He's been there my whole life, you know? He taught me to drive in his old black Caddy when I was twelve. How to hunt, play dominoes. Hell, you've met him. He's funny as hell, right? Always riffing on shit, from the government to Grandma Nola's hens." Sterling tilted back his head and fingered his short dreadlocks as he gazed at the stars. "I just hope he's someplace I can see him again. But who knows what happens when you die? I'm thinking you're just, you know, *gone.*"

"But your soul has to go somewhere," Layla said. "Like, your life spark?"

"Maybe. I don't know." As they followed the tracks across a creek, the air turned cool and damp. Tree frogs chirped and silver ripples glimmered in the dark stream. When they reached the other side, the rails began to vibrate, so they got off the tracks and trudged up a hill shadowed with oaks. Halfway up, Layla turned to watch the train thunder past them. Sterling stood behind her, his hands on her shoulders, his chest warm against her back. When his hands slid to her bare arms Layla's breath caught in her throat. The locomotive roared over the bridge and shook the ground, the air full of wind and tumult. Graffiti-splashed boxcars rattled past and then they were staring at empty tracks and the dim fields beyond them. Sterling dropped his hands. Layla turned to look at him but shadows covered his face and shoulders.

"Guess we should head back," he said. "School night and all." As she followed him up the hill, the heat of his hands lingered on her skin.

ೞ ೞ ೲ ೲ

The bus lurched onto Prince Avenue as Layla groped in her hoodie for her iPod, which she must have left at home. All around her, boys shouted and girls screeched over the opera music that the bus driver, fat old Mrs. Douglas, inflicted on them each morning. This semester was Wagner's Ring Cycle, whatever *that* was. Putting her fingers in her ears, Layla tried to focus on an unfamiliar sensation—happiness and something else, maybe anticipation.

Layla's best friend Stace was slumped on the seat beside her cramming for a French test, because Stace was a good student despite the green hair, her eyes black holes of mascara and eye shadow. Layla thought Stace should lose the dead-white makeup and black lipstick, but she sort of understood. With chubby cheeks, a nervous laugh and bitten nails, Stace yearned to be popular, her goth persona a bid for attention. Half-rising from her seat, Layla shoved down the window and leaned forward, the cool air soft as silk. People kept saying this was the most beautiful spring in recent memory—day after day of blue skies and primrose sunsets, songbirds flitting through leafing trees, dogwood blossoms painting the streets pink and white.

Back in California, Grandma Wenther had planted flowers every spring. Kneeling in the grass with her lank gray hair hanging in her face, she'd pat dirt around a spindly petunia and say, "From miserable beginnings come great things." Like Layla's first miserable months here, when they'd lived with Paul's parents, whose syrupy hospitality couldn't hide their dislike—*Have another biscuit, honey. Didn't anyone teach you girls to say please and thank you? Now you know we love having you here, but didn't I ask you girls not to run in the house?* For nearly a year Layla had despised all things Southern, from the muggy heat and shrill cicadas to the heavy fried food. But life had gotten better when she'd started high school and met Stace. Then she'd met Sterling, a guy friend to bump shoulders with, ride bikes with. And he made her feel safe, watched over, something she hadn't felt since Grandma Wenther moved to a retirement community in Phoenix. But last night had changed things. Layla closed her eyes and the train thundered toward her, Sterling's warm hands on her skin.

The bus jounced up the high school's long driveway, hissed to a stop. The door wheezed open, and a bunch of letter-jacketed boys shouted and shoved their way up the aisle. As Brad Derham sauntered past, he surprised Layla with a quick smile. The cutest boy in the whole ninth grade, he usually stuck to his own crowd. Bemused, Layla followed Stace off the bus.

The first bell was jangling when Layla tumbled books into her locker. As she slammed the metal door, two ninth-grade girls with perfect tans and shiny hair hurried up the hall. The dark-haired one, Brooke Saunders, grabbed Layla's arm and pulled her along, saying, "Mr. P's *so* gonna give us detention if we're late." Amber Wilkins flipped back her blond hair and smiled. Surprised by their friendliness, Layla floated into homeroom in the buoyant bubble of their chatter. As she slid into her seat her phone vibrated. She sneaked it onto her lap and read, LAYLA U GOT ME ON MY KNEES 4 REAL—BRAD D. She glanced up. He was looking right at her—thick blond hair, eyes like a deep summer sky, a bashful smile. She smiled back, then blushed and looked away.

After homeroom Brad fell into step with her in the hall, and she caught a whiff of pungent smoke, probably weed. He pushed back his bangs and asked, "So what do you have next?"

"History. What do you have?"

"English, with Albreizi."

Layla smiled. "Poor you." A few of the kids walking past eye-balled them, probably wondering why he was talking to a social zero like Layla. At her locker she turned to face him. "So what's with the text? Are you pranking me?"

His mouth tightened. "Why would I do that? I mean, what kind of asshole would do that?"

Abashed, she stammered, "It's kind of sudden, is all. It's not like we've talked, or you ever even look at me."

His mouth relaxed into a smile. "You've just never caught me looking at you."

At lunch Amber and Brooke insisted that Layla sit with them. Oh, and Stace too, of course. As Layla sat down, her eyes met Sterling's across the high school's food court. He shrugged and headed over to another table, where he exchanged complicated handshakes with Drew and Marcus, then sat down between Latoya and Michelle. Layla was about to go over and say—*something*—when Brad Derham and Jon set down their trays. Brad squeezed onto the bench beside her and asked what bands she liked.

"The Decemberists, and Neutral Milk Hotel."

Brad nodded. "Yeah, they're cool." He picked up his cheeseburger with both hands. "I'm more into Radiohead, Audioslave."

Stace leaned forward to catch Brad's eye. "I'm *way* into Cruxshadows," she said, "and I *adore* Marilyn Manson." She dipped a French fry into a glob of mayonnaise and licked the end, then closed her eyes and slowly slid the fry into her mouth like she was a porn star. Grinning, she reached for another. "I love mayo fries. You want one, Brad?" He grimaced and shook his head. Brooke rolled her eyes, and Jon snickered. Layla bit into her grilled cheese sandwich, wishing Stace would get a clue. You had to act all nonchalant to be cool. Even Layla knew that.

Between classes that afternoon she went into the computer lab and logged onto Facebook. Amber, Brooke, Jon and Brad had friended her, and Sterling had posted a single line, I want to ride these rails outta here. As she stared at the screen, his words were boxcars clattering away from her. She messaged, emailed, then texted R U OK? As she left the lab she realized that although the morning's happiness had changed, intensified, a dark speck now marred its radiant core.

Brad caught up with her at the buses. Brooke's mom was driving "everyone" to Ben Burton Park, did she want to come? She'd been about to call Sterling, but Brad's smiling blue eyes held her gaze and she nodded, told him where she lived.

When she got home she stood in front of her closet mirror, her thin face staring back at her—stubborn chin, slate-blue eyes and thick eyebrows. Not a face to launch even a tugboat. And her breasts were molehills. Maybe Brad was pranking her after all.

At the park they sat on the flat rocks along the Oconee River basking in the sunshine. Jon lit a joint and passed it around. When it was Layla's turn she handed it to Brad, who inhaled until his eyes watered. Jon shook his head in disgust. "You're such a bogart, dude." Brad grinned, then turned to Layla. "Take a walk with me?"

They strolled along the jade-green river, ducked under overhanging bushes and emerged on a stretch of flat rocks that went
all the way across the water. Layla stopped, mesmerized by shallow
waterfalls and sunlit ripples gliding over submerged rocks. Brad
took her hand, his palm callused from baseball practice. Gazing at
the water, she said, "This is a cool park."

"Yeah, I ride my bike here sometimes just to, you know, chill."
He picked up a stone, skipped it across the water. "And it's awesome
tubing in summer, except the river gets kind of low."

As she gazed at the sunlit ripples she felt him watching her.
When he said, "Look at me, Layla," she turned to him. He took her
face in his hands and kissed her, his lips soft and smoky. She closed
her eyes, heard the river splashing over rocks, birds twittering. His
arms went around her and his tongue twined with hers. Then he
was smiling, saying girl you're so beautiful. She felt hot and shiv-
ery, dazed by the light in his eyes, his warm smile.

"Why me?" she stammered when his hands slid down her arms.

"I don't know, maybe 'cause you're different. Like, you've been
places, done things, you know?"

They sat down on a flat rock and talked haltingly about school,
their families. Last summer at baseball camp in Colorado he'd fall-
en in love with the mountains, wanted to move there after high
school. Layla listened more than she spoke. Even though Brad's
parents were divorced and his mom had remarried, she didn't want
to talk about her reckless mother, the father she'd never met.

At lunch the next day she looked all over for Sterling and finally found him sitting under a tree. As she sat down beside him,
he held up his sandwich. "PB and J on rye. That's what I'm saying."

"Whatever." Layla tore the seal off her yogurt and licked it.
"So, what's up? I tried to get ahold of you last night, to like, see
how you're doing."

"It's all good." He shrugged. "You want to hook up with some
jock, that's cool."

Layla bit her lip, looked away. "I was talking about your
grandpa."

"I miss him, but it is what it is, you know?" He bit into his sandwich, chewed and swallowed. "So are you and jock boy an item?"

It was Layla's turn to shrug, like it didn't matter. She plucked a handful of grass, blew it off her palm. "He kissed me, so I guess he likes me."

Sterling smiled and stood up. "Well, I got people to see, things to do. Catch you later, girl."

భు భు భు భు

Layla went to baseball games now, cookouts and parties. Whenever she could, she invited Stace along, even though Brooke and Amber rolled their eyes at Stace and Jon called her "the Meatwad" behind her back. Sitting with Brad on the bus or walking into homeroom with Brooke and Amber, Layla learned to pretend she didn't see the glances from boys who'd never noticed her before, from girls who resented her sudden popularity. So much had changed in the past month, sometimes Layla felt like a completely different person.

But today her old self was stirring. It was a rainy afternoon and they were hanging out at Brooke's house because her parents were on a Caribbean cruise. Brooke, Brad, and Jon were smoking a blunt and playing Halo on Brooke's computer, per usual, and Layla and Amber were watching a *Desperate Housewives* marathon. Layla glanced restlessly at the rain-streaked windows. Last fall she and Sterling had gone on long rainy rambles while they argued about social justice, whether rap lyrics were sexist, whether the black senator from Illinois had a chance in hell of becoming president. These days she was lucky if Sterling nodded to her in the hall between classes. She bit her lip, glanced at Brad. If you loved someone, didn't you want to know what they thought, what they felt? But although Brad always wanted her beside him, holding his hand, part of his crowd, they were rarely alone, and when they were alone, talking wasn't what he had in mind.

He came over and sat on the couch arm, leaned in to kiss her, his hand on the back of her neck. His soft lips stirred a tingle in her stomach before he pulled away and smiled into her eyes. "After I trounce these fools we're gonna go to the Grill, okay, baby?"

Layla did what a girlfriend was supposed to do. She smiled and nodded, like watching her stoned boyfriend stuff his face with chili fries was what she lived for.

2

Still the same. Still exactly the same. Only Jody herself had changed. In aviator sunglasses, skinny jeans and a white button-down shirt, Jody was cruising down Prince Avenue in a spanking new red Saturn convertible, her black curls whipping in the breeze.

On Barber Street sunlight slanted through the towering oaks, and her former sisterhood sauntered along the cracked sidewalks, some of them leaning on lampposts and cars, their faces eager or dejected depending on how long, and how successfully, they'd been on the street. And there pacing back and forth on the corner was Skinny Molly with her manic grin and raggedy afro. And that was Heidi climbing out of a van, blond and Valkyrie-tall in black thigh boots, her dress barely covering her ass. Jody tapped the horn, then changed her mind. If she stopped, they'd crowd around to bum cigarettes, tell her the hard-luck stories she already knew because they used to be her own.

She turned onto Boulevard and drove slowly under the interlacing oaks. When she spotted Leona's faded purple mailbox she parked and got out of the car, eager to whip off her sunglasses and surprise the hell out of her old friend. After they hugged and exclaimed, they'd have an early dinner at the Red Lobster, then drinks at Foxy's for old times' sake—that is, unless Leona was holding a grudge. *Still the same,* the front yard's shady magnolia trees, white buds unfurling amid the dark glossy leaves. Still the same, but something was wrong. Taking off her dark glasses, Jody stared at a sunlit patch of kudzu where Leona's white clapboard house should have been.

"You looking for Leona?"

A girl, maybe thirteen or fourteen, in a black tee-shirt and rag-gedy jeans stood on the far sidewalk, hands on her hips, head tilted to the side. Jody slid on her sunglasses, then jerked her thumb at the kudzu. "What the hell happened here?"

"Termites," the girl said as she crossed the street. "The whole house, like, collapsed." She stepped onto the curb. "Miss Thalia said it sounded like a freight train. You a friend of Leona's?"

The girl's wary eyes reminded Jody of herself at that age. "Yeah, me and Leona go way back. Shit, she wasn't hurt or any-thing, was she?"

The girl shook her head, then pointed across the street to a blue Victorian house with white gingerbread trim. "That's Miss Thalia's house. And Leona lives over there." She nodded toward a carriage house at the back of the side lawn—a small replica of the blue Victo-rian house in front. Purple wisteria draped an upstairs porch, and a big oak dappled light across the grass. Jody reminded herself that her apartment had cherry wood floors and granite counters, central air. She shrugged. "Trust Leona to land on her feet."

"Just so you know, she misses her house."

"Don't get me wrong," Jody said quickly. "I'm her biggest fan." She stared at the carriage house, wondering if this was such a good idea after all. "Guess I better go on over and say hello."

"You can't," the girl said. "She's at work."

"Is she still at the café? That's where we met, my first job out of high school."

The girl clapped a hand over her mouth. "Oh my god. Are you *Jody*?"

Jody forced a smile. "Guilty as charged. How'd you know?"

"Are you kidding? You're like, a local legend. I'm Layla, by the way. We live over there, next door to Miss Thalia."

"So what did Leona say about me?"

Layla clasped her hands behind her back like she was reciting a poem. "You and these two drug dealers broke into Leona's house. She shot one dude in the hand and there was like, serious blood splatter, and they ran off. Then she let you inside and while the police were pounding on the front door you stole her tip money and vamoosed into the night, never to be heard from again."

"Sounds pretty dramatic to hear you tell it."

"Well that's how Leona tells it."

Jody took a flattened pack of Marlboros from her purse and lit one. Layla made a face and flapped a hand at the smoke. Jody rolled her eyes. "Let me guess," she said. "You're allergic or a Jesus freak or something."

"D. None of the above. So, um, are you still a prostitute?"

"Do you know many hookers driving around in brand-new convertibles?"

"Well maybe you went to Miami and became, like, a high-priced call girl."

"Try Atlanta. And what I became, not that it's any of your business, is an exotic dancer."

"And the difference would be...what?"

"Hello? Giving some schmoe a blow job, versus shaking your booty for football players and music moguls?" Frowning, Jody flicked ash onto the grass. "Though I guess it's a continuum, you know? From waitress to hooker, it's all about making people want what you've got—whether it's sex or a ham sandwich. But dancing at a club in Buckhead, now *that's* the top of the stratosphere. I've got a *sweet* apartment, a fat bank account, and nobody beats me up. Plus, I only put out when I feel like it."

Layla pulled a strand of hair into her mouth and chewed on it, her eyes round.

"I probably shouldn't be telling you things like that." Jody looked Layla up and down. "I mean, you probably think tongue kissing is a big deal."

"*Not* that it's any of your business, but me and Brad, who's like, the coolest guy in the whole ninth grade, we French kiss all the time."

"Wow, all the time, huh? So you must be like, the coolest girl in the whole ninth grade."

Layla lifted her chin. "Are you making fun of me?"

"Just making conversation." Jody dropped her cigarette into the trickling gutter. "Think I'll cruise around the old hood. Wanna come?"

Layla's smile made her thin face almost beautiful. When she got into the car, she stroked the leather seat and said, "I can totally see myself in one of these." As they pulled away from the curb, she peered into the side mirror, touched the lone pimple on her chin. "As a matter of fact, I wasn't popular at *all* till I hooked up with Brad. Then, snap, I'm in with the in crowd, and Brooke and Amber are my new BFFs."

"Like I said, it's all about perception." Jody downshifted for a stoplight. "This Brad dude wants you, and desire drives the market. So your stock's gone up."

Layla's hair blew into her face and she brushed it away. They crossed Prince Avenue and entered a neighborhood of shady streets and old houses. On Hill Street, Jody parked in front of a yellow clapboard house. Behind a neatly clipped hedge the grass was dotted with lawn ornaments—whirligigs, birdbaths, gnomes and plaster animals. Jody took off her sunglasses and stared at the house, her mouth a bitter line. "Home sweet home," she said. "Or not." She opened the door and got out. "You coming or what?"

"Um, maybe I should take off."

"Look, I'm just gonna give my mom a hug, say hi, then we'll split. Easy peasy."

"Nah, that's okay." Layla clicked the lock switch back and forth. "Or I could just wait here."

Jody glanced from the house to Layla. "So, you don't smoke. Does that mean you don't drink either?"

"I used to smoke sometimes," Layla said defensively. "At the commune house back in LA? We used to sneak cigs and wine whenever the moms partied."

Jody leaned into the car with a friendly smile. "A commune, huh? Anyway, if you come with me now, I've got some vodka coolers for after. Interested?"

Layla was interested. Was, in fact, thrilled. But she didn't want to show it. So she shrugged and said, "Fine. Whatever."

Following Jody up the front walk, Layla glimpsed a lawn jockey hunched among the azaleas, its black face chipped to reveal the white plaster underneath—definitely uncool. Jody crossed the porch and pressed the doorbell. They heard voices inside, then footsteps. The door opened, and a woman with dark eyes in a doughy face looked blankly at Jody. "Oh my Lord," she gasped. "You look so nice, well, I almost didn't recognize you, honey." She stepped onto the porch and closed the door behind her. Smiling, she gave Jody a quick hug. Then she noticed Layla and stopped smiling. "Who's this?"

"This is Layla. Layla, this is my mom, Mrs. Johnston."

"Jody, this girl's not a—" Mrs. Johnston looked Layla over, then gave an embarrassed laugh. "No, I can see she's not. Nice to meet you, honey."

After an uncomfortable pause, Jody lifted an eyebrow. "Aren't you gonna invite us in, Mom?"

"Well, I would, honey, but it's Wednesday."

"Oh, right. No daughters allowed in the house on Wednesdays."

Mrs. Johnston's smile thinned. "My Bible study group, dear. And we're going out to dinner at Applebee's after." Stepping closer to Jody, she said quietly, "There's nothing in the house, just a twenty in my purse for dinner."

"Wow." Jody slowly shook her head. "I'm out of here."

Layla mumbled, "Nice meeting you," then followed Jody down the porch steps. At the sidewalk Jody turned and shouted, "Jesus, Mom, I said I was sorry, and I paid you back! And that was *five* years ago. So give it a rest, okay?"

Her mother went inside, quietly shut the door.

Overgrown hedges fenced the sides of Leona's backyard, and a mulberry tree cast its scant shade on a picnic table spattered with dried bird shit. Jody spread a beach towel on the table and they sat down, their feet on the bench, their backs to an alley lined with fences and blank-faced garage doors.

Jody took a joint from her cigarette pack, lit it, then offered it to Layla, who gingerly took it. "You have to hold your breath or you won't get high," Jody said, so Layla held in the smoke until her lungs burned. After a few more tokes, Jody stubbed the joint out on the picnic bench. "That ought to give us a buzz."

Too true, Layla thought. She felt like she was floating or something, and her thoughts were buzzing bees. Frowning, she tried to follow them. "So like, your mom *knows* you were a prostitute?"

"Yep, that's what's so great about living in a small town. She probably knew about it before I finished my first trick. And she's *never*, ever gonna let it go."

"So I take it you and your mom don't get along."

Jody twisted the caps off two vodka coolers and handed one to Layla. "Let's just say it sucks when your unwed teenage mom finds Jesus. I was like this voodoo doll she'd stick pins into to punish herself."

"My mom's like, totally the opposite." Layla took a sip of her vodka cooler, was pleasantly surprised by the tart fizzy taste. "My dad left her while she was pregnant, but the way she goes on about love, it's a frigging miracle I'm still a virgin."

"So are you gonna do it with your boyfriend? Are you guys like, all in love?"

Clasping her knees, Layla searched the puffy clouds for an answer. Brad's body, its maleness, fascinated her—the pale wisps of hair in his armpits, the small ears beneath his thick blond hair, the muscles under his soft skin. "He's a sweetheart, but—I don't know. Not like, *love*, love." She picked at the frayed white knees of her jeans. If getting high meant spilling your guts to strangers, she wasn't doing this again any time soon. Her tongue felt clumsy. "I think I'm wasted. Do I look wasted?"

"Your eyes are kind of bloodshot." Jody dug in her purse, handed Layla a bottle of Murine. "Here. Tilt your head back and don't blink."

Layla put in the eye drops, wiped her wet cheeks. Jody lit a cigarette and offered the pack to Layla, who shook her head.

"You're right, it's a foul habit." Jody slid the pack into her purse. "And I've *tried* to quit. But it's part of the life, you know? Waiting to go onstage, unwinding after work."

"Do you, like, pole dance?"

Jody grinned. "Yeah, but I'm not very good at it. Some of the girls totally pretzel themselves—we're talking serious gymnastics. But I just hook a leg around the pole and bend back, you know?" Handing her cigarette to Layla, who held it at arm's length like a dirty diaper, Jody hopped off the table, wrapped a leg around the mulberry and arched backward. Spreading her arms, she shimmied while staring into Layla's eyes.

Layla burst out laughing. "Oh my god, I'm sorry, but that's so gross!"

Jody grabbed a low branch, straightened up and unhooked her leg. She climbed back onto the table and said, "You may think it's gross, but my customers eat it up."

"What in the hell's going on here?"

Startled, they gaped at Leona, who stalked around the kudzu to stand before them, her arms folded. Jody cocked her head and smiled. "Now don't tell me you don't recognize me, girlfriend."

"Oh, I recognize you, Jody. You mind telling me what you're doing here?"

Jody sat up indignantly. "I thought you'd be all happy and shit. Specially since I've got the money I, um, borrowed."

"You'd better go on home, Layla."

"I can't. I'm wasted."

Leona brushed her auburn hair out of her eyes and glared at Jody. "What did you give her?"

"Just a couple of tokes and a vodka cooler." Jody shrugged. "I don't know why you're making such a thing out of it."

"She's only fourteen is why. And she's not a hooker."

Jody narrowed her eyes. "I was gonna take you out. Dinner and drinks, you know? I thought you'd be glad I landed on my feet."

"Not that I care, but where *did* you land?"

"That club I told you about." Jody licked her lips. "I'm making crazy good money. Got my own apartment." She pointed toward the street. "That's my ride."

"Congratulations. Now how about paying me back that two hundred dollars?"

"Fine." Jody pulled out her wallet, opened it and counted out five fifty-dollar bills. "Here's two hundred, and a tip."

"You can keep your goddamn tip."

"Whatever." Jody handed her two hundred dollars, then turned to Layla. "I booked a room at the Marriott. You wanna go hang out?"

"She's not going anywhere."

"Jesus, what's happened to you, Leona?" Jody asked. "You used to be so cool."

"You and those drug pushers happened to me." Leona jerked her head at the empty space where her house had stood. "That happened to me." Then she sighed and rubbed the back of her neck. "And after Jesse left town, I swore off men, so I'm a little cranky, okay?"

Jody grinned. "It's not my fault you're not getting any."

Leona's lips twitched in amusement. "You'd better come over to my place and sober up. I'll order a pizza, and you"—she pointed at Jody—"can pay for it."

"Now you're talking." Jody hopped off the table. "Pizza and G and T's, right?"

"Can I stay for pizza and G and T's?" Layla asked.

"You can stay for dinner if it's okay with your mom," Leona said. "But you're done drinking. And you ought to thank your lucky stars Miss Thalia's at that church retreat this weekend."

"Who's this Miss Thalius again?" Jody asked.

Layla rolled her eyes. "Miss Thalia, Leona's landlady. She's really cool but she's like a hundred years old and kind of churchy."

They ate on the upstairs porch so Jody and Leona could smoke, and by the time Layla finished her third slice of pizza, the sun was sinking into a bank of yellow clouds, and she felt normal again. When her phone buzzed she glanced at it and said, "It's Brad," then walked into the shadows at the end of the lattice-screened porch. "Hey," she murmured. "What's up?"

"Just chilling, missing you. Wanna come over?"

He lived on the other side of Barber, a five-minute bike ride. But it was fun listening to Jody and Leona talk about the good old days—shooting pool at Foxy's, drinking beer and dancing with men who wanted to sleep with them. Jody had accused Leona of always getting the best-looking dudes, and Leona had laughed, said it was gift, she just knew how to pick them.

"You there, baby?"

"Yeah."

"If you come over, I'll be your best friend."

Layla gave a soft laugh. "Deal."

When she said she was taking off, Jody snorted. "Sounds like a booty call to me."

"Yeah, great meeting you, too, Jody."

"Ah, girl." Jody got up and gave Layla a hug. "Friend me, okay?"

After Layla left, Leona lit a cigarette, smiled at Jody. "If you get that girl in *any* kind of trouble, I will personally hunt you down and hurt you."

Jody pushed aside her paper plate. "Jesus, Leona, you're as bad as my mom. When I went by to see her this afternoon? She wouldn't even let me in the house."

Leona shrugged. "What did you expect? People judge you by your actions."

Jody splashed more gin into her glass, stirred it with her finger. "I haven't turned a trick or stolen a single dime in like, two years. And I don't do meth anymore, not even recreationally."

"What do you want me to say, Jody? How great it is that you're a stripper?" A June bug thudded to the floor and crawled around in a circle, its dark wings buzzing. "You want me to say you're gonna be young and beautiful forever?"

"Anybody home?"

Leona stood up and went to the porch rail. "Hey Janice, come on up." When Leona sat back down, she mouthed, "Layla's mom."

A few moments later Janice pushed open the French doors. Jody would have known she was Layla's mom without any help—the same long brown hair, thick eyebrows and dark blue eyes, the same stubborn mouth and chin. When Janice heard that Layla had gone to Brad's house, she raised her glass and said she was glad that Layla was experiencing the "adventure" of first love.

In Jody's opinion, *adventure* didn't quite cover it. When she wasn't much older than Layla, she'd fallen hard for the guy who ended up pimping her out. But she hadn't made that mistake again—these days her heart was her own. Well, it wasn't her problem if Layla's mom was delusional. She drained her glass, glanced at her watch, and said she had to get going. As she hugged Leona goodbye, they promised to keep in touch, but Jody wasn't sure if Leona meant it.

In her car, Jody sat listening to crickets, a barking dog, a nighthawk's sharp squeak. Then she called the Marriott and cancelled her reservation. Half an hour later she was speeding down the Atlanta highway, Kanye West's *Graduation* blasting through the speakers. It was a warm night, but clouds were spreading across the sky and the air smelled like rain. She was off work till Wednesday, had planned to spend a couple of nights in Athens. But it hadn't turned out like she'd expected. *Welcome home and don't let the door hit you on your way out.* What were you supposed to do when you were homesick for a place where nobody missed you, nobody cared?

As she approached Lawrenceville, floodlit billboards and gas stations crowded out the dark fields. In an hour she'd be home. A whole wide weekend with nothing planned. At the club, music pounded as she strutted onto the stage in spangled pasties and a thong—a star under the glittering lights. Men whistled and called to her, held out tens and twenties so she'd bend over, let them look but not touch. Sometimes they asked her out, offered to buy her things. It was against club policy, but one of these days maybe she'd let a Braves player or a record label exec take her clubbing or out to dinner. If she played her cards right, she could end up a trophy wife.

Lightning fractured the darkness. The CD player changed to Norah Jones singing "Come Away with Me." When she got home she'd put on her bikini, go down to the star-shaped pool and swim in the warm rain. She hadn't done that since she was thirteen, skinny-dipping in the Oconee River with Liz Stanton and Joe Wilson. Lightning flashed in the rearview mirror and she counted to three before thunder rumbled through the clouds. Leona had said Jody wouldn't be young forever, but those were just words. She turned up the music, felt the wind whip her hair. She still had time.

୫~ ୫~ ~୧ ~୧

Brad's house was dark except for the blue glow in his upstairs window. Layla pushed her ten-speed up the steep driveway. As she chained her bike to the porch rail, the light came on and Brad opened the front door, a beer in his hand. "Hey baby." He pushed back his bangs. "Come here and give me a kiss."

Smiling and blushing, she went to him and lifted her face. Beer on his breath, his soft lips on hers, a gloomy Radiohead song throbbing through their kiss. Then he smoothed her hair and smiled. "Mom and the stepdad went to Atlanta, so we've got the place to ourselves." Taking her hand, he drew her inside and shut the door. As he led her toward the stairs she stumbled against him. Her mouth was dry, her heart pounding—excitement or panic, she couldn't tell which.

His bedroom was lit by his computer screen, a lava lamp, and the blue light above an aquarium that was divided into compartments for his fighting fish—two iridescent blue ones, two red ones, and one mottled turquoise and red. The fish flashed along their glass walls, their long gorgeous fins swirling around them. When Layla started toward the aquarium Brad grabbed her hands and pulled her down beside him on his bed. Her nervous laugh turned into a yelp as he pushed her onto her back. Then his tongue was deep in her mouth, his hand snaking up under her tee-shirt. She pried his fingers from her bra and pushed him off her. Still on her back, she readjusted her bra. Brad propped himself on his elbow, his eyes luminous in the blue light. "What's the matter, baby?"

She sat up and smoothed her hair. "Just, slow down, is all. You're making me feel like a ham sandwich."

He gave a soft laugh. "A *what?*"

"Never mind."

He sat up and scooted to the edge of the bed beside her, took her hand in his and played with her fingers. "Um, no offense, baby, but is this the dreaded PMS monster?"

"No, it's just—" Layla slowly untangled her fingers from his, then stood up. Chewing her lip, she studied his tanned face and hopeful smile. "What are you thinking?" she asked, "right this minute?"

"How beautiful you are, how much I want you."

She turned and walked out of his room, down the stairs and onto the porch. Her hands shook as she unlocked her bike. It wasn't that she was upset, or that he'd scared her. She just didn't want to hear any more blasé blah about Halo scores or how much money someone's dad made or how much Brad *wanted* her. As she wheeled her bike down the driveway he leaned out his window and called, "I'm sorry, baby! Come back up, okay? I can slow down, no problem!" She shook her head, tightened her grip on the handlebars. So that was that, she thought. No more soft kisses, no more holding hands at school, other girls' envious glances making her feel like the homecoming queen. At the bottom of the driveway she straddled her bike and looked back, hoping the front door would open, hoping it stayed shut. Then she pushed off and coasted down the street.

Making a wide turn onto Barrow Street, she hit a pothole hidden in a parked car's shadow. A firecracker bang deafened her and the bike lurched sideways, the back wheel dragging. She stopped and jumped off. The back tire was hissing air—a flat. Nothing to do but walk home. With a sigh, she heaved the bike onto the curb and rolled it toward Barber Street. When she reached the corner, a skinny black woman with a shaggy afro reached out both hands and snapped her fingers. "You got any glass, baby girl? Mama needs some candy bad."

Layla shook her head and kept walking. A shit-brown sedan idled alongside her. One glance at the grinning driver and she put her head down and walked faster. When a girl with blond braids darted over to the sedan and leaned in the window, Layla hustled her bike across Barber and onto the root-cracked sidewalk. She didn't slow down until she was back on her quiet familiar street, crickets chirping in the darkness. Walking past Miss Thalia's house, she peered through the gloom at Leona's porch, where candlelight glimmered and Billie Holiday's high, plaintive voice drifted into the night. So they were still there, drinking and smoking and talking in the dark.

Layla leaned her bike against the hedge and sat down on the curb, her elbows on her knees and her chin in her hands. Hard to believe Jody had been one of them, had climbed into strangers' cars so they could fuck her in the back seat, put their dicks in her mouth. But maybe sex was no big deal after you'd done it a bunch of times. Even Leona admitted she'd slept with a lot of men after her husband died—part of the grieving process, she'd said—and Layla's own mom had gone through men like toilet paper, back in the day. Layla chewed her lip. It wasn't like she had anything against sex; she just wanted it to mean something real, was all.

But by Monday everybody would think she'd done it with Brad, because that's what boys said when you broke up with them. And though she couldn't exactly picture Brad telling lies about her, she could *totally* see Brooke and Jon doing it while Brad smiled and let people think what they wanted. The bottom line was, Monday would suck, however it went down.

"Hey, girl."

Layla scrambled to her feet and peered around. Someone was coming up the sidewalk, ambling into the streetlamp's dim light. It was Sterling, probably coming from his cousin Trey's house. She pressed a hand to her heart. "You scared me."

"Sorry." He stopped a few feet away. "What are you doing out here by your lonesome self?"

"I just broke up with Brad."

He squinted at the stars. "You guys have a fight?"

"Not really. It just wasn't going anywhere."

He smiled but his eyes were cold. "Shit happens, I guess. You have a nice night, now." He sauntered past, became a dense shadow in the darkness, then turned the corner.

If she ran she could catch up with him, make him look at her, talk to her. She sprinted a few steps then stopped. Behind her she heard low voices, Leona's throaty laugh. Teetering on her toes, Layla stared up into the night. Beyond the tangled oak branches the crescent moon's silver light curved around its dark side. She took another step toward the corner. Then she turned and hurried across the grass toward the candlelit porch.

WHAT YOU DON'T KNOW

L eona stood at the door, looking into the classroom and wonder-ing just how much she was going to regret going inside. At least the elderly man in the back row meant she wouldn't be the oldest student, though she might still be the worst. Last fall she'd dropped out of watercolor painting because the teacher had sighed, his fin-gers busily unwrapping an antacid, whenever he looked at her crude flowers and misshapen fruit. But a week ago Leona's landlady had talked her into giving the university's Lifelong Learning program another shot. "It is never too late to be what you might have been," Miss Thalia had said. "That's George Eliot, a famous writer. Didn't publish a thing till she was forty."

Two dark-haired young women in the front row glanced at Leo-na, then whispered behind their hands. Tightening her lips, Leona stalked over to an empty desk. As she sat down she glimpsed her blurred reflection in the window—pale auburn hair in a messy bun, her face an ashy streak, her eyes charcoal smudges. Then a stout woman with a mane of gray hair strode into the room and dumped her satchel onto the teacher's desk. "This is Writing Your Life," she announced, "and I'm Elizabeth Borden." She surveyed the class, her gray eyes twinkling above her bifocals. "My dad was a crime novelist, so he named me after the infamous Lizzie Borden accused of murdering her parents with an ax in 1892."

Leaning back against her desk, Ms. Borden said that her own first book (available online and at the university bookstore) was about Lizzie Borden. "I couldn't prove she committed the murders," she said. "But in my heart I *know* she was guilty as hell. My point? That the truth is subjective. *Your* truth isn't the same as *my* truth. In this class, we'll each discover our own truths." Her jovial smile faded under their unresponsive stares. "Well," she said, "let's get to it, shall we?"

After taking roll she asked the students to arrange their desks in a circle as "the first step to building honesty and trust." Then she explained their homework assignment: to list nine things they knew about themselves, then "flesh out" each item with a page of description, anecdote, dramatic scenes. The first three pages of the assignment were due next week, the next three pages the following week, and so on.

Turning to the blackboard, she wrote one column of "concrete nouns" like rain and squirrel and armchair, and another of "abstract nouns" like freedom, peace, and happiness. By matching an abstract noun like "freedom" with a concrete noun like "butterfly," they could make metaphors, which were vessels of truth, containing its essence in myriad forms. Half an hour later Ms. Borden asked them to "share" their metaphors. The elderly man said, "Joy is a silver bell." A skinny tattooed man with sideburns said, "Love is a fire hose." He smugly folded his arms while the man beside him chuckled and a young blond woman muttered, "Give me a break." Ms. Borden said they were off to a good start.

Beaming at her lifelong learners, she clapped her hands. "Let's get to work on that list of things we know. Chop chop! Pens and notebooks out!"

Leona wrote, *One thing I know is I still miss Frank.* Then grief closed her throat. She twiddled her pen and stared at the blank page while fifteen other pens scribbled industriously. At last Ms. Borden dismissed them with a reminder to bring in three pages the following week. "Write what you know," she said. "Then write what you don't know. See you next Wednesday." As the students gathered their things and left, Ms. Borden came over and put her hand on Leona's shoulder. Looking Leona in the eye, she said, "Don't give up before you've really tried."

"I won't," Leona said. "I can't afford to waste money on a class I don't finish."

But as she walked through the cool spring darkness to her car, Leona wasn't sure she'd come back. She felt raw, exposed. And she didn't trust Ms. Borden's jovial smile.

The next morning she sat at the glass-topped table on her upstairs porch armed with her notebook and pen. The wisteria's musky sweetness penetrated her cigarette smoke, and Henry, her big orange cat, sprawled in a patch of sunlight at her feet. Leona opened her notebook, but she couldn't think of a thing to say. She'd thought a memoir-writing class would be easy. After all, she'd kept a journal for years, right up until Frank died. And unlike painting, anyone could write. But now she didn't know how to start.

Tapping her pen on the notebook's blank page, she gazed across the street at the vacant lot where her house had stood. Termites had chewed through its beams and rafters for a decade, and last summer the house had collapsed. Nearly everything she owned was smashed and broken, buried in rubble. So she'd moved into this carriage house, a small replica of Miss Thalia's prim blue Victorian home. Maybe she could write about that.

1. One thing I know about myself is where I've lived

I grew up in San Diego with my parents and my older sister who died when she was eleven. I remember her in brief flashes like the stuttered images of a home movie. We bounce a yellow-striped beach ball on the patio while our dad grills burgers and our mom sets the picnic table. My sister slaps me and Dad smacks her bottom. We plop down on the patio and cry. Mom steps around us like we're whimpering puppies.

*When Frank gets out of the Navy we move into a big
white clapboard house here in Athens Georgia. On summer nights music and light spill into the dark front yard.
Silhouettes dance in lit windows and people pass around
a reefer on the shadowy porch. Inside, Frank and I kiss on
the stairs. We have everything we want. After his death the
house goes dark. For thirteen years the only light is a table
lamp shining on a woman smoking cigarettes, drinking
gin. When she goes outside she blinks in the harsh light.*

*Now I live in a dollhouse at the back of my landlady's
side yard but if I close my eyes I see my white clapboard
house rising from a sea of memories, water streaming from
its rocky shores and the windows blazing with light.*

Leona frowned, reached for her cigarettes. Was that a metaphor? In her mind the wet rocks and white house were as clear as a
photograph, but she couldn't tell if the mental picture was a vessel
of truth. And why was her house surrounded by the sea? Maybe
because she'd lived alone so long, her house a landlocked island.

♥♥ ♥♥♥♥

Just before dawn Leona stood at the curb waiting for Dwight Jordan,
a big blond cop she'd known for years. He'd asked her to go fishing,
and though boats made her nervous she was trying to take Miss
Thalia's advice and "embrace life's possibilities." The sun's first
rays gleamed through the trees as his monster-sized black truck
turned the corner, a trailered motorboat rattling behind it. When
she climbed into the cab he smiled and handed her a big Styrofoam
cup of gas station coffee. She squinted at the overcast sky and said,
"Looks like rain."

He peered through the windshield, shrugged. "An April shower,
maybe."

Outside of town, mist drifted over green fields as they headed south on the two-lane highway. Fields gave way to pine forests,

the highway swooping past roadside stands selling peaches, boiled peanuts. Leona remembered Sunday drives with Frank, the lush green landscape dotted with church steeples and kudzu-shrouded, abandoned barns. Frank would put his hand on her thigh, and as they talked about little things—a new hire at the hardware store, a joke she'd heard at the café—they'd glance at each other and smile. Dwight drove with both hands on the wheel, his eyes on the road.

At the marina she stood on the dock and held the mooring lines while Dwight maneuvered the motorboat down the concrete launch. Shallow waves lapped against the dock pilings, and the reek of gasoline mingled with the dank smell of lake water. When the boat floated free she pulled it in and clumsily looped the lines around metal cleats. Moored at her feet, the red-and-white boat looked like a race car—long-nosed and sleek with swivel chairs for the driver and whoever rode shotgun. Cushioned benches ran along the sides. Dwight parked his truck and lugged a cooler and his fishing tackle down to the dock. Gripping his hand, Leona stepped onto a bench, then into the boat. She sat down quickly and clutched the side. Dwight grinned as he lowered the cooler into the boat. "You want a life vest?"

She eyed the orange vests piled under a bench. They looked moldy and damp. "Do I have to wear one?"

"Nope, not if you want to live dangerously." He stepped onboard, then turned away to free the lines. Leona let her gaze wander up his long blue-jeaned legs to his thickening waist, the silver glints in his heavy blond hair. Last summer on a sweltering night at Foxy's, lust fizzing between them, they'd agreed they'd have a longer shelf life as friends than as lovers. And considering all the women he'd told her about over the years—nurses, teachers, hair stylists, college girls with daddy fixations, single moms, a dental hygienist—Leona didn't regret her decision, at least not much.

Dwight started the motor, and they chugged out of the marina and along the shore, where he said the bass would be feeding. The sky had cleared to a cloudless blue. When he cut the motor the only sound was the hollow thump of water slapping the hull. A fish broke the surface, its splash spreading ripples across a pale drowned sky fringed with dark pines. Leona gingerly took the fishing rod Dwight held out, a plastic worm dangling from the line, and made an awkward cast into the water. He laughed, took it from her and cast it again, then picked up his own rod.

After a while she set down her rod and groped in her canvas bag for *Sense and Sensibility*, the latest of several novels that Miss Thalia said were "a better class of literature" than the romances and murder mysteries Leona usually read. Dwight smiled. "So you're a bookworm, huh?"

The other waitresses called her that. "Always got your nose in a book," they'd tease when she sat on the back steps during a break, a cigarette in one hand, a paperback in the other. Unlike Dwight, they didn't expect a reply, were just pointing out her odd behavior the same way they'd say, *love those fishnets, girl*, if she had a run in her nylons. Wrinkling her forehead, she tried to put what she loved about reading into words. "It's like traveling. To London or Tahiti or Shanghai—all the places I'll never see."

"Why don't you go see them?"

"Yeah, I'll do that, right after I win the lottery."

By noon Dwight had caught three bluegills and a largemouth bass. As he unpacked their lunch Leona hid a smile. Ham sandwiches, a jar of Vlasic dill pickles, half a bag of Doritos and a couple of Snickers bars—a man picnic. He pulled two dripping cans of Pabst Blue Ribbon from the cooler, and they talked and ate while the boat drifted on the current. When they were finished, Dwight leaned back on his elbows and squinted at the water. "First thing I'm gonna do when I retire is buy a lake house down here. Fish all day, sit on my deck and crack open a brew, watch the sunset."

"You're leaving Athens?" Dismayed, she bit her lip, then forced a smile. "What about your poker buddies, all your lady friends?"

"It's only an hour's drive. And maybe I'll get lucky, live next door to someone nice. Someone to go to the movies or out to dinner with. Share my bed with if we feel like that."

Leona wrinkled her nose. "Friends with benefits?"

"Yeah, I guess."

She studied his lined, freckled face, his stubborn mouth and pale blue eyes. "What if she ends up wanting more, or you do? Or one of you gets involved with someone else? You'd be stuck next door to each other."

"If she was like you, I don't think I'd go looking for someone else."

Flustered, Leona balled up the empty Doritos bag. The day was growing dim. Thin clouds veiled the sun, and thunderheads darkened the eastern shore. "We're pretty far out, Dwight."

He smiled. "You want to head back?"

As they sped toward shore, storm clouds overtook the sun, and the lake turned gray and choppy. Heavy raindrops pelted their faces. The outboard motor whined higher as the boat slapped against rushing whitecaps and water sprayed over the prow. When Dwight grinned, clearly thrilled by the rain and their flight across the water, Leona couldn't help smiling back. Her hair whipping in her eyes, she spread her arms, lifted her face to the darkening sky.

ço ço ôo ôo

2. One thing I know about myself is loneliness

Last night's dream

Hidden in the walls and rafters, glowing white termites burst into flames. Fire licks through the floorboards and smoke pours up the stairs. I throw back the covers and run to the balcony. Flames engulf my house as I leap into a fireman's arms. He sets me down with my back against a magnolia tree then he lifts up my nightgown. Heat laps my bare thighs. As he kisses me he turns into Frank. I say thank god you're alright. He tells me Frank's dead—that he's been dead for years. Fire spurts from his scorched eyes.

A Man at Midnight

*I wake up drenched in sweat from a hot flash, which
must be why I was dreaming about a fire. I yank off my
nightgown and hurry out to the porch where it's cooler.
My cat emerges from the vacant lot, trots across the street.
Henry, I call softly. His ears twitch but he ignores me.
Hearing footsteps on the sidewalk I retreat into the shadows. A man strolls by, glances my way and stops. My pale
body must gleam in the dark. When he steps onto the grass
I go inside, listen as his footsteps fade down the sidewalk.
It's been two years since I've felt the heat of a man. Two
years since Jesse left without saying goodbye.*

Leona set down her pen and riffled the stiff new pages of her the-
saurus for synonyms. Blaze, inferno, conflagration, passion. But maybe she was doing the assignment all wrong. Maybe you were supposed
to write about your favorite holiday, your first pet, whether you regretted never having children. But holidays were just something to get
through, and it was too late to regret the children they'd put off having.

"Hey Leona, can I come up?"

Leaning over the porch rail, Leona smiled down at her four-
teen-year-old neighbor, a slim girl with long brown hair, slate-blue
eyes and thick eyebrows. "Sure," Leona said. "Come on up."

Layla thumped up the stairs and onto the porch, where she
flung herself into a chair. "I'm so fuming."

Leona sighed and closed her notebook. "What's wrong?"

"You know my friend Stace? The one with green hair?"

Recalling a chubby girl with dark sullen eyes and livid green
hair, Leona nodded.

"So she's telling everybody I'm a virgin."

Leona raised an eyebrow. "Aren't you?"

"That's not the point. She's telling, like, the whole school that
Brad broke up with me 'cause I wouldn't do it with him. When the
truth is *I* broke up with *him*."

"Yeah, you told me about it the night it happened, remember?" Leona flapped her hand at a bumblebee, watched it zigzag out into the sunlight. "This Stace doesn't sound like much of a friend."

"Oh, I'm *so* not speaking to her. But you know what reeks? There's nothing I can do about it. It's already all over school."

"What do you want to do about it?"

"I don't *know*." Henry leapt into Layla's lap and purred as he turned in a circle. She pushed his quivering tail out of her face. "I want to get back at her but I don't want to get into all the putrid *he said she said* drama."

"Yeah, it's probably better to take the high road."

"Oh, I'm *gonna* take the low road. I just haven't figured out how."

That evening when Ms. Borden asked several students to share their "works in progress," it dawned on Leona that someone else was going to read what she'd written. After class, she approached Ms. Borden to explain her dilemma. She didn't want to stop writing, and she didn't want to change what she was writing about. But she wasn't comfortable sharing her work with the class—wasn't even sure she wanted Ms. Borden reading it.

"You absolutely shouldn't censor yourself," Ms. Borden said. "And I never force anyone to read their work aloud. *I'll* have to read it to comment on it, but I'll focus on the characterization, pacing, images." She beamed at Leona. "Can we live with that?"

Leona gave a polite smile. "We can try."

Ms. Borden held out her hand. "Okay, then, give it here."

Leona reluctantly gave her what she'd written so far—not even close to three pages. "It's not very good."

"I'm sure it's better than you think."

శ్ర శ్ర ఌ ఌ

On her way to work Saturday afternoon Leona stopped by Kroger for cat food and tonic water. The supermarket was cool and dim, a Muzak version of "Johnny Angel" murmuring through the sound system. Leona sang along under her breath as she loaded a dozen cans of cat food into her shopping cart. Then she wheeled the cart into the soft-drink aisle and stopped short. Dwight was lowering a six-pack of Coke into a cart while a young woman with shimmering honey-colored hair clung to his arm. Leona's hands tightened on her shopping cart, but it was already too late to back out of the aisle. Dwight had seen her and was pushing his cart toward her, his head bent to hear what the woman was saying. When they were abreast, he said, "Hey, Leona. How you doing today?"

Thirty years in the South had taught Leona how to deal with *that*. She smiled, kissed the air near his cheek, and said, "Couldn't be better, Dwight." Up close, the woman had acne-pocked cheeks and wasn't so young, probably closer to forty than thirty. Dwight introduced Leona to Pam, who said, "*You're* Leona Davis? Dwight's told me all about you, and my mom's Liz Borden. You're in her class, right?" When Leona nodded, Pam turned to Dwight. "Mom says Leona's a natural-born writer." She leaned across their shopping cart, surprising Leona with a warm smile. "At dinner last night Mom was saying that writing's great therapy for people who, you know, are all alone? She thinks you're doing terrific work, and she doesn't say that about just anybody."

"Oh. Thanks." Leona glanced at Dwight, but he was reading the label on a big bottle of diet 7-Up. "Well, I'd better get going. Nice meeting you, Pam."

"Yeah, great meeting you, Leona." Pam touched Dwight's arm. Startled from his fine-print reverie, he put the bottle on a shelf, nodded at Leona. As they moved away, Pam took his arm and said, "What else do we need, sweetie?"

Pushing her cart down the aisle, Leona numbly wondered how Ms. Borden could tell so much from a scant two pages of writing. And what did Pam mean, *Dwight's told me all about you?* As she reached for a bottle of tonic water, it hit her that Pam had just performed the classic Southern stealth attack: your enemy gushed about how smart or gorgeous or talented you were, how much she *adored* you. Later, the knife she'd stuck in your side twisted, and you gasped at the insult hidden in her compliments.

During the dinner rush Leona was too busy to think about it, but as her tables emptied and she refilled salt shakers, wiped off catsup bottles, her hands trembled and wave after wave of humiliation burned her cheeks. Trapped in the supermarket aisle, coffee splatters on her waitress blouse, her hair in a frowsy bun, she'd had to smile while Dwight acted like they were casual friends and Pam insinuated that she needed therapy. The worst part was, it was her own damned fault for going fishing with Dwight. He'd steered the boat through the twilit downpour into a cove, nosed the prow under overhanging pines. Taking her in his arms, he'd kissed her, then pulled her wet shirt over her head to kiss her upraised arms, her neck and breasts. And she'd wanted it—cold rain on her skin, the boat rocking in the waves. She'd wanted *him*, an aging man with long pale thighs and a reckless heart. To hell with friendship.

On the drive home, the heater on full blast to dry their wet clothes, she'd asked him what it meant, and his eyes had widened in comic anxiety. "Can't we say it was an accident?" he'd asked. When she shook her head, he grabbed her hand, squeezed it. "Let's just let this be whatever it is, okay, Leona? I don't want it to screw up our friendship." She'd nodded, her throat tight with disappointment.

Three nights later her phone rang and the answering machine picked up before she reached it. Shouting over voices and loud country music, Dwight asked if he could come over. She'd glanced at the clock. Nearly midnight—too damned late to be anything but a booty call. She'd fumed for a few days, then left Dwight a message that they needed to talk. But he hadn't called her back. And now she knew why.

She clocked out at nine-thirty, and as the café's back door banged shut behind her, she felt her shoulders relax. It was a cool spring night, only a few stars tangled in the town's pink haze. Thumping music drifted from the back entrance of Foxy's Bar & Grill. She lit a cigarette and strolled down the back steps to the parking lot, then stopped. That big black truck gleaming under a parking lot light was Dwight's. So he was at Foxy's, probably cuddled in a booth with Pam. Leona dropped her cigarette and ground it under her heel. As she stalked over to his truck she pulled four bobby pins from her hair. It took only minutes to squat beside each tire, unscrew the valve cap and prop open the stem seal with a straightened bobby pin. Air hissed from all four tires as she ran to her Thunderbird. Laughing under her breath, she got in and slammed the door.

ဖာ ဖာ ၿ ၿ

When Layla called through the screen door, Leona was in the kitchen marinating three boneless chicken breasts while Henry twined around her legs. It was Wednesday afternoon, and sunlight gleamed on the blue plastic plates in the dish rack. "Back here!" Leona shouted. She tossed the cat a flesh morsel. He gobbled it down, then stared at the countertop. "Don't even think about it," she said, pushing him with her bare foot until he retreated under the table.

Layla trudged into the kitchen, collapsed onto a chair and stared glumly at Leona. "So at lunch today? This random girl I don't even know tells me Billy Webb and Danny Schmitz are taking bets on who'll get in my pants first. And I *still* haven't figured out how to get back at Stace. It just burns me that she's getting away with ruining my life."

Leona smiled. "For one thing, your life isn't anywhere near ruined. For another, they say living well is the best revenge."

"*They* say," Layla scoffed. "*I* think revenge is the best revenge."

Leona studied the girl's thin face, then said, "I'll tell you a secret, Layla. I, um, went out with this guy, and the next thing I know he's dating someone else. So last night I let the air out of his tires."

Layla whooped. "You rock, Leona. No shit, you're my hero."

"Yeah, but now I'm going nuts wondering what he'll do to get back at me. He's got to be pretty pissed off." Leona washed her hands, covered the chicken with plastic wrap and put it in the refrigerator. "My point is, revenge is sweet but it's got consequences."

Layla frowned. "I thought the whole point was to show the other person there's consequences for messing with you."

"I guess that *can* be the point," Leona replied. "But I just wanted, well, some karmic justice. To ruin his day like he ruined mine."

Layla tilted her head, her gaze speculative. "So you gave karma a nudge."

"You could say that."

Their eyes met in a smile. Leona raised a warning finger. "I'd appreciate it if you kept my shenanigans to yourself."

"Hey, my name's not Stace."

3. What I know about love

I was putting away groceries when the phone rang and a stranger told me Frank was dead—rear-ended by a drunk on the Atlanta highway. After I called his folks I went for the gin, drank the whole bottle then passed out under the kitchen table. When I pulled myself off the floor every muscle ached. I took a hot bath, grazed my wrists with a razor, got out and toweled off. In my dreams he comes home, that day like any other day, unremembered.

When grief made room for other lovers, I focused on skin, taste, smell, an infinite variety of men. Once or twice I glimpsed love, but it fled on clattering hooves through a petrified forest.

Leona sighed and set down her pen. Jesse's warm callused hands and dark eyes had made her feel beautiful again. When he'd skipped town without telling her, she'd stared at her face in the mirror, touched the faint lines on her forehead. At forty-six she'd become disposable, a plastic cup to use a few times then toss aside. After Jesse, she'd kept to herself until Dwight.

Maggie, my boss at the café, says she gained ten pounds working at a doughnut shop, gobbling crullers, apple fritters, maple-frosted doughnuts and éclairs, an infinite variety that finally got stale. I haven't lost my taste for men but once you've bitten into love nothing else will do.

She lit a cigarette, screwed up her eyes against the smoke. Before her run-in with Pam, she'd been looking forward to class tonight. But she could just picture Ms. Borden and Pam gossiping about her sex life over dinner. Maybe she should keep writing but not turn in any more work. At least she wouldn't be dropping another class, wouldn't be a two-time loser.

That evening Ms. Borden passed back their graded homework. On the back of Leona's two pages she'd scrawled, *You're a natural-born writer, Leona! Terrific work!* Leona read the margin comments and smiled. So the image of her house had been a metaphor. But picturing Pam's honey-colored hair soured her pleasure. After class she asked Ms. Borden if they could discuss something. Ms. Borden glanced at her watch. "Of course, Leona. What's on your mind?"

"You talked about me. To your daughter."

Ms. Borden's forehead wrinkled in a puzzled frown. "I'm afraid I don't know what you're talking about."

Leona stared at her, nonplussed. "Pam said you told her I'm a natural-born writer." She held out her homework. "And see? That's exactly what you wrote."

Ms. Borden blanched. "Honestly, Leona, I had no idea Pam knew you, and—"

"She *doesn't* know me. She dates a friend of mine, is all."

Ms. Borden busied herself packing up her satchel. "All I said was I had some talented students in this class. I'm sure I didn't mention you by name."

"But you *must* have."

"I'm sure I didn't. But I *was* grading papers before she came over, and I *did* leave them on the coffee table. But she shouldn't have looked at them. And I'm shocked that she repeated something I told her in confidence."

Leona crossed her arms. "So what exactly did you say? I mean, I'm glad you think I'm a good writer, but why did you tell Pam I need therapy? Because I wrote about that dream?"

"I don't remember saying you needed therapy, but if I *did* say anything like that, well, how long ago did you lose your husband? Nine or ten years ago, right?"

Leona's throat tightened. "It'll be fourteen years this September."

"That's a long time to grieve, dear."

Leona hugged her elbows and stared at the floor as she tried to swallow her anger. Then she looked up and said, "Did you ever have someone you loved ripped out of your life without warning?"

"Well, no, but—"

"Anyway, how I feel is private. It's *my* business, and I don't appreciate hearing about it in the middle of Kroger."

"Oh dear." Ms. Borden took off her bifocals, her large gray eyes suddenly naked. "Sometimes I forget what a small town this is. And I should know better—I was the butt of some very cruel gossip after my divorce." The corners of her mouth turned down. "My ex went around saying I was an unfit mother, and a surprising number of our friends believed him."

Looking at Ms. Borden's flushed, unhappy face, Leona felt her anger ebb away. Bad enough when the horrid things people said about you were true, even worse when they were lies, or flat-out wrong. Like Pam ambushing her in the supermarket with her artless bit of gossip. *By the way, my mom says you need therapy.* Though actually, when she thought about it, it was Ms. Borden who'd first ambushed Leona. "You told me you'd only look at my imagery," Leona said. "Stuff like that."

Ms. Borden winced. "You're right, I did say that. I'm *very* sorry, and I promise that from now on I won't discuss your work with a living soul. Will that do?"

"I guess it'll have to. Or I can drop the class."

"I hope you won't. I'd feel terrible if I thought I'd derailed your progress."

Your progress. Like Leona was in rehab, or seeing a shrink.
"Well, thanks for talking to me."

"Thank *you* for sharing your concerns."

Fearing a hug, Leona thrust her latest assignment at Ms. Borden, then wanted to snatch it back. As Ms. Borden slid the single page into her satchel Leona said goodnight and hurried out.

On the drive home her thoughts shifted from Ms. Borden's perfidy to Dwight's. Just as she'd feared, sex had wrecked their friendship. And though she still thought Dwight had deserved it, the psychological cost of her prank crept higher every day. At this point she wasn't sure if he realized she was the culprit. And if he did know, was he angry, flattered, plotting revenge? But letting the air out of his tires had felt good, even exhilarating. A drunk could kill her husband, termites could destroy her home, and Jesse could leave her, but she'd gotten even with Dwight Jordan.

A few days later he strolled into the café and spoke to the hostess, who nodded and led him to one of Leona's tables. Leona retreated through the swinging doors to the waitress station—a dim alcove between the dining room and kitchen. Telling herself to calm down, she picked up a coffeepot and touched its side to make sure it was hot before she went back out to refill her customers' cups, drop off the check at her four-top, scoop up tips from an empty booth.

"Afternoon, Dwight." Smiling, she poured his coffee and said she'd be right back. She whisked herself through the swinging doors and set down the coffeepot, then returned to his table, her order pad and pencil at her chest like a tiny shield and sword. "Ready to order?"

"Yeah, I'd like a side of flat tires." His eyes hard as agates, he opened his fist and let four straightened bobby pins fall onto the blue-checked tablecloth. "Look familiar?"

Leona bit back a smile. "A lot of women use those. I use them myself."

"You think this is funny?"

"Oh, no," she said earnestly. "There's nothing funny about bobby pins."

He scowled at the table, his face dull pink. "Damn it, I thought we were okay."

"So did I—until you didn't call me back and started parading around town with a woman half your age."

"Pam's thirty-eight."

"That's not really the point, is it Dwight?"

"I thought we were just gonna let this be whatever it is."

She looked him in the eye. "That's exactly what I'm doing."

"So what do you want, Leona?"

She observed the tic in his jaw with the satisfied eye of a connoisseur. "I'm through wanting anything."

He picked up a bobby pin, twirled it between his thumb and forefinger. "So that's it, then? We're through?"

Dismayed, she tried to backpedal. "I just meant, I didn't get what I wanted, so I gave you something you didn't want."

He cocked his head. "If I'm following you, you're saying we're even, right?"

"Right."

"And we're still friends?"

"We'll see about that. You want to order something?"

Dwight grinned as he got to his feet. "Nah, I ate at the Waffle House."

That evening Leona sat on her front steps wishing she'd brought up his midnight booty call before he flung down his ultimatum—call it even or call it quits. But mostly she just felt relieved. She tucked an auburn strand behind her ear and leaned back, her elbows on the porch. Pink clouds gleamed through the oak branches, and robins foraged in the grass. Beyond the hedge a screen door slapped shut. Layla came around the hedge and crossed the lawn, the robins taking flight before her hurrying feet. Leona smiled and said, "Hey Layla, what's up?"

Layla sat down on the steps. "I got my revenge today."

"Wow, really?"

"So at lunch I'm in the quad bathroom when Stace and her little goth squad come in and she starts *screeching* that she's *dying* to hook up with Brad—you know, my ex? So I crack open the stall door and catch the whole thing on my cell phone." Layla bent forward to pick at the flaking porch paint, her long dark hair hiding her face. "Then I sent it to Jon Forbes and by sixth period everybody was talking about it."

"So, sweet revenge."

"I guess so." Layla clasped her hands between her knees, her thin face perplexed. "I went by her locker after school, and she's shoving stuff into her book bag, and there's like, black mascara tears on her cheeks? So I go, 'How's it feel to have the whole school into your personal shit, Stace?' Then she calls me a bitch, and I'm like, 'You're the one who started this shit.' She's all, 'Just leave me alone I hate you,' and slams her locker so I say, 'I thought you were my friend.' She gets all quiet, then she says, 'You ever think maybe I got tired of guys panting after you and looking right through me?'"

"So she was jealous, huh?" Leona sat up and absently brushed flakes of peeling paint from her elbows. "I guess I was, too. That's why I let the air out of that guy's tires. But maybe Stace was afraid to do anything to those guys who ignored her, so she hurt you instead." Leona smiled, shook her head. "Whatever that means. So then what?"

"She said she was tired of being enemies and could we be friends. And that was the hard part. Because it sucked being enemies—my stomach knotted up every time I saw her. But I don't trust her anymore, and how can you be friends with someone you can't trust?"

Leona sighed. "Good question."

"So I said I'd have to think about it, but in the meantime at least we could stop being enemies."

"You're a wise soul, Layla."

Layla nodded. "Yeah, I think I acted pretty mature. And now she knows how it feels. But honestly? It wasn't all that fun. Her crying and all." She glanced at the darkening sunset, got to her feet.

"I'd better get home. The stepdad's making meatloaf and he acts like it's major hot cuisine."

Layla got up and hurried across the lawn to the sidewalk, where she turned and waved. Watching her go, Leona wondered what life would have been like if she'd been pregnant when Frank died. Would taking care of a baby have led her out of grief sooner, or by a different path than she'd taken? If she'd had a child, maybe she wouldn't be so desperate for love now that she'd once again ignored the voice whispering that Frank was a fluke, a miracle, and every misfortune in her life was exactly what she deserved.

Darkness crept across the grass and the streetlights glimmered on. Leona went inside and climbed the stairs to her bedroom. She found her notebook on her unmade bed, switched on the porch light and went out through the French doors to sit at the glass table. Moths swooped around the light bulb. When she opened her notebook shadow wings fluttered across the page.

4. *What I don't want to know about myself*

Squatting on the beach patting damp sand into castle walls I saw my sister inside a wave—a mermaid draped in seaweed, her long red hair fanned out around her. She sank into the foam and as she rose in the next wave silver bubbles streamed from her mouth like a fountain. When the bubbles cleared, her eyes were white. I screamed and ran down to the water. Then my mom grabbed me and my dad ran past us into the waves. I never told anyone that I'd knelt in the sand watching silver bubbles while she drowned.

When my dad trudged out of the waves he left God behind him in the sea, though he never told us, kept going to church as the light went out of our house. But I was young, didn't need his god to light my way into the world. I turned my back on him, on my dead sister. But years later she returned to me—a shadow in the corner, a whisper in the dark.

*After Frank died I drifted in grief's black sea. When I
surfaced the sun was white fire, guilt the current pulling
me under. Even now I feel the tug of those dark waves. But
each day I set my feet on the rocky shore, climb toward my
white clapboard house. From its windows a light flashes in
slow intervals, shining a bright path on the water. This is
what I know and what I don't know. The intervals of light,
the dark sea.*

Her fingers trembled as she closed the notebook. She'd stirred
up the old grief and guilt but it was what she'd needed to say—a
confession to herself, maybe to the god her father had left in the sea.
That god had punished her for thinking her sister's death beautiful.
Since Frank's death she'd felt like a shadow in the sunlit world, her
feeble attempts to live misdirected, futile. Still, there was nothing
to do but keep trying, and who knew what the future held? She
could only see as far as tomorrow, when she'd sit in a circle with
the other students while dusk grayed the windows and Ms. Borden
urged them to find their own truth, her jovial smile masking her
private pain.

A warm breeze whipped Leona's hair as she crossed the café parking lot to her car. She was groping in her purse for her keys when
she glanced up and saw Dwight leaning on her Thunderbird, his
arms folded, sunglasses hiding his eyes. Forcing a smile, she said,
"I swear, Dwight, you have more time off than any cop I know."

"You must not know many cops."

"So, what's up?" On the far side of the parking lot a red-tailed
hawk flapped up from a pine, circled upward until it was lost in the
sun's white glare.

"Want to go fishing tomorrow?"

Leona stared at him. "Is that supposed to be funny?"

"Not really. I guess I thought if we went back to where things
got complicated, maybe we could figure out how not to mess it up."

"We did what we did, Dwight. Sex in your boat, you blowing me off, me letting the air out of your tires. Going fishing won't change what's happened."

"But it might change what's going to happen." He took off his sunglasses, squinted into the sunlight. "You ready to hear my side of the story? I'd started seeing Pam before we went fishing—"

"So you told her about us? Is that why she asked her mom about me?"

Dwight rubbed a hand over his mouth. "I mean, sure, I've mentioned you from time to time. But I didn't tell her what happened on the boat. Anyway, when I called you and you didn't call back right away, I thought you weren't interested. To tell the truth, I was relieved. I'm no good at juggling women."

"I'd say you're piss poor at it."

"Thanks."

"And what if I *had* called you right back? What were you gonna do, Dwight? Start juggling?"

"It's not like I planned it, Leona."

"You don't know what it's like—" She bit her lip.

"What what's like? What don't I know?"

"Nothing. Never mind." She'd be damned if she'd tell him how much he'd hurt her.

"Anyway, I didn't mean to make a mess."

"Is that supposed to be an apology?"

"If that's what you want, then yeah, I'm sorry. So you want to go fishing?"

How could she like him so much when she didn't trust him? "I'm filling in for Deb tomorrow. Maybe next week. If it doesn't look like rain."

He smiled at the ground. "Right. No rain." Then he pushed himself off the Thunderbird and headed toward his truck. As he walked away, Leona realized she didn't really blame Pam—at least, not much. After all, Pam was there first.

"Dwight?" she called after him. "Don't mess things up with Pam on my account."

He stopped, his back to her. "You mean that?"

She took a deep breath, then let it go. "Yeah. I do."

He nodded and kept walking. Leona got into her car, rolled down the window and started the engine. He waved as she bumped over the potholes to the back exit. She turned onto the road that wound past a low field and over to Boulevard. At the creek she heard a sudden thump as if she'd run over something. When the thumping continued she stopped and got out. Sparrows twittered in the reeds as she followed a low hiss to the right rear wheel. Kneeling beside the flat tire, she pulled a bobby pin from the stem valve.

She stood up, whipped out her phone and flipped it open. When Dwight picked up she said, "I'm at the creek. You'd better get your ass over here." She snapped the phone shut, leaned against the hood and looked across the field, a smile in her eyes. In the distance a black truck bounced over the parking lot's potholes and onto the road.

THE BLUES PALACE

The airport shuttle stopped under the motel portico, and the driver ran around to open the door. Clutching his hand, Thalia climbed out of the van into muggy heat and screeching gulls, the salt tang of the Gulf. Beyond the seawall the ocean heaved under a darkening sky, and heat lightning flickered on the horizon. So this was Galveston, she thought, the place she'd imagined for so many years. And tomorrow, God willing, she'd finally see Will. He was in the hospital recovering from a heart attack, and his daughter Gwen wouldn't let Thalia see him until he was out of intensive care.

Gwen had called with the news yesterday—a double shock because Thalia hadn't known that her brother had any children. In his rare letters, usually scrawled notes on the back of a postcard of his saloon, he'd never once mentioned having a family. Not that Gwen was acting like family. She hadn't invited Thalia to stay with her, hadn't even asked her to dinner tonight. Maybe the woman lived in one room with a hot plate and couldn't afford to go out to a nice restaurant. Or maybe she just didn't have any manners.

But Thalia would do just fine on her own. The white motel looked clean and inviting, and across the parking lot a Denny's sign glowed in the dusk. She could have stayed someplace nicer, of course, but she'd be spending most of her time at the hospital with Will, so why waste money on a room she'd barely see?

"Here you go, ma'am." The driver set down her bag and raised the handle for her. She smiled and tipped him five dollars, then wheeled the suitcase into the lobby. Yes, she'd be fine on her own.

∾ ∾ ∽ ∽

Lying awake in the dark motel room, Thalia's mind was a glaring chamber where busy thoughts bustled to and fro. Even with the long ride to the airport in Atlanta and the even longer ride from the airport in Houston, it was only six hours from Athens, Georgia, to Galveston, but in another sense this trip had taken fifty years. And if her older brother Clay had gotten his way she *still* wouldn't be here. On that horrid speakerphone in his law office in Charleston, Clay had insisted she was too old to go gallivanting off to Texas, especially to see Will. When she'd refused to back down, he'd tried to foist his middle-aged son on her. That's when she'd raised her voice, speakerphone or no. Harry was a dutiful, affectionate nephew, but a dull traveling companion, and lately he'd been pestering her to move into an assisted living home. To her mind, *assisted living* was only a step away from *life support*, something she didn't hold with. When the body couldn't support life, it was time to let the soul go home to God. But not, dear Lord, her brother's soul, not yet.

She switched on the bedside lamp, took her worn black bible from the nightstand and flipped it open. Closing her eyes, she planted her forefinger on a passage, Romans 3:23. *For all have sinned, and come short of the glory of God*—truth, not comfort. As she turned off the lamp she hoped God would forgive her, even if Will didn't.

At dawn she found the breakfast room and forced down half a sweet roll with her coffee. Then she hurried upstairs to bathe and dress before meeting Gwen in the lobby. Her hands trembled as she applied lipstick, fastened a string of pearls around her neck.

Sitting in the lobby, she watched people come and go but nobody looked like an unknown niece. She picked up a *USA Today* and read the headlines—those White House nincompoops were clamoring to invade Iran, as if the war in Iraq wasn't already a train wreck. When Thalia glanced up, a light-skinned black woman in a green pantsuit and gold jewelry stood before her—tall and big-boned, probably in her forties, her straightened hair in a stubby ponytail. The woman held out her hand. "Aunt Thalia? Is that what I should call you?"

After a stunned moment, Thalia closed her mouth, stood up and shook the woman's hand. "You must be Gwen." Good Lord, this *couldn't* be Will's daughter. "I'm so glad you called me. How is he?"

"Better. He's out of intensive care. You ready to go?"

Thalia followed her niece out to the parking lot. Eight in the morning and already muggy, just like home. Glancing at Gwen, Thalia saw Will's dark eyes made fiercer by a jutting nose and strong chin. Maybe some Indian blood there, on the mother's side—whoever she might be.

Gwen drove a white Honda Civic with zebra-print seat covers, its back seat strewn with glossy red brochures imprinted with *Galveston Island Realty* in white letters. As she drove out of the parking lot Gwen explained that she was a real estate agent and her husband Sam was a building contractor. Thalia smiled. "So he builds things and you sell them?"

"Not really. Most of Sam's jobs are commercial. I specialize in residential and vacation properties."

When Thalia asked if they had any children, Gwen said they had a son, Nolan, who went to college in Houston but was home for the summer. Then she tuned the radio to a news station and didn't say another word until she'd pulled into a spot in the hospital parking deck. Thalia opened her door, then turned to her niece. "Does he know I'm here?"

Gwen hesitated. "I didn't want to say anything. In case you didn't come." After that, Thalia was too nervous for conversation.

As they approached Will's room, someone inside shouted, "God damn it, I told you to take this shit away!"

A sharp little voice said, "You need to keep your strength up, Mr. Henderson."

"*You* eat it if you think it's so goddamned good."

A chubby girl in lilac scrubs came out of the room with a breakfast tray. She smiled at Gwen and rolled her eyes. Gwen smiled back, then leaned in the door and said, "Someone's come to see you, Daddy. Someone you haven't seen for years and years." Then she gestured for Thalia to go in. Thalia's heart thudded as she crossed the threshold. A frail man with big brown eyes and thick white hair glared at her from the hospital bed. His gown was slipping off his shoulder, and intravenous tubes snaked out of one gaunt wrinkled arm. "Who the hell are you?" he demanded.

"Oh, William." Thalia stepped closer. "You're so *old*."

Struggling up on his elbows, he stared at her. "Good God, Thalia?" Then he grinned. "You're pretty damned old yourself."

Tears blurred the room as she sat down in the bedside chair. "I hope you aren't mad. I so wanted to see you."

"Of course I'm not mad."

Thalia touched his hand. "I came as soon as I could."

"For Christ's sake, Thal, I'm not dying."

Gwen came over and kissed his cheek. "How you feeling, Daddy?"

"Weak is all. The pain's gone."

"I'm going downstairs for a cup of coffee, okay? Let you two catch up."

"Don't be long, hon. I want you here when the doctor comes by to poke at me."

Alone with Will, Thalia fiddled with her purse strap, realized what she was doing and set her purse on the floor. "Thank God you're alright," she said. "What happened?"

"Well, I was sitting in with the house band—Friday night and we had a good crowd, not too many tourists—when I got a bad pain in my stomach. It kept getting worse so I let my sax fade out and got off the stage. I figured it was indigestion, but Gwen took one look at me, hustled me into her car and drove like hell to the emergency room." He lifted a hand, let it fall to his lap. "The doctors are calling it a mild cardiac event, probably a spasm in one of my arteries. If that's all it was, they won't have to operate, and I can get the hell out of here in a day or two."

"You don't still smoke, do you?"

"Don't preach at me, Thal. I'm not up to it."

"Sorry." She bit her lip, then blurted out exactly what she hadn't wanted to say. "Why didn't you ever come back home, Will? Or let me come see you? Why didn't you tell me you had a family?"

He looked past her, his dark eyes thoughtful. "I don't know that I tried to keep you away, exactly. And it's not like I swore I'd never go back home." He scratched his bare shoulder, tugged up the hospital gown. "It's just, after a time my life back there seemed like a long-ago book I'd read. A good book, mostly, but not one I felt compelled to read again."

"Do you—do you read my letters?"

"Of course I do." His eyes softened as he met her troubled gaze. "It wasn't a matter of forgiveness, if that's what's been bothering you. I'll admit I was bitter at first, but I got over it. Still, you can't blame me for not telling you about June and Gwen."

"June?"

"My wife. Cancer took her, fifteen years ago now."

"Oh, I'm sorry. But if I'd never said...what I said about you and Ettie?"

"The fact is, you did say it. And that led me to the Blues Palace and my June. So if anything you did me a favor." He cocked his head. "That's the first real smile I've seen since you walked in, Thal."

Then Gwen returned and the doctor came in. A short, bustling man, he nodded and muttered to himself as he examined Will. Feeling weak with relief, Thalia retreated to the window to gaze down at the entrance plaza. For two days now she'd been terrified that something or someone would keep her from Will. Now she'd actually touched him, looked into his eyes, and she couldn't understand why she hadn't come here years ago, with or without an invitation.

As soon as the doctor left, a nurse came in to check Will's vital signs and change an intravenous bag. Then Gwen helped Will to the bathroom. By the time she got him back in bed the skin under his eyes was gray, his mouth slack. But he patted Gwen's hand and said, "You heard the doctor, kiddo. I'll be out of here before you know it."

"That's right, Daddy. You're gonna be fine." Gwen kissed his forehead and sat down beside him, gesturing for Thalia to take the other chair. When his eyelids fluttered, Gwen whispered that it was time to go, she'd bring her aunt back later. Thalia opened her mouth to protest, but the look in Gwen's eyes changed her mind. Her lips set in a thin smile, Thalia picked up her purse and followed her niece out of the room.

In the car, Gwen's tight lips confirmed Thalia's suspicion: her niece didn't like her one bit. As Thalia gazed out the window at the lush lawns flowing between hotel driveways, the bicyclists spinning along the boardwalk, she wondered how Will had explained their long estrangement to his wife and daughter.

৯৯ ৯৯ ৯৫ ৯৫

A shock to see Thal's anxious eyes in that wrinkled old face. Her visit had tired him—made him remember things he hadn't thought about in damned near half a century. And maybe because he hadn't exposed those memories to the corrosive air, their sharp edges could still cut. He recalled his mother's gardenia scent, her soft arms and gentle smile; his father's cold eyes and thin lips—a mean-spirited Henderson through and through, just like Clay.

But Thalia, two years older than Will, had been his protector and playmate, the only one who shared his love of music. Though it was music that drove them apart when his sax led him to the Hot Corner, what everybody called the black business district on Washington and Hull streets. For the price of a beer he could sit in the storefront bar on Hull Street listening to the old-timers reminisce about the great jazz and bluesmen—Blind Willie McTell and Clifford Brown, Armstrong and Dizzy Gillespie—who'd all played the Morton Theatre in its heyday. And sometimes old Johnny Carter

even let Will sit in on a set with the house band. When Thalia found
out she was horrified. If he didn't care about himself, she scolded,
he should have some consideration for his family. It wasn't pleasant
to hear people call her own brother a nigger lover.

All hell broke loose the day after Thalia rejected a marriage
proposal from Clay's best friend, Tom Gordon. Even now, lying in a
hospital bed and stuck full of tubes, Will could see his father carv-
ing the Sunday roast, hear silverware clinking on bone china. Clay
had pointed his fork at Thalia and said she was a fool to turn down
Tom. Now she'd likely end up an old maid. When Will pointed out
that Tom kept half the town's whores in high heels, their father
slammed his fist, asked Thalia if she'd rejected Tom because of
Will's filthy sneers.

Her cheeks flushed with humiliation, Thalia had stared at
her plate. Then she'd smiled at Will, her eyes bright with malice.
"Wasn't that Ettie you were kissing behind the oak tree?" she asked.
That was when all the hell broke loose.

Slender, with soft brown eyes and even softer lips, Ettie was
their maid, and Will's first love. No doubt some of it was the lure
of forbidden fruit, but mostly it was their eyes meeting in shared
laughter, her flashing smile and effortless grace. Back then it was
illegal to marry the other race. In fact, any relationship that went
further than a white man taking what he wanted from a black woman could get both people hurt. So of course his parents fired Ettie.
When he went to see her the next day, her mama came out on the
porch before he'd stepped foot in the yard. Respectful but with an
edge to her voice, she said they didn't want any trouble. She was
sure he understood.

A nurse came in—a dumpy blonde who checked his blood pres-
sure, poked a thermometer under his tongue, and asked if he needed
to use the bathroom. He shook his head and closed his eyes, hoping
that when he opened them she'd be gone.

That evening Thalia sat at Will's bedside catching him up on things she hadn't mentioned in her letters, which were, she thought ruefully, usually confined to local news, family gossip and church goings-on that probably hadn't interested him. A waitress named Leona now rented the carriage house at the back of their property, she said, and a harum-scarum family had moved in next door. And though the Barber Street brothel was long gone, streetwalkers paraded up and down Barber in broad daylight now—just two blocks from the house. But yes, the interlacing oaks still made a canopy over Boulevard, the wide quiet avenue where they'd grown up together.

Gwen sat on the other side of the bed reading a mystery and passing her father a plastic cup of water whenever he wanted a sip. Thalia longed to ask him about his life—about June, and how he'd managed to buy the Blues Palace—but he'd shut her out for so long she didn't dare. And she couldn't bring herself to say a word about Ettie.

Two black men came in, one of them stout and balding, the other a younger, thinner version of the first—the same broad cheeks and flat nose, though the older man had big brown eyes while the younger one's eyes were almond-shaped. Will broke off in mid-sentence to say, "Hey, Sam. Nolan, come here and give your granddaddy a kiss."

With a curious glance at Thalia, the young man edged around Gwen and bent to kiss Will's cheek. "How you doing, Grandpa? You ready to get out of here?"

"Damn straight. I'd leave this minute if your mama would let me."

Gwen tightened her lips. "You're not going anywhere till the doctor says so."

"Nolan, this is my sister, your great-aunt Thalia."

Nolan wiped his palm on his baggy jeans and reached across the bed to shake her hand. "Nice to meet you, ma'am."

"And this is my son-in-law, Sam."

Another brown hand to shake, this one with callused palms and scarred knuckles. They all smiled awkwardly. Then Nolan challenged his dad and grandfather to a poker game and the women gave up their seats. "I'll take your sister back to the motel," Gwen said. She frowned at Sam. "Don't let Daddy get riled up."

Sam heaved a sigh, shook his head. "You see who's giving the orders here, Will?"

"I know," Will said. "She's just like her mama."

The next day Will was sent home with strict instructions to quit smoking, get plenty of rest, and avoid undue exertion—no saxophone till after his three-month checkup. His legs were weak from three days in bed, so Nolan helped him out of the hospital wheelchair into Sam's gray sedan. Thalia rode with her niece down Harborside Drive, past oil storage tanks and corrugated metal sheds with white-hulled cruise ships looming behind them. When they reached downtown, Thalia peered up at the old cast-iron and brick buildings. Then Gwen found a parking space, and there it was, the Blues Palace, its year-round Christmas lights glowing wanly in the sunshine. Open windows lined the building's long wooden front, and music drifted into the street, a tenor singing "Sitting on the Dock of the Bay." Inside, sunburned tourists drank beer and margaritas, leaned out the windows and called to passersby.

"Will lives *here?*" Thalia asked as they got out of the car.

"After Mama died he converted the upstairs into an apartment, to keep an eye on the till, he said."

Keep an eye on the till, indeed. What had happened to the aloof, intellectual boy she'd so loved? They crossed the street and walked past the Blues Palace to the corner, where Thalia saw Sam's car parked in front of a side door on Moody Street. "Looks like they already got him upstairs," Gwen said. When they reached the side door, she opened it and led Thalia up a narrow, shabby staircase. At the top of the stairs another door led into a big sunny room with a hardwood floor, a few bright abstract paintings on the white walls. Large windows looked toward the harbor, where wheeling seagulls flashed white in the sun.

"Don't come back yet!" Nolan called. "Grandpa's naked."

Gwen folded her arms and stared out the windows. When Thalia asked if there was a picture of June anywhere, Gwen's face tensed. "She was black, if that's what you want to know."

"I guessed as much, dear."

Gwen picked up a framed photograph from a bookshelf and handed it to Thalia. A lanky woman with marcelled curls and almond-shaped eyes stood in a lush garden, a giant fern behind her. It was a candid photo, the woman smiling at something beyond the picture's frame. Thalia glanced at her niece. "It seems all you got from your daddy was your eyes. And your ears—close to your head like his."

Gwen held her hand out for the picture, then hugged it to her chest. "You've got Clay's kids to pass on the Henderson looks."

Thalia stared at her. "If you don't want me here, why did you call me?"

Gwen looked away. "You're his sister. You sent him those letters. I thought you should know." Her lips tightened. "To tell the truth I didn't think you'd come. Daddy said you were all a bunch of racists, and until I introduced myself I thought you knew about us."

Thalia gave a rueful grimace. "Was it that obvious?"

"You were all right once you picked your jaw up off the floor."

"You know, dear, it was nineteen fifty-five when Will ran off. Attitudes about race were something we just didn't, well, question back then." Thalia took a breath, made herself go on. "But times change, and so do people. Will was right. And we were wrong."

Gwen raised an eyebrow. "Would you have come if you'd known about us?"

"I've been waiting more than fifty years to see Will. Nothing would have kept me away." Feeling a twinge in her arthritic hip, Thalia lowered herself onto the leather couch and peered around at the life Will had hidden from her. The clean, low lines of the mahogany furniture, bookshelves crammed with novels and poetry, Mr. Faulkner's *Go Down, Moses* lying open face-down on the coffee table—this room was more in harmony with what she remembered of Will than the honky-tonk downstairs, its muffled music thudding under the floorboards

Nolan came in to say they could go on back. As Thalia struggled up from the couch he hurried over to help her. She held onto his arm for a moment, her hand a wrinkled white crab on his smooth skin. "And what are you studying, Nolan?" she asked.

"I'm getting a business degree, ma'am, and when I'm done I'll go into construction with my dad." He smiled. "People always building something in Galveston."

Will's bedroom was as sunlit and airy as the living room. Propped up by pillows, he was wearing tea-colored satin pajamas, and with his thick white hair and dark eyes he looked like an Italian duke, a silent film star—until he spoiled the impression by glancing sharply from Gwen to Thalia and saying, "You two aren't cat fighting, are you?"

Gwen smiled reluctantly. "We're trying not to, Daddy."

"I bet that's wearing you both out," he said. "But I'm grateful nonetheless."

After Will had some chicken noodle soup, he and Nolan said they wanted to watch *CSI* on the bedroom television. In the living room, Gwen flipped through a magazine while Sam ordered a pizza. When Thalia offered to pay for it, Gwen said, "We're not *poor*, Aunt."

"I realize that." Thalia gave a soft laugh as she pulled her wallet from her purse. "But neither am I."

"I'm sure you're not. Especially since Daddy was disinherited for loving a negro."

Thalia's hands tightened on her wallet. So Will had told them that story, including her own treachery. Although her smile didn't falter, she couldn't meet Gwen's accusing eyes. But it really wasn't her fault Will was disinherited. There'd been his disreputable friends, his scandalous behavior, his refusal to go to law school. And worst of all, that cold gray afternoon he'd slipped out of the house, never to return. There'd been times when they hadn't known if he was dead or alive.

Hanging up the phone, Sam smiled, shook his large round head. "Now you know I can't let you pay for dinner, ma'am. You know I can't do that."

"Well." Thalia slid her wallet back into her purse. "I'll admit I wouldn't let you spend a red cent if you came to visit."

Gwen glanced up from her magazine. "But that's not very likely, is it?"

"You'd be welcome anytime," Thalia said with forced cordiality. After all, it might be worth it just to see Clay's face. He always did call Will the black sheep of the family. And if Will came with them, came home at last, her cup would runneth over. But then he'd find out her secret. Years ago she'd rehired Ettie at twice the usual wage for domestic help. Of course by then Ettie was Mrs. Ester Johnson, married with four children. Would Will be shocked, angry, to see Ester, now a wrinkled old woman, mopping Thalia's floors, polishing her silver? Across the room Gwen was watching her with a sardonic smile, as if she'd guessed at least some of Thalia's thoughts.

৽৽৽৽

Shouts and laughter floated in through the windows. Louis Armstrong's husky voice smiled above clinking glass and scraping chairs. How strange to be in bed while right downstairs his life went on without him. *And I think to myself, what a wonderful world.* Will groped under his pajama top, felt his heart's faint beat beneath his skin. Reassured, he turned his head toward the window to watch an airplane's blinking lights traverse the night sky. Years since he'd been on a plane, or traveled any farther than Houston or Beaumont. The week before June was diagnosed, they'd gone to New Orleans to hit the jazz clubs, eat good food, wander the French Quarter. He'd always been glad they'd taken that trip before the long awful months of pain that ended in a coffin. *The bright blessed day, dark sacred nights.*

Sam and Nolan were in the living room talking about a construction job out by Scholes Field, and Gwen was taking Thalia back to her motel. They probably thought he was asleep, but Thal had stirred up too many memories of the old Victorian house he'd fled so long ago. He remembered he'd stuck it out till December to finish college, then he'd packed some books and clothes and gone into his parents' bedroom. The little curio he'd loved as a child—an African violet made of jade and amethyst—was on his mother's dresser. He'd taken it back to his room and wrapped it in a sock. Valise in one hand, saxophone case in the other, he'd walked out of the house into the dusk.

Riding the bus through drizzling winter fields, he went to New Orleans, then on to Houston. He didn't want his family's money, had never intended to be a lawyer. While he tried to figure out the future he got a bartending job, lived in a boarding house, saved his money. Running downstairs, hands in his pockets, a day off ahead of him, he'd felt free, no one disappointed or angry because he couldn't live up to their expectations. He'd wandered the libraries and art museums, browsed used bookstores. In the Fifth Ward's blues clubs he was often the only white face in the room, protected by his skin color until resentment faded into indifference, maybe because all he wanted was their music.

On a weekend trip to Galveston in 1963, he'd met June in a crowded bar in Kempner Park. She was sitting with her friends, her head flung back in laughter, her eyes shining. When Smokey Robinson's "My Girl" came on the jukebox Will asked her to dance. She shrugged, smiled, and slid off her barstool. The moment he touched her silky skin, breathed her cinnamon breath, the rest of the world slid away. He moved to Galveston and got a bartending job at the Blues Palace.

Ettie and June were different as sunshine and lightning, but once he met June he craved lightning. The trick was getting it to strike. He knew better than to chase her. A lone white tree in a storm-dark field, he tempted the lightning into his arms. A year later they moved into the small house on Avenue K, where Gwen was born in 1965—the same year Will bought the Blues Palace from old Mr. Remy. By the time the Supreme Court overturned the laws against interracial marriage in Texas and fifteen other states, it was 1967. Will was thirty-three, his bride twenty-four, their daughter two years old.

When he woke at dawn, Thalia was reading in the armchair by the windows. How gray her face was in the cloudy morning light—gray lips and gray skin, a long thin nose. Then she looked at Will, and a smile lit her eyes. Closing her book, she asked how he was feeling.

"I feel like a cup of Joe, if there's any made."

Thalia frowned. "Is that a good idea?"

Will sat up, pushed back his tousled hair. "The doc said a cup in the morning wouldn't hurt me."

"Well, if the doctor says so. How about some oatmeal to go with it?"

"Fine, after I get some coffee."

While he drank his coffee Thalia explained that Gwen would spend the afternoon with him and Nolan would spend the night.

"Damn it, I don't need a babysitter."

Thalia sniffed. "Gwen thinks you do, and far be it from me to argue with her."

Will grinned. "I knew you two were cat fighting."

"Well I'll be out of her hair tomorrow. In fact I'll be long gone before you-all wake up."

"I know you've got your own life to get back to, but I hate to see you go, Thal."

She smiled, her eyes luminous. "I'll be back. That is, if I'm welcome."

"Of course you are." While Will finished his coffee she gazed at the morning light seeping through the clouds. Then he set down his cup and asked, "You ever been in love, Thal?"

"Once," she said tranquilly. "I was in love once. We would have married. But he moved to Chicago, and I couldn't bring myself to leave the South."

"I'm glad."

"That I never left home, or that I never married?"

"Why the hell would I care whether you moved away or not? I'm glad you were in *love.* Everybody ought to feel that, at least once."

"Like you did with June?"

Will nodded. "Like me and June."

After lunch Gwen asked Nolan to drive his aunt back to her motel so Thalia could rest a while. And Thalia had to admit she *was* tired. She'd missed yesterday's nap, and last night she'd woken up around midnight startled and disoriented, her heart clamoring in her chest, and it had been a long time before she went back to sleep. But as Nolan helped her into his truck she asked if he'd mind giving her the nickel tour before they went to the motel. His almond eyes amused, he asked what she wanted to see. Thalia stammered, "I'd like to see where Will and June lived. And maybe your family's house? So when I think about you-all I can remember the places, too."

On Moody Street Nolan slowed to point out the Grand Opera House, then turned onto a busy thoroughfare lined with palm trees and dusty oaks. A few minutes later, a left turn took them into a neighborhood of old apartment buildings and small houses. The sun glared on the cracked sidewalks and the scuffed lawns littered with trash and plastic toys. They parked on Avenue K, got out and crossed the street to a craftsman bungalow with a sagging roof, its porch crowded with potted plants. "That's it," Nolan said. "That's where they lived."

Thalia squinted, picturing Will and June sitting on the porch, Gwen a stern little girl with tight pigtails playing hopscotch on the sidewalk. A palm tree towered behind the house, and she wondered if the giant fern still grew back there in the lush garden. "Thank you for bringing me here, Nolan."

As they walked back to his truck he said, "Mom remembers more trees when she was coming up. Kids running all over the place, old men playing dominos on the porch." He did a quick two-step and chanted, "A bar-ber shop, and a corner gro-cer-y store."

Thalia glanced at him. "Your mother doesn't like me."

"No, ma'am." Nolan gave a soft laugh. "She can get herself real worked up about some white folks. Not grandpa, of course."

Thalia laughed too, not because she understood what was funny but because Nolan's laugh was young and without meanness. His world was shiny and new, everything in it a wonder, including his rancorous mother.

"But it doesn't make sense," he said, "not really. Grandpa's not bitter, and I don't remember Grandma June real well, but Grandpa says she got a kick out of every day, and that doesn't sound bitter. So I don't know where Mom gets it from." He helped Thalia into the truck, hurried around and got in. When he started the engine, heat blasted through the air vents. Nolan turned up the air conditioning. "You sure you don't want to go back to your motel, ma'am, rest a while?"

She shook her head. "I want to see more."

Thalia stood under the motel portico at dusk and watched her niece drive off. Then she crossed the wide boulevard to the seawall. The sea glinted like crinkled tinfoil in the fading light, and music wafted from a bar down the road. She was glad she'd come, but she was ready to go home. Tomorrow was one of Ester's days, and her old cleaning woman would fuss over her, insist she put her feet up. And Ester had been there when Gwen called, so she'd want to know about Will. But should Thalia say anything about his family? She pictured Ester's eyes and realized she'd have to tell the truth. But that was for tomorrow. Tonight her cup really did runneth over. She even felt kindly toward Gwen. Before getting out of the car Thalia had looked at her and said, "I hope you won't try to keep me away."

Her niece had stared straight ahead, her arms resting on the steering wheel. "I wouldn't do that," she finally said. "I wouldn't do that to Daddy."

ᏇᏇᏁᏁ

Walking in her front door, Thalia breathed in the lemon furniture polish and bleach. It felt like she'd been gone longer than four days. When the floorboards creaked overhead she went to the stairs and called, "Ester?" But it was her nephew Harry who smiled down over the banister. "What on earth are you doing here?" she asked.

"Dad asked me to pop over to make sure you were okay."

"You don't just 'pop over' from Charleston, Harry. And there's nothing wrong with me that a good night's sleep in my own bed won't cure."

He came downstairs, pink-faced with a middle-aged paunch and jowls, not a bit like his long lean daddy. Thalia went into the parlor and sat down in her wingback chair. The lace curtains dappled sunlight on the faded Persian rug. Outside, insects hummed in the summer air. Harry came in and poured two glasses of tawny port from the decanter. "How's my uncle?" he asked.

"He's out of the hospital, on the mend, we hope."

Harry cocked an eyebrow. "We?"

"He has family. Good people, though his daughter doesn't like me much."

"Well, I'm glad he has people to look after him. Any grandkids?"

"A boy, in college." Thalia shifted her weight. She was tired, wanted to go upstairs and lie down, and she resented his inquisition.

"In college, huh? Pretty good for a bartender's grandson."

"Will *owns* that bar. And the rest of the family isn't hurting for money either."

Harry handed her a snifter and sat down on the couch. "Why doesn't the daughter like you?"

"Because her daddy was disinherited, of course." Thalia raised her eyebrows. "Anything else you want to know?"

"I'm just curious, Auntie. They're family, after all."

"I thought Ester would be here."

"She finished up a while ago, so I sent her on home."

"I wish you wouldn't meddle, Harry."

A deeper pink tinged his cheeks, and he tucked in his chin—his hurt, offended look. "I was just trying to be helpful. I mean, you pay her by the hour, right?"

She leaned over and patted his hand. "If you want to be helpful you can take my suitcase upstairs, and when I've rested a little we'll have dinner at Harry's Bistro." She returned his perfunctory smile at their old joke; as a child Harry had thought he owned the restaurant. "And tomorrow you can scoot on home and tell your daddy that I'm fine and Will's fine."

"No problem, Auntie." He slapped his knees and got up, humoring her, no doubt.

Over dinner Harry resumed his interrogation. What did his cousin Gwen look like? She favored her mother, Thalia said, but she had Will's eyes. Yes, Nolan was a *very* nice boy. He'd shown her the beach house on stilts where his parents lived. Describing the house, she didn't mention the African print lampshades, the primitive masks on the walls. When Harry asked about the Blues Palace she talked about the tourists who crowded in for oysters and catfish po-boys, margaritas and live music, rather than the autographed photos of tuxedoed black men on the walls.

When they got home Thalia said she was tired and went upstairs. Glancing down from the upper landing, she caught Harry staring up at her, his receding hairline giving him an innocent, astonished look at odds with his narrowed eyes. He smiled and said, "Sleep tight, Auntie." She gave a noncommittal nod. In her bedroom she put on her nightgown and climbed wearily into bed. A breeze stirred the curtains, and crickets chirped in the darkness. As sleep took her she heard waves lapping against the seawall, the faint cries of gulls.

After Harry left the next morning, she called Ester, then drove over to the house on Hancock Avenue. Ester was sitting in a cane rocker on the front porch. She lifted a hand in greeting as Thalia got out of her car. Thalia climbed the front steps, sank into a rocking chair and said, "A warm one, isn't it?"

"It's all of that. How you doing, Miss Thalia?" Ester poured a glass of iced tea for Thalia, who sipped it and smiled. "You make the best sweet tea, Ester. I'm fine, glad to be home. How's Clifford?"

"He doing good. He took the grandkids fishing today."

Thalia set down her glass. "I wanted you to know that Will's okay. He's back home and his family's taking care of him."

Ester nodded. "That's alright then. That's good."

"Ester." Thalia laid a hand on Ester's knee. "I never, well, apologized for what I did to you and Will, betraying your secret."

Ester frowned. "I ain't studying that, and you shouldn't either, Miss Thalia."

"Well, I am. I knew it was wrong then, and I've felt bad about it ever since."

Ester gripped the arms of her rocker and leaned forward. "Listen here, Miss Thalia. A long time ago me and Will were sweet on each other for a short spell. And how long have I been taking care of you? Forty years? Anyway that was back before civil rights, remember? We both knew what we felt for each other couldn't go nowhere."

Thalia cleared her throat. "He ended up marrying a black woman he met in Galveston."

"And I married a black man I met in Athens. Pardon my saying so, Miss Thalia, but so what? That's water under a long-gone bridge. You don't need to be worrying about it, you hear me?"

Thalia gave a faint smile. "I hear you."

Ester's rocking chair creaked, a contrapuntal rhythm to the thrumming ceiling fan. "I never told you how Will came to see me—after your mama said I couldn't work for you-all no more. But Mama came out on the porch and asked him to leave us be. And the scolding she gave me?" Ester sucked her teeth. "Messing up a good job, carrying on with a white boy. And my daddy didn't speak to me for weeks, not till Clifford started coming around. Then Daddy was all smiles again."

"Clifford's a good man."

"Amen to that. The Lord was looking out for me when he sent that man my way."

ぬぬぬぬ

Thalia sat in a booth sipping port while all around her people drank, wept, laughed, raised their glasses one last time to Willy Henderson. It was early afternoon but the lights were on, the windows closed against the bitter wind. When Nolan slid into the booth to see how she was doing, Thalia asked what would happen to the Blues Palace.

"Oh, we've got to keep it going, ma'am. Grandpa would never forgive us if we didn't. Mom and Dad will take care of insurance and stuff like that, and Jeannette will manage it." He nodded toward a burly redhead serving drinks behind the bar. "She's almost as much of a fixture here as Grandpa was." He looked away, tears in his eyes.

"And how are you doing, Nolan?"

When he shook his head, she said, "It's hard to lose the people who've been pillars in our lives, our parents, grandparents. When they pass on, the world shifts on its axis. It's never the same again. And when you lose a brother or sister, the world shifts another ninety degrees. You lose the witnesses to your life, one by one."

When his dad called him over, Nolan gave Thalia a strained smile and got up. She finished her port, then slipped through the crowd to the door and stepped outside. Clouds darkened the October sky, and the wind skittered an empty beer can down the sidewalk. She hurried around the corner to the side door and went inside. At the top of the stairs she eased open the door and walked into the living room. A truck rumbled down the street, shaking the room. She heard a faint, familiar tinkling and looked around. There on an end table was the jade-and-amethyst African violet she and Will had loved when they were children. Only four inches high, it stood in a miniature brass flowerbox, its jade leaves and milky purple petals connected by brass wires. Clusters of tiny yellow beads formed the pistil of each flower. As she picked it up she murmured, "Mama always wondered where you got off to."

"What are you doing here?" Gwen came down the hallway into the galley kitchen and stood with her arms folded, her eyelids swollen.

Feeling like she'd been caught shoplifting, Thalia hurriedly set down the African violet. "I wanted"—she swallowed—"I wanted to be where he lived, one last time."

Gwen bit her lip, then shrugged. "I noticed my uncle Clay didn't bother to come."

"Well, he's not in good health. His son, your cousin Harry, wanted to come with me, but luckily he caught the flu." Thalia raised a hand to forestall Gwen's rebuke. "I'm glad, but not for the reason you think. I wanted to be let alone to grieve, not have Harry fussing at me." She picked up the little stone plant. "This used to sit on our mother's dresser. Could I take it back with me?"

"That was Daddy's wedding present to Mama."

"Oh, well, of course then." Thalia's eyes filled with ridiculous tears.

"You want your letters back, too?"

Thalia stared at her. "You don't understand, do you?"

"Don't I?"

"I want this because Will loved it, because it's been with him all the years he wouldn't let me come near." The stone plant trembled in her hands, purple petals clicking against jade leaves. "What if I promised to leave it to you in my will?"

Gwen rubbed her arms, her eyes wide and unseeing. "He's never walking back in that door."

"I know, dear. He's gone home to the Lord." Was it rage or grief turning Gwen's dark face to stone? "You have Nolan," Thalia heard herself say. "And Sam."

"I know what I've got." Gwen closed her eyes. "Please, just take the damn thing and go."

Thalia put the African violet in her handbag and went down-stairs to find Nolan. He'd promised to take her back to her motel, where the airport shuttle would pick her up in an hour.

When they reached the motel, Nolan parked under the portico and turned to Thalia. "You'll come see us again?"

She hesitated, then said, "I'm getting too old for all this gadding about, but I hope you'll come for a visit before I'm much older. I'd like you to see where your grandpa was born. You could sleep in his old room—it hasn't changed a bit since he left."

"Maybe I can come for Thanksgiving break."

"It would mean a lot to me if you did."

That evening the African violet trembled in its plastic tub on the airport conveyer belt. Throughout the flight Thalia held it on her lap, the stones tinkling as the plane shuddered and dipped, then droned on through the wind-whipped starry night. Tomorrow she'd see about changing her will to return a portion of her brother's inheritance to his grandson, Nolan, who'd been kind to an old white woman he barely knew. As for the niece, she'd get what she'd wanted—milky purple petals and jade leaves, years of love and grief carved into stone.

THE TREE THAT OWNS ITSELF

From the moment Layla hooked up with Brad, Sterling had retreated into a world that excluded her. She'd see him sitting with his black friends at lunch, and if their eyes met, he gave a cool nod and looked away. That had been hard to take, but later that spring things had gotten a *lot* worse. When Layla broke up with Brad, all his friends had posted hate messages on her Facebook wall, unfriended her in droves. Even *her* best friend, Stace, had turned against her. Now it was September, the start of tenth grade, and though Layla and Stace were tight again, Sterling was still making her pay—he was friendly one minute, then the next minute he'd look right through her like she wasn't there.

So when Layla woke to pebbles clattering against her window screen on Saturday morning, she groggily pulled on her clothes, scribbled a note for her mom and crept downstairs. She eased open the front door to find Sterling squatting in the corner of the porch, examining a dew-spangled spider web. He stood up and said he had something to show her, a surprise. That could mean anything from a vivid slash of dumpster graffiti to a litter of feral kittens in his uncle's toolshed. But Layla didn't care what the surprise was. It was enough that he'd asked her along.

They headed down the driveway to the sidewalk, his shoulder-length dreadlocks swaying with his long strides. Hurrying to keep up, Layla felt tongue-tied and awkward, but apparently Sterling didn't because as they turned onto Barber Street, he launched into a rambling story about a big gray possum that had climbed in through his cousin Trey's window and down onto the couch where Trey was dozing in front of the television. Waking to a possum on his thighs, Trey had screamed like a little girl while the possum hissed and bared its long teeth. Suddenly the animal keeled over onto its side and stiffened, its lips curled back, its beady dark eyes lifeless, its anus secreting a stench like rancid meat—because playing possum meant not just looking dead, but smelling dead too. Trey said there was a lesson there. He just hadn't figured out what it was.

Birds twittered and the sun glinted through the trees, speckling light on the shady sidewalk. But as they approached Hancock Avenue the trees became sparse, the houses shabbier—a poor black neighborhood Layla wouldn't normally venture into. At Broad Street they sprinted across the four empty lanes to the far curb, where a cobblestone street climbed a steep hill. Overgrown gardens shaded the curb on one side of the street, and ramshackle cottages crowded the opposite sidewalk.

At first Layla thought the cobblestones were the surprise. But Sterling pulled her up the lane, his palm warm and damp around her wrist. One night last spring she and Sterling had watched a train thunder past and his hands had slid down her bare arms, but he hadn't kissed her. At the top of the hill, a quiet, sunny street dead-ended at the cobblestone lane, which turned to asphalt and snaked downhill. On the far corner, islanded between the street and a long driveway, a towering tree stood in a dirt oval encircled by a low stone wall. Sterling pointed at it. "You know what that is?"

"An oak tree. Duh."

"It's a landmark, girl. You're not a true Athenian till you pay your respects to the Tree That Owns Itself."

"Ooh, an Athenian," Layla teased as they crossed the street. "That's special."

Just inside the low stone wall, a ring of knee-high concrete obelisks were linked by a black chain that smeared rust on Layla's fingers when she touched it. She stooped to read a granite marker set in the dirt:

For and in consideration of the great love I bear this tree and the great desire I have for its protection for all time, I convey entire possession of itself and all land within eight feet of the tree on all sides. —William H. Jackson.

Layla looked over her shoulder at Sterling. "So what's the story?"

"Like it says, back in the day this Jackson dude loved a tree so much he gave it to its own self, so no one could cut it down. That was in like, the 1830s. A hundred years later that tree blew over in a storm, when it was older than Athens is now—and that's *seriously* old. This tree started out as an acorn from the first one."

Layla pushed back her dark bangs and peered up at the sunlight flickering in the leaves. "So the first tree was born wild, and then Athens grew up around it, and now this tree's wild but the trees around it aren't."

"I don't know that this one's wild, but it's free. You got a smudge on your forehead." He licked his thumb and rubbed above her eyebrow, then wiped his thumb on his jeans. "I used to come sit here," he said. "Ponder what it means to own yourself."

Layla stepped onto the low stone wall and tightrope-walked along its curve, then pivoted to face him. "What *does* it mean, to own yourself? That guy set it free. Like—what's that word when they freed slaves in their wills?"

Sterling's thin black eyebrows twitched. "Manumitted."

"Uh-huh. But the tree's still in chains."

"Those are to keep *you* out, not keep it in. And it's a *white* oak. Why you got to turn it into something sinister?"

"Hey, you're the one who says toilet paper's racist because it's white."

"Yeah, I like to think about that when I wipe my ass. Anyway that's who I am, not who you are."

Layla lifted her chin. "What's *your* problem?"

"Maybe I don't like you appropriating my ideas. Maybe I'm sick of being the black guy who gives you street cred."

She stared at him, then laughed. "Street cred from Honor Roll Sterling? I so don't think so."

His hands in his pockets, he smiled at the tree. Then he turned and walked away. Layla hopped down from the wall and followed him into the middle of the street. "That's right," she shouted. "Run away like you always do."

He turned to scowl at her. "I brought you here to show you something—I thought you'd understand. I was maybe gonna kiss you, but forget it."

"Oh, right, like I'd *let* you kiss me."

"The way you've been chasing me, girl? I thought you wanted some."

"Fuck you, Sterling." She stalked back to the tree, then turned and shouted, "I can't believe you're still mad about that! That was months ago. Get over it already!"

"You mean your brief reign as hotness queen of the ninth grade? I am over it." He glanced around the empty street like he was searching for a crowd that wasn't there. "Looks like everybody else is too, except you." He backed away, then turned and ran toward the cobblestone lane.

Layla sat down on the low stone wall, her elbows on her knees. Maybe she *had* been a little giddy. So what? All the ninth-grade girls had spent last year dreaming about Brad's vivid blue eyes and shy smile, his nonchalant grace when he caught a fly ball or vaulted a low fence. And when Brad kissed her at her locker, Layla was no longer a grubby latchkey kid, didn't have to remember the nights her mom didn't come home. Hungry and frightened, Layla and her half-sister Summer would show up at school the next day with unwashed faces, half-combed hair and mismatched clothes, so unkempt that the other kids picked on them and the teachers kept their distance.

And their mom's brilliant childcare solution? Start a feminist commune in the Los Angeles suburbs. That little experiment had catapulted Layla from latchkey kid to full-blown freak when the neighbor kids asked if the commune moms were dykes, whether the commune kids were sperm-bank babies or adopted. The boys asked if Layla wanted to fuck, if she could score them some weed.

But Sterling just didn't get that. He'd grown up in a big old house with a normal family—two smart, pretty sisters at Spelman, lots of aunts and uncles and cousins, his dad a doctor, his mom a school nurse. He'd *always* belonged. And did he *really* think she'd kiss him after he'd treated her like dog shit for months now? He'd *had* his chance that night beside the railroad tracks, and he hadn't taken it.

A breeze rustled the oak leaves; an acorn dropped into the dirt. Layla stood up and brushed off her jeans. Squinting up at the fluttering leaves, she wondered if she'd ever be happy for longer than a couple of months, or if she was going to be a lifelong screw-up, just like her mom.

ဟေ ဟေ ဟေ ဟေ

Summer half-rose from the desk chair to peek through the blinds at her stepdad, who was dozing in the hammock under the backyard trees. Her mom was out running errands, but any minute Layla might burst into the den and demand the computer just because she was three and a half years older.

There were hundreds of Michael Burnetts on Google. Summer clicked one link after another, searching for a photo that matched the pictures her mom kept in a scuffed shoebox. Half an hour later she gasped. Her own soft blue eyes were staring at her from a middle-aged man's face. The accompanying article was about his software company in Santa Cruz. The writer praised Michael's new computer game, Surf 'n' Safari, for its state-of-the-art graphics and nonviolent content, "so rare in this age of first-person shooter games."

Summer gnawed her thumbnail as she read about Michael's wife Caitlyn and their two children, seven-year-old Emily and five-year-old Max. Their existence ruined the fairytale ending she'd concocted for her favorite bedtime story: once upon a time in Venice Beach, her mom met Michael on a canal bridge, a surfboard under his arm and sand in his bright gold hair. A sweet infatuation, her mom always said. She called Michael her "gentle dreamer" but she wasn't so nice about Layla's dad—a bird dog who'd knocked her up, then trotted off wagging his tail. All her life Summer had hoped her dad would come back, and that hadn't changed when her mom married Paul. Because as much as Summer loved Paul, he was a stepdad, disposable. If her mom got restless, he'd end up as another photo in the shoebox, another story with an unhappy ending.

She found Michael's email address on his company website and copied it into the send bar. Her fingers hovered above the keyboard as she wondered how to start—*Dear Dad, Dear Michael, Dear Mr. Burnett? I think you're my father,* she finally typed.

My name is Summer and I was born in Venice Beach California on March 5 1996. My mom is Janice Beauvais but she used to be Janice Wenther. She has long brown hair and dark blue eyes but I have light blue eyes and blond hair just like you. We have a school assignment to make a family tree so I decided to look for you. All I had to go on was your name, some photos and what Mom said—that your summer romance ended before she knew she was pregnant. That's why she named me Summer. I hope this isn't too bad of a shock but I thought you'd want to know you maybe have another daughter. I'm eleven and a half and I live in Athens Georgia. We moved here about two years ago when mom married Paul Beauvais who's great and I love him but I think you're my real dad. I don't want to bother you but it would mean a lot if you wrote me back.
Probably your daughter,
Summer

The front door slammed and footsteps pounded up the stairs. Summer glanced at the ceiling with a sour smile. She'd heard the clattering pebbles this morning, knew what it meant. An upstairs door banged, and *that* meant Layla and Sterling were fighting again, and it was probably Layla's fault, per usual.

Layla slammed her bedroom door, flung herself onto her bed and pressed her face into the scratchy yellow bedspread she'd chosen when she was thirteen and getting her own room for the first time. In fact the only good thing about moving here was having her own bedroom, and of course Miss Thalia, who lived next door and knew about art and books and the theater, knew how to listen. Last Sunday they'd sat on Miss Thalia's front porch while the streetlights flickered on. Wrapped in her black shawl, her wispy white hair in a bun, Miss Thalia had said, "Sounds like Sterling can't forgive you, but he can't let you go, either." Then she'd touched Layla's arm and said, "Look, here it comes." They'd fallen silent as a bright moon rose through the magnolia trees in the vacant lot across the street. Too bad Miss Thalia had gone out of town to visit her Charleston relatives.

When the television came on downstairs, upbeat guitars and girls trilling a pop tune, Layla pictured Summer slack-jawed in front of a *Hannah Montana* rerun. Her sister's dad must have been a total moron, because Summer sure didn't get the drooling-idiot gene from their mom, just the immaturity gene. Layla got up and wandered over to the window. Her sister was a retard, her mom was a flake, and *everyone* at school hated her. She cast a look of loathing at her bedspread, grabbed her backpack and ran downstairs.

On the front porch she unlocked the ten-speed Paul had given her for Christmas—another vain attempt to buy her love. The Christmas before that, Janice, Layla and Summer had driven through rain and snow across the desert and the endless Texas plains until they entered a strange country called the South, where the sky became a narrow blue strip above highways hemmed in by swamps and pine forests. All so her mom could marry Paul, whom she'd met during his brief stint as a Hollywood screenwriter. For nearly a year Layla had despised all things Southern. But last summer they'd moved into this big brick house on Boulevard. Two stories high, with a tall chimney, and basement windows that peered up from the ground, it felt solid, like a real family lived in it. And last fall she'd met Sterling and Stace, and things had gotten better for a while.

She bumped the bike down the porch steps, swung her leg over the seat and wobbled down the driveway to the street. At the corner she turned onto Barber Street and pedaled hard past the hookers loitering under the oaks. Warm air fanned her as she sped by the liquor store, the laundromat, the old stone church on Prince Avenue. She stood on her pedals to climb Clayton Street into downtown and was sweating by the time she chained her bike to the rack outside the Grill.

College Square was busy—panhandlers, a drum circle, sidewalk cafés full of people basking in the late September sunshine. At the Espresso Royale Café she bought a chai iced tea and sat at a window table. If a passing college boy saw her—pensive and all alone—he might come in and strike up a conversation. Then Sterling would walk by and see that she was into older guys now.

She pulled Cormac McCarthy's *The Road* out of her backpack and set aside the gray feather she used as a bookmark. But after a sentence or two, the novel's charred hills and ash-laden winds parted like curtains to reveal a quiet sunlit street where she yelled at Sterling, trapped in a quarrel she didn't understand. Beyond the plate-glass window vague human shapes moved through the sun's glare; this time last year she and Sterling would have been among them. They'd hung out on weekends, studied together, rode their bikes to Dudley Park, tickled and tripped each other. Now he only spoke to her to pick a fight. How did that add up to *I was maybe gonna kiss you?*

Two vague shapes crossed the street and became horrifyingly clear—Sterling, and bouncing along at his side was Megan Kolowski. Gangly and pale with stringy blond hair, she was from Detroit and talked like the kids from the projects. Layla bent her head and opened her book. Ashes blew past blackened trees in a twilit world.

On her way home she stopped at the little green house on Dubose Avenue where Stace lived with her mom and a fat, wheezing black lab named Roscoe. Stace's mom was at work so they sat on the back porch and smoked a bowl. Layla didn't usually indulge, but she thought maybe the weed would lighten her mood, and she was right. After a few hits her thoughts slowed and her jittery glance settled on a crepe myrtle tree by the fence.

"Like, he leaves the door open when he's taking a dump."

Mesmerized by the crepe myrtle's puffy pink flowers, Layla asked, "Who does?"

Stace passed her the little glass pipe. "Jesus, Layla, you're not even listening. Travis, my mom's new boy toy."

Layla sucked on the pipe, held her breath, exhaled a pungent cloud of smoke. "Back in LA? My mom dated this guy like, half her age who strutted around our apartment in his tighty-whiteys. And can I just say his favorite band was Abba?"

Stace nodded. "That sounds just like Travis. I swear, sometimes I wish I could live with my dad, except the stepmom's such a bitch, and Eatonton's such a shithole."

"And don't forget the step-bro crawling buck naked into your bed last Christmas."

Stace rolled her eyes. "God, he's *such* a rodent. Last time I was there? He tried to stick his hand down my pants."

"I guess it sucks to be us. But at least you *have* a dad."

"You know what, Layla? The man doesn't give a shit about me." Anger flickered in Stace's dark eyes. "He's lumped me and my mom together as this big fat mistake. It's like I don't even *have* a dad, not a for-real one."

Layla took the pipe. "As far as I can tell, my dad feels the same way about us."

ဖွ ဖွ ဖွ ဖွ

Summer walked home from school on Tuesday in a stream of chattering girls that trickled off into side streets until only her shadow walked beside her, sharp and black in the fierce sunshine, a tan blur in the warm shade. When she reached the leafy cave of oaks arching over the south end of Boulevard, the air cooled and she glimpsed their red brick house through the trees. She walked faster, trying not to hope. Michael Burnett *still* hadn't answered her email. Now she was glad she hadn't told anyone, her disappointment a secret shared only with her diary.

In the front hall she shrugged off her book bag and went through the kitchen to the back porch. Paul was on the patio grading math papers in a green plastic Kmart chair, his coffee cup on the low green table. He set aside his clipboard and smiled. "How was school?"

"Lucas Watkins gave me a friendship bracelet." She came down the porch steps and crooked her arm to display the braided green and blue thread around her wrist. Paul bent his head to look, his scalp gleaming through his ginger-colored hair. Layla kept nagging him to chop off his straggly ponytail, but Summer didn't mind it. His thinning hair was just part of who he was, like the way he blinked his pale eyelashes when he was nervous or excited.

He squinted at her. "So what does a friendship bracelet mean?"

"It means in a couple days Lucas will walk me home and try to kiss me."

His eyelashes fluttered. "Um, do you let boys kiss you, Summer?"

She flipped back her hair and said, "Not a chance." Abandoning her pose, she bumped his knee with hers. "You sounded like a real dad when you said that."

"Believe me, I felt like one. Now let me get back to work, hon. I want to finish these before dinner."

Summer went into the den and closed the door. Sunlight slanted through the blinds, slicing the gloom with blazing stripes. When she opened her inbox her breath caught. Gnawing her thumbnail, she clicked on Michael's message and read,

Dear Summer,

I've often wondered if you were growing up somewhere, and what, if anything, you knew about me. Now that you've found me I think I owe you an explanation. The short version is I always meant to look for you but I kept putting it off, in part because I wasn't sure you'd ever been born.

Do you remember the little house in Venice? Or maybe you've seen photos? It was on a walkway off the Venice Boardwalk and there were flowering vines on the front porch. Janice's mom, your grandma, was keeping Layla that summer, so we had the place to ourselves. It was one of the happiest times of my life.

When I got offered a job up north I couldn't wait to tell Janice. But when I went to see her she was upset, distracted about something, and before I could ask her to come to Santa Cruz with me she rushed to the bathroom and threw up. All I could think was oh shit, she's pregnant, oh shit, I'm not ready for this. So I snuck out of the house, and that was the last time I saw her. She never called to ask what was wrong. It was like she knew without me saying anything.

When Caitlyn and I got serious I told her about Janice. But like I said to Caitlyn, I didn't know for sure that Janice was pregnant—it might have been the flu for all I knew. Caitlyn said I should find out for sure, and I swear I always meant to.

I'm glad you found me. And I hope we can meet someday soon. Caitlyn wants to meet you too, and she wants to know if you've told your mom you've found me. Maybe next summer you can fly out here for a visit. Until then, we can get to know each other this way. —Michael

Paul crossed the patio, his shadow a drifting cloud blotting out the white strips of light. Summer clicked *print* and closed her email, snatched the page from the printer and ran upstairs.

In her bedroom she lifted a feathered Mardi Gras mask from her dresser and peered through the eyeholes at her white four-poster bed, her little white desk, the rainbow stickers on her mirror. None of it was comforting or even familiar. The kitchen radio came on downstairs and pans clattered, Paul starting dinner. Setting down the mask, she picked up her Disneyland globe in both hands, gently shook it. Glitter swirled around Sleeping Beauty's castle. She'd thought the castle was real, but when she went inside on their Disneyland trip, she found only some low-ceilinged rooms with glass-cased scenes from the Sleeping Beauty movie. Not a real castle at all. Still, that trip was one of the best days of her life—running from ride to ride with her mom and Layla, eating corndogs and popcorn and messy grape popsicles. When night fell, fireworks exploded above Sleeping Beauty's castle, its turrets lit pink and blue against the black sky.

Still holding the globe, she stared through her window at the maple tree's dense green leaves. The tree's single red leaf turned into a cardinal that ruffled its feathers, then stretched its throat and twittered a sweet, piercing refrain. Miss Thalia said cardinals mated for life, like swans. And weren't people supposed to mate for life, too? But if Layla's dad had married their mom, then she, Summer Wenther, wouldn't exist—or if she did, she wouldn't be herself. Right now, her self felt like a dull confused ache. The wish she'd made on a thousand shooting stars had come true, but it didn't feel like that, not at all. Her dad had thought *shit shit shit*, and then he'd run away.

ℒℴ ℒℴ ℴℒ ℴℒ

During last period someone had sprayed shaving cream all over Layla's locker and wrapped her padlock in a huge wad of duct tape. By the time she got the tape off, she was near tears and her bus was gone. No one offered her a ride as she trudged down the long driveway to Milledge Avenue, the quickest way home—except that it meant going past the Varsity, where Brad's clique hung out these days, and they might have some shaving cream left. At the next corner she turned onto a quiet side street to detour around the danger zone. Walking slowly past sunny lawns and antebellum houses, Layla remembered Miss Thalia's advice: to hold her head up and act like none of it—not the ostracism, the pranks or nasty graffiti—bothered her. Easier said than done.

Lost in her thoughts, Layla didn't notice the tree until she was standing under it. She hesitated, then took off her book bag and sat down on the low stone wall. Sunlight slanted through the oak leaves. A chipmunk with bulging cheeks scurried across the dirt driveway and dove into a dark gap in the wall's stones. Squinting into the street, Layla pictured Sterling scowling, his forehead puckered as if he were about to cry. He'd brought her here because it meant something to him. Why hadn't she kissed him instead of quarreling with him? If her life were a novel she'd get a second chance, because just like a Jane Austen girl, she had let other people's opinions push her into Brad's arms, hadn't realized how lonely she'd feel there until it was too late.

She got to her feet and looked around, wishing Sterling would come walking up the cobblestone lane. He'd stop on the corner, a question in his eyes, and she'd run to him, their kisses like the ones mothers give cut fingers to make them stop hurting. Slinging her book bag onto her shoulders, Layla plodded across the street to the empty space where Sterling wasn't waiting for her. She'd been more miserable than this lots of times, but her heart had never ached like a clenched fist. And maybe Miss Thalia would say that was part of growing up.

When Layla got home she trudged upstairs and flopped onto her bed. She put another pillow under her head, picked up *The Road*, set it down. That cardinal shrieking outside her window needed to find a frigging mate already, except it was the wrong time of year. Someone tapped on her door. The cardinal took flight, a red flurry of feathers, and the door opened a crack. "Can I come in?" Summer whispered. Without waiting, she slipped inside and tiptoed over to the bed.

Layla sat up, absently scratched her arm. "And we're tiptoeing *why?*"

Summer sat cross-legged at the foot of the bed and picked up their mom's old Raggedy Ann doll. She peered at the doll's grubby face, rubbed the bald spots in its yarn hair. "I've got a problem."

"Besides being a brainless twerp?"

Summer's face puckered and she scrambled to her feet. Layla grabbed her sister's arm and pulled her back onto the bed. "Damn," she said. "Can't you take a joke?" She thrust the rag doll into Summer's lap. "I'm sorry already. So, what's the problem?"

Summer spoke in a breathless rush. "I found my dad and he emailed me and I'm afraid to tell Mom."

"Okay, he emailed you. What did he say?"

"We look *exactly* the same." Summer wound her fingers into the doll's red hair. "Just like you and mom do."

Layla rolled her eyes. "So what did he *say?*"

Summer pulled Michael's email from her pocket. Layla read it through twice, then wrinkled her nose. "We're talking way too much information."

"I thought...Mom said Michael didn't know about me, but he did."

"Yeah," Layla said. "She'll *love* finding out he scampered off instead of asking her to come to Santa Cruz with him."

"You think she'll be mad?"

"Oh, I'd say you can count on that." Staring at the rag doll in Summer's lap, Layla saw Janice at the kitchen table in their old apartment, her feet propped on the empty fourth chair, a tumbler of red wine in her lap as she bitched about menstrual cramps and guys who didn't call back, the rent check bouncing, the lecherous shits at work who stared at her tits—as if Layla and Summer were her girlfriends, not children struggling to bridge the gulf between her words and their ignorance. "You know what?" Layla said. "Screw Mom. She can just deal."

"But she'll be mad. And Paul might have hurt feelings." Standing on a kitchen chair to get a can of spaghetti from the cupboard when Janice worked late, telling bedtime stories about their dads so Summer wouldn't get scared the nights Janice didn't come home at all, getting parked with strangers when Janice took off for the weekend, that was Layla's childhood. Now when Janice was late it was Paul who made dinner, helped Summer do her homework, told her to brush her teeth and go to bed. Layla chewed her lip. Janice was their mom so she couldn't stay mad at Summer forever, but a stepdad didn't come with a warranty. "Paul might be a *little* hurt," she said. "But if you tell him you love him, and this is just something you have to do, I bet he'll understand."

Now that Janice and Paul were learning the dance steps of their marriage they liked to take their wine out to the patio for an hour of "grownup time" that the girls usually respected. But that night after dinner Layla dragged Summer outside to interrupt them. They were talking quietly on the far side of the patio. Pink and gold clouds gleamed through the oak branches, and a beeswax candle burned on the low table. "Mom," Layla said. "Summer wants to tell you something."

Janice glanced at them, her thick eyebrows bunching in a frown. Layla gave Summer a shove that propelled her halfway across the patio before she stopped and covered one bare foot with the other. She looked back at Layla. "You tell them."

Layla heaved a sigh and sat down on the steps. Summer sidled over to Paul and leaned against his chair while Layla broke the news, omitting the part about Janice being pregnant. "Summer thought you guys might be all hurt that she wanted to find her dad," Layla concluded. "But it's not like it changes anything, right?"

Janice's frown deepened. "I want to see that email, Summer."

Summer reluctantly pulled it from her pocket. As Janice read through it, Paul patted a chair. "Sit down, honey. You didn't hurt my feelings. Of course you wanted to find your dad."

Summer sat on the edge of the chair. "Mom?" she asked in a small voice.

Janice crossed her legs, one foot jiggling as she narrowed her eyes at Summer. "You could have told me," she said. "I don't know why you had to sneak behind my back."

Layla rolled her eyes. "You think *maybe* she was afraid you'd throw a tantrum, just like you're doing?"

"Oh, sweetie—" Janice gave an angry laugh. "This is so not a tantrum." She swirled her wine. "And by the way? That bullshit about him knowing I was pregnant? I didn't even know I was pregnant until *after* Michael left town." She nudged Summer's leg with her toe. "I thought you might be Rollo's baby until you came out looking so much like Michael."

Paul blinked rapidly. "It's funny how people remember the same things differently. Mama and Aunt June both swear that when my grandma died—"

Janice stood up. "I'm afraid this *could* change things, sweetie. Michael could sue me for joint custody, make you go live with him part of the year. But maybe that's what you want."

"Mom!" Layla jumped up. "Enough already."

Paul pulled Summer's thumb away from her mouth. "It's okay, hon. Your mom's a little upset, is all."

Janice set down her wineglass and pressed her fingertips to her temples. "I've got a headache," she said. "You'll have to finish playing gang-up-on-Janice without me." She stalked past Layla and went inside, banging the door behind her. Layla strolled across the patio, took her mom's empty chair and cocked an eyebrow at Summer. "So, mission accomplished?"

"That didn't go so good, did it?"

"Don't sweat it," Layla said. "She'll sulk in her room until Paul goes upstairs. Then she'll pick a fight with him and get it out of her system. Right, Paul?"

He gave a wry smile. "That's the usual drill."

"And nobody's gonna sue anybody for custody," Layla added. "In fact, a couple more emails and the whole thing will probably peter out."

Paul frowned at Layla. "I don't know about all that," he said, "but Michael's not going to sue us, that's for sure." He stood up and held out his hand to Summer. "I bet you girls have some homework to do."

Layla said she'd already done hers. Paul gave her a skeptical look, then shepherded Summer into the house. As the screen door slapped shut, a light came on upstairs and Janice appeared in the master bedroom's open window, her hands over her face. When Janice dropped her hands and swept out of sight, Layla leaned sideways to blow out the candle. The flame guttered out, the dusk suddenly loud with frogs and crickets—a pulsing chorus that muffled the medicine cabinet banging in Janice's bathroom, pill bottles clattering, water hissing angrily into the sink.

That night Layla lay in bed listening for Janice's fierce whispers, Paul's placating murmur. Risking the creaky floorboards, she got up and tiptoed down the dark hall. Her ear pressed to their door, she heard Paul ask, "Doesn't it matter that *I* love you?"

"Of course it matters," Janice said, a shrug in her voice. "But everything's not about you, Paul."

The next day Janice was deaf to her daughters, distant with Paul. After work she went straight to her room and refused to come down for dinner. Later she came downstairs to shiver on the patio with a bottle of wine, her eyes stricken. And she kept it up all week long. On Sunday morning when Summer pilfered a fistful of daisies from Miss Thalia's garden and put them beside her mom's coffee cup, Janice brushed the flowers to the floor. Summer's face crumpled as she crouched to pick them up.

Layla followed Summer upstairs to her bedroom and sat beside her on the four-poster bed. "She can't stay mad at you forever, you know."

"You don't know that," Summer said. "She might stay mad for years."

৯৽ ৯৽ ৶ ৶

At lunchtime Layla and Stace found an empty table in a corner of the high school food court. While Layla hungrily forked up pasta marinara, Stace drank a Slimfast shake and provided a running commentary on the action. That new girl from Detroit, Megan what's-her-name, was sitting with the black cheerleaders, and *no way!* Jon Forbes had a Mohawk. Oh my god, he was cute—even cuter than Brad, in Stace's opinion. Oh, had Layla heard that Brad and Brooke had finally hooked up?

Layla glanced up from her food in time to see Megan plop down on Sterling's lap and kiss him on the lips, then hop up and swagger back to her table while Veronica pumped her fist and yelled, "Go, girl!"

Stunned, Layla stared down at her plate. So Megan and Sterling were together. Except it hadn't been that kind of kiss—eyes closed and tongues tangled, your body limp in the boy's arms. So maybe Megan had kissed him on a dare. And even if Megan *was* crushing on Sterling, that didn't necessarily mean *he* was into *her.*

"Oh my god," Stace said. "Is Sterling *with* her now? She's like, this starved albino rat. Did I tell you Danny Kincaid asked Jenna if I was with anybody?"

"Um, about ten times." Layla glanced at Stace, who'd pretty much dropped her goth persona—no whiteface on her plump cheeks, less mascara fringing her eyes, her short dark hair streaked blond instead of green. The old Stace wouldn't have made that dig about Brad and Brooke, meant to recall Layla's spectacular nosedive from homecoming-princess frontrunner to the most loathed girl in the tenth grade. Layla could have said something pretty cogent about friends who kicked you in the teeth when you were down, but she didn't. Stace was the only friend she had left.

When Layla got home that afternoon, her mom's car was in the driveway, but Paul's truck was gone. The house was quiet, no zombie sister watching television, no radio muttering about the war in Iraq, the latest natural disaster in Haiti or China or wherever. She dumped her backpack on the stairs and hollered, "Mom?"

"Out here!" Janice called.

Layla went through the kitchen to the back steps. Her mom was slouched in a patio chair, her bare feet on the low green table. On her lap was the shoebox of jumbled photos that she called "my life in a box."

"How come you're home?" Layla looked at the glass of red wine on the table. "You get fired?"

"Have I *ever* gotten fired? That god-awful Southern cooking show's finally in production, so I took the afternoon off."

Layla nodded. Whatever else went wrong, Janice had always held down a job. Back in LA she'd even worked her way up from the oldest, lowliest D-girl to head of script coverage at Galaxy Studios, and now she worked for a local television company. "So where's Paul and Summer?"

"Getting a bucket of KFC."

"Oh, that's healthy." Layla turned to go inside.

"Hold up a minute. I want to talk to you."

Layla slogged across the patio and collapsed into a chair. "What?"

Janice lifted a picture from the shoebox, held it between her fingertips. "Did you know Summer was looking for Michael?"

"I didn't have a clue. Are we done here?" Layla started to get up.

"I suppose you're going to track down Scott now."

Layla sank back into her chair. "The way I look at it? The man's out there living his life—or not. It's not like we've got anything to say to each other."

"Why do you think she did it? Why now?"

"Um, because Google made it possible? But just so you know, Mom? Summer's been crying herself to sleep like, every single night, so you might want to rethink the whole I'm-gonna-take-out-my-bitterness-on-my-daughter thing. I mean, she's only a kid, and it took a lot of guts for her to write Michael, but you're acting like she committed some heinous sin."

Janice hunched a shoulder. "She shouldn't have gone behind my back. Some pervert could have kidnapped her—or Michael could drag us into the courts."

"Why don't you just admit that his email pissed you off?" Layla jerked her chin at the photograph. "Is that Michael or my dad?"

Janice handed it to her. "Careful, don't smudge it."

In the photograph Michael and a younger Janice stood with their arms around each other on the Venice house front porch, their mouths wide with laughter. Michael's face was sunlit, but morning-glory vines cast inky shadows on Janice's face and throat. Layla handed back the photo. "There's your answer."

Janice frowned at the picture. "What?"

"If *you* weren't so old, we'd look like sisters. And who does Summer look like? Nobody. It's what Sterling says about white people adopting black babies—the kids grow up without a validating reflection of themselves."

"Spare me the lecture, Layla. I'm not in the mood."

Layla shrugged. "I'm just saying. You and I *get* each other, even when we're fighting, you know? But Summer's different." She propped her feet on the table and grinned. "So what would I find out if I got in touch with Scott? Because honestly? I don't think Michael made up that shit about knowing you were pregnant."

Janice sighed. "I would have sworn on a bible that he moved away before I knew I was expecting. Just like I'm goddamned certain Scott knew I was pregnant, and in love with him, when he rode off on his Harley with my best friend behind him. The thing is, I've always known Scott rejected me, but I never realized Michael did, too."

"So," Layla said slowly, "our whole lives would be different if Michael hadn't figured out you were pregnant."

Janice shrugged. "Who knows? Things might have turned out worse. I mean, we're fine now, aren't we?"

❧❧❧❧

The sky was incandescent blue in the day's last light. Colorful lights whirled all around Summer—the Ferris wheel's high revolving circle, the octopus ride's spinning arms, the white-lit carousel. The roller coaster rumbled overhead, and its riders screamed and flung up their hands. Sizzling hot dogs, frying funnel cake and spilled soft drinks made the air feel sticky as cotton candy. It wasn't Disneyland, but this parking-lot carnival cast its own shimmering spell.

Summer was waiting with Layla and their mom while Paul stood in line at the ticket booth. Layla kept rising onto her toes and craning her neck, probably looking for Stace. Summer wasn't looking for anyone. She'd found her dad, and her mom had forgiven her, though she insisted on seeing all Michael's emails "for Summer's own good." But Summer was keeping some of those emails to herself. Like Layla said, what their mom didn't know wouldn't hurt her.

Michael's latest email had included a picture of his family, one of those posed photos people sent as Christmas cards. Max and Emily looked like Caitlyn, olive-skinned with smooth brown hair and doe eyes, so Summer had Michael's looks all to herself. His golden child, he'd said when she'd mailed him her class photo. Now she had two dads. One dad wrote to her, telling her little stories about when he was her age. He'd even confided in her about Emily still wetting the bed, which made Summer feel all grown up. And Paul was the dad who put his arm around her and was there when she got home from school. Her mom said Michael's emails "bordered on inappropriate," and Layla said he had logorrhea, which meant diarrhea of the mouth. But after years of no father at all, Summer felt like she'd won the lottery.

Paul hurried over, a roll of red tickets uncoiling in his hand. He tore off about twenty and gave them to Layla. Janice frowned at her watch and said, "Meet us back here at nine-thirty, Layla. And don't make us wait, you hear me?"

"Yeah, nine-thirty, don't be late, I got it," Layla called as she plunged into the crowd. Paul smiled, his eyelashes fluttering. "What do you want to do first, honey?" Summer pointed at the carousel, her favorite ride. As they strolled toward it, Janice put her arm around Summer, keeping her close. Paul said merry-go-rounds upset his stomach, so Janice and Summer stepped onto the platform and chose their mounts. Summer picked a prancing white stallion with a yellow mane while Janice climbed onto a curveting black steed. The warning bell clanged, then calliope music blared and they were floating around and around, rising and sinking and rising again. Summer clutched the gold pole with both hands, the breeze in her hair. Every time they passed Paul, she waved, and he smiled and waved back.

The midway was crowded with squealing kids, couples holding hands, boisterous teenage boys and screeching girls with green glow necklaces wound around their necks and arms. The carnival lights sparkled brighter as the sky darkened. It was warm for October, but Layla was shivering. When she didn't find Stace at the gravitron or the tilt-a-whirl, she headed toward the roller coaster. Cutting around a pretzel stand, she almost walked into Sterling, whose eyebrows shot up as he gripped her arms to fend off their collision. She took a deep breath and leaned in to kiss him, but he stepped back and she stumbled forward. He grabbed her shoulder, steadying her, then raised an eyebrow. "What's up, Layla?"

Her cheeks hot, she glanced into his eyes. "I was trying to kiss you," she blurted out. "I wanted to, you know…"

"No, I don't."

"I want to, you know, be with you."

Sterling sighed. "Jesus, Layla."

"I, I thought that's what you wanted."

"Damn." Fingering his dreadlocks, he looked up at the dark sky. "A month ago, even a couple weeks ago? You wouldn't have had to ask me twice, girl. But now, shit."

"It's just, I got confused, you know?" As Layla searched his face for forgiveness he looked past her, a smile in his eyes. She turned as Megan bounced up to them holding a long strip of tickets, glow necklaces like green snakes around her pale arms.

"Y'all know each other, right?" Sterling asked.

"Yeah, we *habla español* with Mrs. Finch, second period." Megan punched Sterling's arm. "Ready, Freddie?" She turned to Layla. "First stop's the roller coaster. You in, girl?"

"Um, thanks, but I'm meeting up with Stace."

Sterling looked at Layla, his smile so tender and sad that she didn't quite believe it when he said, "Catch you later, then."

As they walked away Megan clutched Sterling's arm as if this lame parking-lot carnival was the frigging high point of her life. Layla turned and hurried through the crowd, her face hot with shame. Faces swarmed past her. The chair-o-plane whirled overhead. She blinked back tears. Was this how her mom had felt, standing alone at the curb while the man she loved straddled his Harley and rode out of her life?

There wasn't a line for the Ferris wheel so Layla gave three tickets to a skinny roustabout with a cobra tattoo on his neck. She climbed into the car and he shoved down the safety bar. The warning bell buzzed. Her chair jerked, then swept backward, lifting her above the asphalt and music and milling crowds into the cool night. The carnival lights blazed below her. She spotted her goldilocks sister and dark-haired mother walking away from the carousel. Jenna, Stace and Danny Kincaid were ambling down the midway while Megan and Sterling hurried toward the roller coaster. As her car reached the top, the Ferris wheel halted. Suspended between the earth and sky, Layla knew that Sterling had found a way to forgive her, and now she had to find a way to let him go.

WHAT GIVES LIGHT

Wet skin dripping hair a fuzzy yellow something in her hands—
a towel. To dry with. This green tile floor and fogged mirror
a bathroom. Yes, it was Christmas Eve in Charleston, a thin cover
of snow on the ground, and she'd better keep her wits about her or
they'd lock her up. They'd find a lovely place with gardens, a restaurant and caring attendants, but no less an institution. No less a
prison for the old.

Goodness, she wasn't *that* old, only seventy-five. And this awful
confusion had assailed her only once before, last summer in Galveston. The air conditioner roaring in the pitch-black motel room, her
heart pounding, her hand clutching her throat, she couldn't think
what gave light, couldn't think *lamp* or *light switch*, until language—the names and uses of things—swooped back inside her like
a homing pigeon. Now it had happened again, and in unfamiliar
surroundings, just as before. So why risk further episodes by moving someplace entirely unfamiliar, like a retirement home? A solid
argument, but if she told people that her mind wobbled every time
she took a trip, they'd probably lock her up.

An hour later Thalia descended the staircase in a gray crepe dress with ruffles at the throat, her sparse white hair in a chignon. Gripping the banister, she took each step with care. Why was it only in this house she felt her age? Back home in Athens, Georgia, in the blue Victorian house her grandfather had built, she met her adolescent self on the stairs, glimpsed her childhood self in the garden, saw her adult self in the parlor after her mother's funeral, a mournful stick figure in black.

Standing at the foot of the stairs, portly pink-faced respectability in a bow tie, her nephew Harry said, "Ah, there you are, Auntie. Let me—"

Thalia raised her hand to stop him. "Stay right where you are, Harry. I don't see you helping your daddy down the stairs, and he's nearly eighty."

"Well, Daddy's—"

"Don't explain. You'll bore me and I don't want to hear it."

Harry tucked in his chin—his hurt, offended look. Nevertheless he waited for her, his hand held out as if she were royalty. When she reached the bottom step he crooked his elbow, and she took it gladly. The foyer's slick marble had been scheming for years to break her hip, which would no doubt send her into a swift decline ending in the family's marble vault. The brethren of marble was plotting against her, but if she breathed a word they'd lock her up.

Framed by the living-room archway, Harry's two sisters—thin blond Madison and slender dark-haired Claire—and their families were gathered around a Christmas tree glittering with gold ornaments and lights, its monochromatic elegance a poor substitute, Thalia thought, for the rude gaiety of popcorn strands and tinsel. In frilly pink dresses, Madison's three girls were circling the tree, the older two pointing at their presents while the toddler wobbled after them. Madison was sitting on the couch, and Claire, who'd flown home for the holidays with her husband and their two little boys, was placing a bulky package under the tree while her sons watched intently, their hands clasped behind their backs. "I don't see what the big deal is," Claire said in a bored voice.

"Well *I* think we had a right to know," said Madison. "Aunt

Thalia should have told—oh, Auntie!" Madison jumped up to hug Thalia and explain her husband's absence. His mother had come down with pneumonia, poor thing, and on Christmas Eve, too.

"Aunt Thal." Claire kissed Thalia's cheek. "Was it an awful drive?"

"Nearly five hours. And the traffic into Charleston was terrible."

Harry brought Thalia a glass of sherry. "I said I'd come get you, Auntie."

"Thank you dear, but I was fine." She hoped he wouldn't notice the dent in her front bumper—a mere fender bender in barely moving traffic, the highway slick with melting snow. It could have happened to anyone.

Claire's husband James was gazing out the large front window. It was dusk, the snow-covered lawn ghostly in the streetlamp's thin light. He turned to greet Thalia with the sweet smile his sons had inherited. A good thing, too. Tart was what the Hendersons were, from Thalia's father to Thalia and her brothers Clayton and Will, to Clayton's three children, though Harry wasn't as acid-tonged as his sisters.

As Harry settled Thalia in an armchair by the fire, Clayton strolled into the living room. He let his daughters kiss him, shook hands with James and accepted a glass of port from Harry. Lowering himself into an armchair beside Thalia, he asked how she was holding up. Then he leaned forward, a malicious grin deepening the wrinkles in his gaunt face. "You just had to do it, didn't you, Thal?"

Thalia raised her eyebrows. "Had to do what?"

"Invite that boy to stay with you. I bet you thought we wouldn't find out about it. And we wouldn't have if it weren't for Harry."

Thalia tightened her lips. "I *told* Harry I had company that weekend."

"You should have known he'd hotfoot it over to Athens to find out who it was."

"It's none of his business—or yours—if Will's grandson pays me a visit."

Clayton's grin deepened. "Admit it. You didn't want me to know that our little brother married a negro. That their daughter married the darkest man she could find so nobody would mistake her son for a white boy." He shrugged, leaned back in his chair. "Probably instinct, survival of the race."

"For pity's sake, Clayton, you sound like a character in a Faulkner novel."

"Please tell me you didn't put that boy in my bedroom."

"He slept in Will's old room. But I've been thinking." Thalia gave a sly smile. "What with this sub-prime loan fiasco, Nolan's parents may be in for a rough spell, so I've offered to pay his tuition and expenses next year."

Clayton smiled right back at her. "From what Harry says, this boy's mama—"

"Her name's Gwen. She's your niece."

"Anyway, she sounds too uppity to let you pay for her son's education."

"That's where you're wrong. She thinks we owe them something because Will was disinherited."

"Well she won't get a penny from me."

Grace Malone, the housekeeper, came in to announce dinner. Thin and twitchy as a greyhound, she winked at the little girls but ignored Harry's weak smile. Thalia wasn't supposed to know about Grace and Harry, but Claire had regaled her with the story one tipsy New Year's Eve: their affair began when Harry was only twenty-eight and had lasted three years. When Grace started hinting at marriage, a flustered Harry broke things off and moved out of his daddy's house to the condominium in Battery Park where he still lived.

Claire had said her brother was such a snob, he couldn't bring himself to marry the housekeeper. Thalia had wondered if Harry knew that his uncle Will's sins included kissing the family maid, a black girl who was fired over the incident. In any case Claire was right. Harry was a snob, with a snob's inferiority complex. The result, no doubt, of growing up in his daddy's shadow. What a waste, poor Harry's life. Fifty years old, a partner in Clayton's law firm, and he spent his days fretting over his spinster aunt and cantankerous daddy. Some people weren't meant to live alone, and she feared Harry was one of them. He should have married a nice dull girl from a good family, had a passel of nice dull children.

In the exodus to the dining room Thalia found herself beside Claire, who was herding her sons, her hands stretched out in front of her. Claire's tight mouth relaxed as her husband stepped between the boys and laid a hand on each small head. Taking Thalia's arm to cross the foyer, Claire asked, "Was Daddy giving you grief about our new cousins?" When Thalia nodded, Claire leaned close to whisper, "Harry *still* hasn't gotten over meeting Nolan."

Thalia grinned. "You should have seen his face, dear—like he'd swallowed a cutworm." She'd been coming downstairs from her afternoon nap and had paused on the upper landing when Nolan opened the front door to Harry, who'd gaped at him, then said, "Who the hell are you?"

"I'm Miss Thalia's grand-nephew," Nolan had drawled. "And you'd be?"

Harry's mouth opened and shut like a fish. "I'm her nephew, Harry Henderson."

"Well now." Nolan had sounded amused. "I guess that makes us cousins."

Thalia came downstairs then, and they went into the parlor, where Harry asked Nolan where he went to school, what he wanted to do when he graduated. Harry nodded approvingly when Nolan said he was going to work for his dad's construction company. No, Harry said, he wouldn't spend the night. He'd just dropped by to see his favorite aunt—as if, Thalia had thought indignantly, anyone ever just "dropped by" Athens from Charleston.

In the dining room Claire hurried over to her sons, and Madison carried her toddler into the kitchen to be fed and amused by Grace, who kept hand puppets in a drawer. Thalia took her seat on Clayton's right. When Harry sat down beside her, she set her lips in a thin smile and prepared to be bored.

She was equally bored the next morning when she went downstairs for coffee. Harry was eating breakfast, and after wishing her a merry Christmas he asked about the dent in her bumper, then pestered her about assisted-living facilities. He knew of several fine places here in Charleston, had some brochures in his car if she was interested.

Thalia sipped her black coffee, his words buzzing mosquitoes. Her old house on Boulevard sat on a spacious corner lot, a wide lawn sweeping around one side and a carriage house at the back—every inch of the place familiar, beloved. When Harry paused for a bite of ham, she set down her cup. "I've was born and raised in Athens. I've lived my whole life there, and I'll be buried there. I'm too old to uproot myself."

"But you don't *have* to leave Athens. There's a real nice facility over by the hospital—Sunset Gardens, I think it's called. And there's the Carleton House just off the Lexington Highway."

Thalia held up a hand. "I know you worry about me, and I'm grateful. But I'm not ready to be locked up."

"No one's talking about locking you up, Auntie."

"That's exactly what you're talking about. And from what I can see you're the only one talking about it. At least wait till I'm wandering around naked or collecting stray cats. Now, that's my last word on the subject." She patted his freckled hand. "Let me live out my life the way I choose, dear."

ৎৡ৯ ৎৡ৯ ৹ৡ৯ ৹ৡ৯

In early March Thalia was driving home from the beauty parlor when she slammed into the back of a pickup truck. The seat belt dug into her collarbone as the airbag exploded around her. She was badly shaken, with a bloody nose from the airbag, and the front end of her Lincoln looked like an accordion. Unfortunately, Harry was coming for the weekend and was bound to fuss about it. And this time she had no excuse. She simply hadn't noticed the traffic light turning red.

When Harry arrived on Saturday, Thalia was standing on the side lawn chatting with Leona, the waitress who used to live across the street and now rented Thalia's carriage house. It was a cold dim afternoon, the sun pearly in the gray clouds. Leona was excited about taking a trip to the north Georgia mountains with Dwight Jordan, the big blond cop she'd been seeing for the past year. Thalia smiled, remembering a trip to Dillard when she was twelve. The road had climbed into the mountains past steep slopes of leafless gray trees streaked with pine trees. When her father rolled down his window cold air blew in, and a stream rushed over rocks below the road. Then and there, Thalia had decided that the Blue Ridge Mountains were the perfect spot for a honeymoon. "It's time you and Dwight thought about getting married," she said. "Make things right with the Lord."

Amusement flickered in Leona's dark eyes. "It's not that kind of relationship. We're together when we want to be, no strings attached." Then she grinned. "But honestly? We don't want to be with anyone but each other."

"Then why not get married?"

Leona shrugged. "What's the point? At our age it's not like we're going to start a family."

"There's the legal benefits, and don't forget the wedding presents." But Thalia didn't have the heart to press it. No doubt Leona had expected more from life than she'd been given, had probably assumed she'd live submerged in the mundane, hectic flesh of marriage and children, like her mother and grandmothers. But when her young husband was killed in a car accident, Leona started drinking hard and sleeping around, though perhaps even then she'd expected a second chance. Instead her house had warped around her, a wooden carapace. Within its walls Leona drifted on rivers of gin and cigarette smoke while termites devoured the house's old bones. When the house finally collapsed in a cloud of dust and squawking birds, Thalia had grudgingly let Leona rent the carriage house. And after twenty-five years of mutual enmity they'd become friends.

"Besides," Leona said, "I'm used to living alone—no socks to pick up off the floor, no shirts to iron, no meals to cook unless I feel like it." Her voice flattened. "Your nephew's here."

Harry got out of his car with an overnight bag and headed toward the front porch. When he saw them on the lawn, his smile faded. Suddenly Thalia saw Leona through her nephew's eyes. In skintight jeans and a sequin-trimmed sweater, reeking of cigarettes, her auburn hair a tangled mop to her shoulders, Leona looked every bit the trashy widow that Clayton and Harry thought she was.

Harry hurried up the side lawn's brick path to hug his aunt and urge her to come inside out of the cold.

"In a minute, dear. You remember Leona."

"Of course." He gave a curt nod. "How you doing, Leona?" He gestured toward the gravel driveway behind Thalia's house. "Where's the Lincoln, Auntie?"

"Didn't I tell you? It's in the shop. For some minor repairs."

"What's wrong with it?"

"Well, a few things, actually."

Leona smiled. "I have to get ready for work. Nice seeing you, Harry. Say hello to your father for me."

"Yes, well." Harry took Thalia's arm. "Let's get in out of the cold."

Thalia usually looked forward to Harry's visits. You wouldn't call him scintillating, but he was cheerful, glad to change a light bulb or get something down from a high cupboard. And they had their little rituals: the occasional concert or movie, dinner downtown at Harry's Bistro, church on Sunday morning before Harry drove home. Thalia enjoyed their outings, was grateful to her dutiful, affectionate nephew. But by Sunday morning she felt positively un-Christian toward him. He was treating her like a naughty child—as if she'd purposely wrecked her car, wouldn't move into a retirement home out of sheer contrariness.

When they got back from church she sat in her parlor enduring another lecture. In Harry's book, two accidents in three months meant she shouldn't be driving. He got up and put another log on the fire, frowned at the flames. "And I don't like to mention it, Auntie, but you're getting a bit absent-minded. Well, not so much absent-minded as erratic."

Thalia gripped the arms of her wingback chair. "What on earth do you mean?"

"Well, offering to pay Nolan's tuition without consulting me, for one thing. And at Christmas I heard you tell Claire that after forty-odd years as a staunch Republican you've switched parties. What's next, Auntie? Converting to Judaism?"

"I suppose I'm allowed to change my mind, the same as the next person."

"It's not just that." He sat back down with a heavy sigh. What would happen, he asked, if she had a heart attack or stroke and it wasn't one of her housekeeper's days? She might lie helpless on the floor for hours, even overnight. It preyed on his mind, he said, his favorite aunt living so far away and all alone.

"I can always get one of those medical-alert thingamajigs Adelaide Wilkins wears. Besides, Leona's always stopping by, and Layla's right next door. They'd notice fast enough if anything was wrong."

"I'm supposed to feel better because a trashy teenager runs in and out of your house like she owns it? As for Leona, she smokes like a chimney, dresses like a hooker and drinks like—"

"If you want to see how hookers dress, just take a walk down Barber Street." Thalia held up a peremptory hand. "Not another word, Harry. Layla's stepdad takes out my trash barrels every single week, and Leona's been a good friend, an obliging termite. Tenement." Her heart pounded as she peered at the round blob hovering before her. It moved closer, its soul-things—eyes, they were called eyes—staring at her. A face, yes. Harry's pink fleshy face, his mouth making sounds, *Auntie, are you alright?*

"I'm fine, dear."

"You looked like you blanked out for a minute there."

She forced a smile. "Don't tell me you never forget what you're about to say."

"Actually, I don't think I do." Harry frowned. "Did you hit your head in that accident? Did the doctors do an MRI?"

"I did *not* hit my head. Now stop fussing, dear." She leaned forward and patted his hand. "I'm fine, and you've got a long drive ahead of you."

৶৽ ৶৽ ৶৽ ৶৽

Glimpsing Leona walking up the brick path to the carriage house, Thalia came to the front door and asked her in for a glass of sweet tea. It was a lovely afternoon, so they sat on the screen porch overlooking the side street. Birds twittered, and leafing maples cast a pale green light on the pavement. After they talked about Leona's trip to the mountains, Thalia set down her glass and said, "Now I want the truth, dear. Do you think I'm getting senile?"

Leona's eyes widened in surprise. "Of course not. Whatever gave you that idea? Don't tell me—Harry's been giving you a hard time, right? No offense, Miss Thalia, but he's the biggest killjoy I've ever met."

Thalia made a wry face—part protest and part agreement. "He thinks I'm losing my mind. And I *have* been forgetting things lately."

"Everybody forgets things now and then. That doesn't mean you're senile."

"Well, I don't *feel* senile, but what if I *am* losing my marbles? I'm worried about what will happen to you if I have to let Clayton and Harry take over my affairs."

Leona grimaced. "They'd kick me out so fast I wouldn't know what hit me."

"Yes, I'm afraid they would."

Leona sighed. "In my worst nightmares I never thought I'd end up homeless."

"Well it's your own fault." Thalia sniffed. "Feckless, that's you, Leona. Never thinking ahead, never planning for the future."

"I *made* plans. They didn't work out."

"It's fifteen years since you lost Frank. Plenty of time to come up with a plan B."

"Well, it's too late now."

"It's too late when you're dead and buried, not a moment before. If you take my advice, you'll sell your property and put the money into an IRA account. Then you'll have something to live on besides social security when you're my age." Thalia glanced at Leona, wondering if she was listening. "You could rent an apartment with what you'd save on property taxes, not to mention what it must have cost to heat your drafty old house before it fell down."

Leona looked away. "I was thinking about putting a trailer on the lot, but the man in the zoning office said Boulevard's a historic district, not a trailer park."

"I couldn't agree more. I don't want to end my days living across the street from a doublewide."

"Well it looks like you'll be spared that horrible fate."

Thalia patted Leona's hand. "You've got plenty of time to think things over, dear. I just wanted you to know, so it wouldn't come as a shock."

That night Thalia knelt by her bed, as she'd done as a child in this very room, and asked God to help her keep the promise she'd made two years ago—that Leona could live in the carriage house for as long as she wanted. But God was silent, and the calmness that usually came with prayer eluded her. She got to her feet, wincing at a twinge in her arthritic hip. As she switched off the lamp and climbed into bed she pictured Leona and her big orange cat huddled in a drab apartment, neighbors arguing, televisions blaring through the thin walls, the hope of rebuilding her house gone for good. And if Leona wasn't going to marry Dwight Jordan, she needed *something* to hope for.

When Thalia turned away from the dim moon and shut her eyes, the china clock on her nightstand ticked louder. With an exasperated sigh, she rolled onto her back and shoved another pillow under her head. Beyond the low mound of her feet, the dresser's oval mirror glimmered. Something swam in its silvery shadows—a finned creature rising from the deep, the holy spirit, her own pale eyes seeking an answer in the dark.

The next morning Thalia called Bruce Werner, and after lunch she took a taxi to her daddy's old law firm on Jackson Street, where Bruce ushered her into his office. A sullen young man with shaggy eyebrows and deep-set eyes, he reminded Thalia of a bear, slow but ferocious. He was the grandson of old Max Werner, one of the firm's original partners, whom her daddy had apostrophized as *a brawling, ham-fisted Kraut*. Sitting on the edge of his desk, his arms folded, Bruce listened to her scheme, then said, "Your nephew won't like this."

"No," Thalia said as they exchanged conspiratorial smiles. "Not one bit."

"Didn't you offer to rebuild Leona's house a while back?"

"I did indeed, but she turned me down." When Leona had first moved into the carriage house, Thalia had offered to rebuild her old house if Leona would attend a weekly bible study class. Thalia had thought she was doing the Lord's work, but she should have known that you can't shove religion down someone's throat.

Bruce sat down behind his desk and pulled a legal pad toward him. As he scribbled he said, "So we're talking about a life estate. In exchange for rebuilding Leona's house and granting her lifelong occupancy, she'll deed the property over to you, to revert to your estate upon her death." Frowning at his notes, he added a few touches of his own. Thalia's estate could pay for new furniture, homeowner's insurance, taxes and maintenance, most of which, he said with a bland look, would increase the property's value in the long run.

When Thalia got home, she went up the brick path to the carriage house. Leona was on the upstairs porch fouling the air with a cigarette, another reason to get her back across the street where she belonged. Shading her eyes with her hand, Thalia said, "Could you come down for a minute, dear?"

While she waited, Thalia wandered over to the flowerbeds on

the side of her house. The roses had leaf spots, needed deadheading. Leona came out and hurried across the lawn. She looked tired, gray shadows under her eyes and her mouth drooping. Thalia impulsively took Leona's hands, gave them a gentle shake. "Good news, dear. I just saw my lawyer, and I think we've found a way to rebuild your house."

As Thalia explained her scheme, Leona's eyes brightened. "I can't thank you enough—"

"You don't need to thank me. It's a good investment. And it'll give both of us more peace of mind, don't you think?"

"But I *do* need to thank you. No one's ever been this kind to me—*no* one."

"Maybe you could show your gratitude by stepping foot in a church one of these days even if I'm not asking you to go to bible-study classes." Thalia pointed at a dandelion. "Could you yank that up for me, dear? If there's one thing I can't abide, it's dandelions in my lawn."

శ్రీ శ్రీ శ్రీ శ్రీ

On Harry's next visit they attended an afternoon concert at the university chapel, a lovely old building with Doric columns. As the string quartet began to play, Thalia closed her eyes so she could watch the music forming shapes in her mind. Beethoven's Opus 59, No 7, was followed by Schubert's "Death and the Maiden," which stirred Thalia to tears, the melody evoking her grief over her brother Will, who'd died this past October. Although they'd been estranged for fifty years, when he'd had a heart attack she'd flown to Galveston, where she'd been shocked to learn that his wife had been a black woman. Nevertheless, they'd reconciled, and now she felt his absence from this world. She surreptitiously dried her eyes with a tissue, hoped Harry hadn't noticed.

After the concert they strolled along a walkway on the north campus lawn toward the parking lot. Squirrels scampered between the trees and students sprawled on the grass, some studying, some talking. On the drive home Thalia wondered what it was like for the girls she'd seen on the lawn. They'd looked so relaxed, so comfortable in their skin. Her old friend Adelaide had gone to the university, and several of their friends had gotten teaching degrees. Why hadn't it occurred to Thalia to go to college? Perhaps because she hadn't needed to earn a living, or because she'd assumed she'd get married someday. Like Leona, she hadn't thought she needed a plan B.

As he waited to turn onto Boulevard, Harry said, "I saw a construction company sign in Leona's yard. Don't tell me she's got a bank loan to rebuild."

"No, she didn't get a bank loan." Gazing serenely at the streetwalkers loitering under the oaks, she ignored his fingers drumming on the steering wheel. He turned left and drove slowly under the canopy of oaks, then parked in front of Leona's empty lot. His hands clenching the wheel, his jaw tense, he studied the white-and-red sign emblazoned with the names of the architect and construction company. No, Thalia thought, this wasn't going to be pleasant.

He took her elbow as they crossed the street and went up the front-porch steps. When they got inside, she went into the parlor and sat down in her wingback chair. Harry walked over to the sideboard and picked up the decanter. As he handed her a glass of port, she said, "Sit down, dear. I have something to tell you."

He raised an eyebrow. "That sounds ominous. Should I pour myself a double?"

Thalia gave a thin smile and waited while he filled his glass and sat down on the couch. His hands clasped his paunch. "You want to know what I think this is about?" he asked.

"No, dear. I want you to listen." As she explained her decision to rebuild Leona's house, he slowly hunched forward, his hands between his knees.

When she finished, he said, "Are you out of your mind, Auntie?"

"I was reading the *Wall Street Journal* before you were born, Harry. We both know this is a solid investment."

"What we *know* is that the bottom's just fallen out of the housing market."

She nodded. "It was due for an adjustment, just like the stock market's due for one. The estate will come out ahead in the long run."

"What bothers me is the principle of the thing."

"Oh, I won't touch the principal, dear."

He sat up straighter, his hands on his knees. "You can laugh if you want, but if you think I'm going to let an unscrupulous widow take advantage of your—"

"Leona's had her troubles, but she's hardly unscrupulous."

Harry snorted. "Preying on a rich, lonely old woman—"

"I'm not lonely, Harry."

"No, not with half the neighborhood sniffing around for handouts. Next thing, you'll be setting up a college fund for those hookers on Barber Street."

She tilted her head as though considering it. "I don't think I will. But I really should do more for Nolan." Gracious, Harry's face was nearly purple. It was wrong to tease him, but he'd had his britches in a bunch ever since she'd come back from Will's funeral full of praise for Nolan (though she hadn't mentioned the boy's skin color). But after all, Nolan was as sweet-tempered as his mama was sour, and in the middle of his first real grief he'd been kind to an old white lady he barely knew.

She patted Harry's knee. "I'm getting old, and truth be told, so are you. We both have plenty of money and no one to leave it to but nieces and nephews." She paused to let that sink in. "So I don't know why it upsets you that I'm practicing a little Christian charity."

He gave a tight smile, but he wouldn't meet her eyes. Her voice sharpened with apprehension. "I've already signed the papers, Harry."

"Then all I can say is, I wish you'd discussed it with me first." He picked up their glasses and carried them to the sideboard. "We used to talk everything over, Auntie, but these days you're so impulsive I can't keep up with you."

"Maybe you should stop trying. Now if you'll just hand me that magazine, yes, that's the one, I think I'll read a while before dinner."

ഏ ഏ ഏ ഏ

Hands on her hips, Thalia stood on her front porch and glared at the overflowing dumpster across the street. Machinery grumbled from dawn to dusk. Hammers pounded, chainsaws screeched, boards clattered and workmen shouted above the din. Fast-food wrappers and cigarette butts littered Leona's unkempt yard. Even worse, Thalia had spied more than one construction worker relieving his bladder against Leona's overgrown hedge. A whole summer of dust and trash and racket to look forward to. Too late to stop it, and she supposed it would be over soon enough. Leona said now that they'd finished the frame and floors and roof—the rough construction, she'd called it—things should quiet down. Gracious, how long had the phone been ringing? Thalia hurried inside, almost tripping on the parlor rug in her haste to reach the phone. "Hello?" she quavered.

"First off," a deep voice drawled, "you didn't hear it from me."

"Clayton?"

"I was passing by Harry's office just now, and I overheard an interesting conversation—a *very* interesting conversation. He's petitioning for a conservatorship of your estate. On the grounds that you're getting senile."

"Good God." Thalia abruptly sat down.

"Exactly. He'd better not try that shit on me, that's all I've got to say."

"I'm *not* senile."

"I *know* you aren't. But he'll say you're a vulnerable old woman being victimized by your neighbors. And it's your own damn fault for giving him the rope to hang you with, Thal. I'm referring," he drawled, "to a certain real-estate transaction involving a shady widow. I'm not saying he'll win, mind you. But you'd better get your ducks in a row."

"Thank you, Clayton. I mean that."

"Don't say I never did anything for you. And don't you go telling Harry I called. He doesn't know I overheard him, and I don't

want him yapping at me. To tell the truth, I'm sick of his sancti-
monious crap—always bleating that he's got your best interests at
heart. I'll bet he's worried you'll squander all your money on Leona
or that black boy."

"His name's Nolan," Thalia said wearily. The enormity of it hit
her again. "Why does Harry care what I do with my money? He's
got plenty of his own."

"Well maybe it's not about the money. Maybe you've hurt his
feelings, liking that black boy better than him."

"Now that's just not true, Clayton. I'm very fond of Harry, and
I'm grateful—"

"That's not the same as liking him, is it? And you've got to
remember, Harry grew up hearing about nasty old uncle Will who
whored and drank and ran around with nig—you know what I mean.
Hell, I remember I felt like dancing in the streets when Will ran
off. I was *glad* he never came back. So how do you suppose Harry
feels, watching you cozy up to Will's family? And don't even get me
started on what he says about Leona—not that I don't agree with
him on that."

Thalia was utterly still. Not only was her irascible brother con-
fiding in her, he'd made her realize she'd been insensitive, unkind.
"I never meant to hurt his feelings."

"Well, you did, and now he's on the warpath. You take my advice, Thal, and call that sourpuss lawyer of yours."

"Oh, I plan to, the minute we hang up."

Leaving Bruce Werner's office the next day, Thalia was so angry she
could hardly speak. Outrageous that the court didn't have to notify
her when someone tried to usurp control of her life—a flagrant vio-
lation of her civil rights was what it was. Worse, if Harry could get
her declared incompetent, the probate court could decide her fate
without her knowing a thing about it until it was too late. When
Bruce explained that little fact, she'd used his phone to make an
appointment with her doctor.

ക്കൈ ക്കൈ

Thalia's mouth was dry, her heart lurching as she sat in the waiting room. She believed in facing up to things, yet she'd been putting this off since Christmas, telling herself that she'd had only two, then three, attacks, and *always* in stressful circumstances. It didn't mean she had Alzheimer's or some other horrible dementia. But now the moment of truth loomed, and she was afraid.

On her visit two weeks ago, Dr. Frost had asked her some simple questions, such as her telephone number and mother's maiden name, then she'd read aloud from a diabetes pamphlet. Holding up a pencil, a comb, a clock and a cup, he asked her what they were called. Then he ordered blood tests and an MRI and told her to come back to discuss the test results in two weeks.

Thalia glanced at her watch. She'd been waiting half an hour, and she couldn't focus on her book, *Girl With a Pearl Earring*, about one of Vermeer's models. Finally the nurse ushered Thalia into an examination room. A few minutes later Dr. Frost came in and sat down. He'd been her doctor for twenty years, a courteous silver-haired man with kind blue eyes. He was smiling. Was that a good sign or just good manners?

"Well," he said. "It's not Alzheimer's."

Thalia hadn't known she was holding her breath until it erupted from her lungs, expelled by her relief. So she'd be spared that particular death sentence—the dying brain abandoning the body to the care of strange hands, bewildered old eyes peering into unfamiliar faces.

He explained that she was suffering from a vitamin B12 deficiency caused by achlorhydria, a condition that limited her body's ability to absorb vitamin B12 from food. Its symptoms included disorientation and aphasia—the loss of language—but it was treatable. He gave her a stern look. "I thought you were taking a daily multivitamin, Thalia, but your tests suggest otherwise."

Avoiding his gaze, she stared at a pain chart (those idiotic happy faces in various stages of agony). "I *was* taking them. But the capsules were so big, half the time I gagged and spit them into the sink. So I, well, I stopped."

"Why didn't you tell me? I want you to go straight to the pharmacy and get some chewable multivitamins and a big bottle of vitamin B12 supplements, which you'll just have to find a way to choke down." He gave her a green sheet of paper with information about B12 deficiency, which she folded and tucked into her purse.

"There's something else I need to talk to you about," she said. "My nephew wants to become my legal guardian. No doubt he'll be sending you a letter full of legalese asking you to declare me incompetent."

Dr. Frost smiled. "I'd have to say you're terrifyingly competent. I've thought so for years."

"Thank you. I think."

"You're welcome. But next time you're worried about something, don't wait till your nephew threatens to haul you into court to come see me." He stood up, patted her shoulder and strolled out of the room.

ৎৡ৽ ৎৡ৽ ৵৵ ৵৵

All through June, hammers pounded in the vacant lot and the muggy heat kept people indoors, fans whirring, hands reaching into refrigerators for pitchers of ice water. Taking refuge on her shady side porch, Thalia tried to figure out how to thwart Harry without appearing in court or betraying Clayton's phone call. She was *sure* his petition would be denied, but she dreaded the prospect of pleading for her freedom in a courtroom—Harry's turf. Nor did she relish the thought of airing the family's dirty laundry there. But her surly lawyer was no help; Bruce *wanted* to go up against Harry in court.

In the end, the law came to her rescue. The court didn't have to inform *her* when Harry filed a petition, but it *did* have to notify her closest living relative, and that was Clayton. Ever the devious lawyer, he "accidentally" faxed the notice to Claire in San Francisco, and she promptly called Madison, then Thalia. "Madison knows all about it," Claire sputtered. "And she never said a word to me. I don't care if she *is* my sister. She's a ferret-faced little weasel. And Harry's a fat pompous weasel. You want me to fly back there and testify for you, Aunt Thal?"

Thalia was silent, staring at a gray little germ of an idea.

"Better yet," Claire said, "I'll call Harry right now, put a stop to this shit—sorry, Aunt. This crap."

"Thank you, dear, but I'll take care of Harry myself."

A few weeks later Thalia twitched aside the parlor curtains to watch Harry's black sedan pull up to the curb. Would he broach the subject, or had he convinced himself that Dr. Frost would declare her incompetent, and therefore the court would grant his petition without Thalia's knowledge? In that case, he'd want to spring it on her as a fait accompli, after which he'd become a benevolent dictator, indulging her whims, curtailing her freedom.

He didn't bring it up at lunch, and he was his normal, cheerful self as he fixed the leaky kitchen faucet. That evening they went to Harry's Bistro and sat at their usual window table overlooking a spindly tree lit with white Christmas lights. A busboy brought them warm crusty rolls while the sommelier poured their Sauvignon Blanc. When the waiter came, Harry ordered shrimp jambalaya, and Thalia, whose stomach no longer tolerated the spicy Creole dishes she loved, settled for the grilled salmon in caper sauce. As Harry slathered butter on his roll, she said, "So you think I'm senile, do you?"

His roll skittered down his shirtfront. Grimacing, he retrieved it from his lap, then dipped his napkin in his water glass and dabbed at the oily smears on his shirt. "I don't know who you've been talking to, Auntie, or what they've been saying, but I hope you know I'd *never* do anything to harm or upset you. I'm just worried, is all."

"So worried you can't look me in the eye?" Fascinating to

watch the minute adjustments, muscles shifting under his coarse pink skin to create a pained, patient smile. Was it the muscles around the eyes or the gelatinous orbs themselves that infused his smile with warm sincerity? He was giving her his best, she realized, dissimulating far more, and far more convincingly, than when he'd seen her merely as a character—a rigid old Southern lady whose behavior he could predict. And that was the problem. His case against her was based on the assumption that old people were incapable of growth, that any change in her behavior must be senility.

His smile turned rueful, and he spread his hands in self-deprecation. "It's just, I'm seeing a pattern of increasingly rash and highly uncharacteristic decisions. The aunt I know doesn't rent her carriage house to a promiscuous, chain-smoking alcoholic. The aunt I know would *never* become intimate with a woman like Leona—"

"Become *what?*"

"And the aunt I know doesn't run off to Galveston to meet a bunch of strangers claiming to be family."

"But they *are* family." She winced at her pleading tone—she sounded like a guilty child.

"You didn't know that when you flew off to Galveston just because some stranger called and said she was Will's daughter." He held up a finger. "Let me finish. The aunt I know does *not* siphon money from her estate into the pocket of a woman I wouldn't introduce to my mother, god rest her soul. Lastly, that aunt wouldn't let greedy relatives con her into squandering her money on a black boy she doesn't know a thing about."

Thalia glared at him, her spine a ramrod, her thin nostrils dilated. Leaning back, she sipped her wine, then shaped her lips into a smile that quelled the anger in her eyes. So that was how it worked. You simply banished the fury from your heart, and the anger left your eyes. It lingered only in your mind, where it could do the most good. Or, if you preferred, the most harm.

Harry touched her hand. "Please, I don't want to quarrel with you, Auntie. I'm just trying to protect you. Aren't we supposed to protect the people we love?"

"But not smother them, Harry."

Their salads arrived. The waiter fluttered the pepper mill over Harry's plate, then effaced himself. Thalia's warm spinach was excellent, but Harry barely touched his spring greens. Well, she might as well get it over with. She pulled a folded sheet of notebook paper from her purse and handed it to him. He perused the list, then glanced up with a quizzical smile—the tolerant nephew again. "What is this, Auntie?"

"People who'll testify on my behalf. Your own sister, my doctor who saw me just last month, my priest, police officer Dwight Jordan, most of my congregation and numerous friends." She tapped his forearm. "Even your daddy says if push comes to shove he'll testify, though he thinks I'm a blamed fool. He knows—as you do in your heart, dear—that I'm completely compos mentis."

"That's just it. I *don't* know. And are *you* sure? I mean, would you know if you were losing your, your—"

"My marbles? Maybe not. But the people on that list would know." She plucked the paper from his grasp and slid it back into her purse. "You've been foolish, dear. And if you don't withdraw that petition first thing Monday, I'll hotfoot it to my lawyer and leave every red cent I've got to Nolan."

Harry pushed aside his salad. "A boy you've met, what? Two or three times? He could be in a gang for all you know, a drug dealer. And all these years I've—"

"I'm fond of you, Harry, and it's not that I don't appreciate all you've done for me, but I *won't* be dictated to. More evidence of my erratic behavior, no doubt. My lawyer's expecting to hear from you first thing Monday. Ah, here's our dinner. Let's talk about something more pleasant, shall we?" So they discussed the painful recrudescence of Clayton's gout; Madison's girls, who were starting ballet lessons; and Thalia told him about Layla's starring role in her high school's production of *A Doll's House* this past spring. But neither of them had much appetite, and for once Harry didn't order dessert.

On the drive home she said, "I made a reservation for you at the

Marriott. I'm extremely angry with you, Harry. You've been scheming behind my back—something I find hard to forgive."

He didn't say a word until they were parked in front of her house. Then he folded his arms on the steering wheel and rested his cheek on his arms, his eyes seeking hers. "I didn't mean for it to be like this, Auntie."

"I know you didn't, dear." Beside her in the shadowy car she saw the little boy who'd run to her when his daddy's anger scared him, the child she'd hugged, comforted with oatmeal cookies warm from the oven. Was he remembering that—the deep, unselfconscious love between a woman and a child who was her flesh and blood?

With a groan he raised his head and unlocked the car, no doubt intending to walk her to the door, maybe coax his way back into her house and her heart. She put a hand on his knee. "Just watch me to the door, then scoot on over to the Marriott."

"But Auntie—"

"Harry. I insist."

Trying not to fumble, she heaved open the passenger door. Goodness, she was tired. She gripped the seatback and hauled herself to her feet. "Good night, Harry. My love to your daddy." She shut the car door and went up the dark front walk. The porch light was on, and a lamp glowed behind the parlor's lace curtains as if someone were waiting for her. She almost turned around, almost called for Harry to come inside.

The rising sun swept the sky with pink light and a mockingbird warbled a lilting aubade. Thalia yawned and stretched, too contented to get out of bed. No doubt Harry would lock her up someday, but maybe by then she'd be too old to care. In any case, she'd already arranged her revenge. When her will was read, Harry would find she'd left the bulk of her estate to Nolan, who unlike Harry could actually use the money. But picturing Harry's chagrin involved seeing her own body laid out in a casket, a depressing thought. Better to think of Jesus. Jesus who would take her hand

and lead her through the pearly gates to kneel dazzled and blissful in God's radiant light.

She got up, poked her feet into her slippers, her arms into her robe, and went downstairs. The table lamp in the parlor was still on. Maybe she *was* getting senile. But no, everybody left a light on now and then. She switched off the lamp and went into the kitchen, where the coffeemaker gasped puffs of steam.

When she took her coffee out onto the front porch, the screen door slapped behind her, and a startled rabbit zigzagged across the lawn. As she sat down she heard voices. Across the street, Leona and Dwight were strolling down Leona's front walk, her big orange cat trotting ahead of them. They stopped under the magnolia trees. Leona said something and Dwight laughed and pulled her into his arms.

Thalia's hand crept to her throat in sudden yearning—for dogwood blossoms in spring, a man touching her naked body, hard wet sand under her feet as she ran through a summer cloudburst on Tybee Island. Her lips rounded in astonishment. Was life simply this, the hunger for more life despite the body's frailty? She reached for her coffee, quietly thrilled that the world was still mysterious, that middle-aged lovers kissed under magnolia trees with white blossoms like stars among the dark leaves.

Lauren Cobb's short fiction has appeared in literary journals such as the *Beloit Fiction Journal, Arts and Letters, Eclipse,* and *Green Mountains Review.* Her fiction awards include the *Another Chicago Magazine* Chicago Literary Award and second place in the *Southern California Review* Fiction Award. Born and raised in Los Angeles, she earned her doctorate at the University of Georgia, Athens. She now lives in northern Minnesota, where she is currently working on a literary mystery novel set in Southern California.